STORM AT SEA

Bragen marched Nichole toward the cabin, vowing he wouldn't underestimate the little vixen again. She'd bested him twice. That was enough.

"You're hurting my arm."

"Be thankful I don't break it."

"You started it," Nichole huffed as he dragged her inside and slammed the door.

"And I'll finish it." Bragen swung her around, his gaze landing on the tantalizing mounds of flesh rising above her bodice. Desire spread through him, and it angered him even more. She had no right to unbalance him like this.

He jerked her against him, their mouths so close he could feel her breath on his lips. "If I'm going to be accused of fathering your bastard child," he rasped, "then I'm damn well going to enjoy some of the pleasure."

Books by Sue Rich

The Scarlet Temptress
Shadowed Vows
Rawhide and Roses
Mistress of Sin
The Silver Witch
Wayward Angel

Published by POCKET BOOKS

Sue Rich

Wayward Angel

POCKET BOOKS

New York   London   Toronto   Sydney   Tokyo   Singapore

This book is a work of fiction. Names, characters, places and incidents are products of the author's imagination or are used fictitiously. Any resemblance to actual events or locales or persons, living or dead, is entirely coincidental.

An *Original* Publication of POCKET BOOKS

POCKET BOOKS, a division of Simon & Schuster Inc.
1230 Avenue of the Americas, New York, NY 10020

ISBN: 0-671-89807-8

First Pocket Books printing August 1995

10 9 8 7 6 5 4 3 2 1

POCKET and colophon are registered trademarks of Simon & Schuster Inc.

Printed in the U.S.A.

Heather Nicole Rawlins, my granddaughter:
Thanks for the use of your name.

Caroline Tolley, my editor:
You made this book possible.

Dianna Crawford, my friend:
Your support goes far beyond writing.

Jim Rich, my husband—my very own hero.

Chapter 1

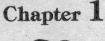

Charleston of the Carolinas, 1783

Bragen Alexander reined his mount to a halt on a rise overlooking the ocean. The scent of sea and kelp drifted on the breeze as he watched waves slap at the shore. It had been three years since he had crossed that ocean—three years since he'd escaped the hangman.

Clayton Cordell rode up beside him and stopped, but Clay's attention wasn't on the ocean. It was on a distant, sprawling community—Charles Town.

The wind gusted through the spruce and slapped the fringe on Bragen's buckskin shirt. The roan beneath him side-stepped with impatience. "Easy, boy," he soothed, running a hand over the animal's powerful neck. "We'll be on our way soon."

"Your horse is as eager to end this journey as I am," Cordell remarked.

Bragen smiled. For all Clay's wealth and station, he never complained. The man had been a rogue and a pirate far too long to let a few weeks in the saddle bother him. "I pray Jason was right when he said Gabriel Bodine was in Charles Town."

"Charleston." Clay shoved a lock of dark, reddish brown hair out of his eyes. "The city's residents recently changed its name. And I can't imagine why Kincaid would tell you Bodine was there *and* engaged to his half-sister, Nichole, if it weren't true."

"You're right, of course. And I can't blame Jason for being worried. He doesn't even know Gabe, and he's concerned over the hasty engagement."

"With good cause."

"Yes," Bragen agreed, unable to conceal the bitterness in his voice.

"Then there's no doubt Gabe's there."

"None. It's just hard for me to believe I may actually catch him this time. I've been close before, yet he always managed to disappear before I arrived."

Clay flashed his notorious smile. "That may have been true in the past. But not so on this occasion."

"I know." Bragen's stomach knotted with anticipation— and a trace of fear—because of what he might learn when he finally came face to face with the man he'd once called friend.

Nichole watched Gabriel as she brushed a long curl away from her cheek. His gaze was fixed on the scant bodice of her gown, the one Miss Fender had insisted she wear. The woman would stop at nothing to get Nichole married off.

With an inward sigh, Nichole returned her attention to the package she'd just received. "I can't believe it, Gabriel," she said, trying to keep her voice level. "Jason sent a gift."

"Is that so unusual, my dear? After all, he is your brother, and we are to be married soon." He smiled, but the action was forced.

Nichole peered across the small expanse of Miss Fender's stylish parlor at the stocky man who would soon be her husband—the displaced English baronet who'd courted her into making a decision she regretted but could do little about. Her guardian, Miss Fender, had given her an ultimatum: find a husband before the end of the summer, or find another home. But Nichole had no other place to go. Her parents were dead. And her half-brothers, Jason and Nick, had cast her out.

Her only hope was to marry Gabriel, the man who coveted the fortune he thought she possessed. His poor financial status was no secret among Charleston's elite. But hers was. She wasn't about to tell anyone the Heathertons' relatives, the Wentworths, had petitioned to claim her inheritance, or that the majority of her brothers' money had been spent furthering the colonial cause.

She traced the edge of the package with her finger, wishing she could tell Gabriel the truth. But she couldn't—first, because he wouldn't believe her, and second, if by some miracle he did, he'd refuse to marry her. Then how would she live? Even the allowance her brothers sent each month was a strain on their finances. She couldn't burden them by asking them to support her.

Settling her gaze on the toe of her slipper, she reflected on her childhood in England with the Heathertons. She hadn't known they weren't her real parents, but seven years ago, when she turned fifteen, they'd told her the truth of her birth. Her unwed mother, a woman of loose morals, had died during childbirth, and her uncle had ordered the midwife to get rid of the child.

The shocking news had explained so much: why the Heathertons had never believed her when she tried to tell them about their neighbor, Lord Wimpleset, and how he'd made indecent advances; why they hadn't been concerned over her governess's cruel treatment of her, or the cook's vicious slurs. After all, she was a whore's whelp, not blooded aristocracy.

Not long after the discussion with the Heathertons, she had received a letter from her real brothers, Jason and Nick

Kincaid, who had learned about her existence just months before and had set out to find her. They had asked her to join them in the colonies. At the Heathertons' urging, she had done so.

When she reached the Americas, she learned the real truth about her birth and her mother. She hadn't been a woman of profession at all, but a lady of quality who'd fallen in love with a married man—Beau Kincaid, the son of a duke.

But her pleasure in learning about her real family was overshadowed. She'd just arrived in Williamsburg when she received word the Heathertons had perished in an accident.

Never having been on amicable terms with the rest of the family, who'd treated her as if she had the pox, she'd had no choice but to stay in the colonies with her brothers. Besides, she was penniless. The Heatherton relatives, Amelia and Fredrick Wentworth, had laid claim to the estate since Nichole wasn't a blood relation.

She fought tears at the memory of the only parents she'd ever known, and then addressed Gabriel's question. "Yes, I'm surprised my brother sent me a gift, Gabriel. Jason was so angry when I last saw him, I didn't think he'd ever contact me again. He sent me away because he thinks I burned down his stables."

Instead of being shocked, as she'd expected, a smirk curved one corner of Gabriel's mouth. It was apparent that he'd heard all about her misadventures—at least those that had occurred since she arrived in Charleston. The look in his eyes promised those mishaps would cease the minute they were married. "Did you set fire to them?"

"It was an accident."

Gabriel's mouth flattened into a grim line, and his fingers tightened around his thick leather belt, almost as if he considered using it on her. "How many horses did he lose?"

Nichole squirmed in her seat. "None. I managed to get them all out, but that didn't cool Jason's anger any, since he'd just built the stables. I'd never seen him so furious."

4

"As any man would have been. Women must understand the importance of obedience."

Now why did he have to say that? Nichole wondered, afraid of how forceful he might be once they were wed. He didn't look like a man who would beat his wife, but one never knew.

He straightened his ruffled cuff. "Did you not say you have another brother?"

Right now, she wished she didn't. The reason he had thrown her out was just as bad—and that was why she'd said so little about them to Gabriel. "Nick lives in Williamsburg."

"Why were you not sent to him rather than here, to a mere acquaintance?"

She didn't want to answer that question, so she hedged. "Miss Fender isn't an acquaintance, she's Mother Heatherton's sister. She took me in temporarily—out of a sense of duty." *And she's the one who's forcing me into an unwanted marriage.*

Nichole curled her fingers around the twine. She couldn't stall any longer. "And I wasn't sent to Nick's because he'd already cast me out. He thinks I sank one of his ships."

Gabriel's hazel eyes widened. "Another accident, I presume?"

She hadn't been anywhere near the docks, but she'd taken the blame to save a young cabin boy from the lash. She knew Nick wouldn't beat her, but she'd never expected him to ask her to leave. "Yes. And because of it, Nick packed me off to Jason's."

"And Jason sent you here after the stable incident," Gabriel concluded in a tired voice, brushing a piece of lint from the leg of his dove-gray breeches. He admired the shine on his buckle shoes. "You are quite a troublemaker, my dear."

Why was it so easy for people to believe her when she admitted to mischief, yet not when she told the truth? She had sworn to Jason that she hadn't started the fire in the stables. She had begged the Heathertons to believe her about Lord Wimpleset. "Yes, I suppose I am."

Gabriel knotted his fists at her insolent admission. Then he gathered himself and gestured at the parcel in her lap. "Are you going to open that?"

Nichole watched him as she untied the gift, wondering at the spark of cruelty she saw in his eyes. Then her attention drifted downward. She gave a reverent sigh when she saw a magnificent statue lying in a bed of tissue. Carved out of the finest polished ivory, a scantily dressed woman sat astride a stallion, her hair streaming behind her, her elfin features a mixture of innocence and rapscallion. Nichole knew it was how Jason envisioned her. "Isn't it lovely?"

"Well, that for certain is not what I expected from someone as wealthy as your brother—and really, my dear, do you think it appropriate for a nuptial gift?"

"I think it's wonderful," she defended, certain she'd never be able to live under the same roof with the pompous ass. Wishing she had a choice, and struggling with waves of unhappiness, she again examined the present in her lap. "Besides, the price isn't important, only the fact that my brother cared enough to send a gift at all."

Gabriel conceded, albeit without sincerity. "You are right, of course. Please forgive my momentary lapse. And I do think the piece is quite striking."

Not in the least appeased, she began riffling through the tissue.

"What are you looking for?"

"A note. Surely he sent one." Sheer paper fluttered out of the packet and to the floor, displaced by her search. "Here it is!"

Gabriel eyed the fat envelope with anticipation. "Perhaps Kincaid saw fit to include a spot of cash to offset the paltriness—er—to purchase finery for the nuptials."

Nichole clenched her teeth. The man had interest in two

things, money and obedience, neither of which she could give him. Concerned about how she'd manage to survive under his control, and praying he took a mistress without delay, she opened the letter.

As she read, she reached for the gold, pearl-trimmed locket she always wore—the one that had belonged to her real mother—only then realizing she'd neglected to put it on in her haste to dress for Gabriel's unforeseen arrival. Not that *that* should surprise her. His unscheduled visits had ceased to upset her weeks ago. Sometimes she wondered if he wasn't expecting to find her with another caller.

She felt a well of emotions as Jason's words touched her heart. A tear slid down her cheek and dropped onto the exposed swell of her breast.

She glanced up to see Gabriel's eyes fixed on the glistening spot.

Nichole shifted. "Jason says he's sorry he sent me away, that he's always had a devil of a time with his temper." She gave her betrothed a weak smile. She herself had inhrerited that bothersome trait. "He didn't invite me to return to his home in Virginia, though. He's painfully stubborn. And I'm certain Samantha and the boys had something to do with his apology. They were quite distraught when he sent me to Charleston. Knowing Samantha—Jason's wife—I'm sure she made his life miserable. We were friends in London long before we became sisters-in-law."

"Another willful chit," Gabriel mumbled.

Ignoring him, she read on. "Listen to this: a friend of Jason's is going to pay a call. Must be someone important, too. He urges me to show this Bragen Alexander the utmost courtesy."

Gabriel stiffened, and she thought she saw a flash of panic in his eyes. "Good heavens," she continued, "Mr. Alexander left for Charleston the same day this package was posted. Why, that means he could arrive at any time." She came to her feet, darting a critical eye around the parlor.

"I'm afraid you'll have to excuse me, Gabriel. I really need to inform Miss Fender about Jason's friend."

She placed the statue on the mantel over the fireplace, then gave him an apologetic smile. "You can see yourself to the door, can't you?"

Without waiting for a response, she hurried from the room.

"Calm down, Hallie. And do stop that babbling," Miss Fender commanded the young servant in a sharp tone. The matron's narrow features were pinched into a perpetual scowl, most of which was due to Nichole's presence. Even her high, pointed crown of silver braids looked pinched. "Now, what is this about Mr. Bodine?"

"I seen him comin' down the stairs. And the door to Miss Nichole's room was open. Then he run out, fast as you please, like he done somethin' sneaky."

"When?"

"Right after you and the missy here dashed off to the merchant's for them fancy candles for the guests. I seen him. I did!"

Nichole watched the girl's plump brown face as she flapped her hands, though her excited revelation wouldn't mean one whit to Miss Fender. Gabriel could have set fire to Nichole's room and the woman wouldn't have cared. Besides, there was nothing of interest to him in her chamber. Nothing at all. Still . . . his actions were curious. It was possible, she concluded, that he hadn't been able to find the footman, and had gone in search of his tricorn. A rather feeble concept to be sure, but she couldn't think of any other reason for him to be upstairs.

Hallie pressed her point. "I tell ya, that fella was up to no good."

Miss Fender's curveless chest puffed out in indignation. "How dare you speak of your betters in such a manner. Get out of here and get to your polishing before I take a strap to your backside. And mind your tongue. I'll not have you spreading your vicious gossip about Miss Heatherton's betrothed."

Contrite, the servant's shoulders slumped, and she gave a halfhearted curtsy. "Yes'm."

Nichole's sympathy stirred as she watched the young woman scamper out the sitting-room door. There had been no need for Miss Fender's cruel barbs. Her dislike for her hostess grew, but she forced herself to remember that the woman *had* given her a home ... however temporary. Feeling as dejected as Hallie, unwanted, and painfully unloved, Nichole sought her own escape. "If you'll excuse me, Miss Fender, I'd like to change before Mr. Alexander arrives."

Determined not to feel sorry for herself, Nichole hurried to her room, then scanned the chamber for signs of Gabriel's presence. The armoire doors were closed, the small four-poster bed undisturbed. The white pitcher and bowl still sat in the center of the washing stand, a clean towel draped over a bar protruding from the side.

She glanced at the mahogany bureau, noting the colorful bottles of bath scents, tins of white powder, her silver-backed brush, and her pearl-rimmed jewelry box with a gold angel on the lid, which remained closed. Nothing was out of place.

Satisfied, she summoned the only friend she'd made since coming to Charleston, her personal maid, Chelsea, a middle-aged Negress with a saucy mouth.

Through mumbles of protest about the hurried pace, Chelsea helped her bathe and slip on her chemise. The gown she planned to wear was carefully spread out on the bed. It was a silvery blue concoction that matched Nichole's eyes, with tight sleeves that ended at the elbows, then flared out with long, dripping white lace. The lace-trimmed bodice was so low, the tops of her nipples were sure to show, bringing to mind Miss Fender's suggestion of using rouge to accentuate them even more. Embarrassed by the mere thought, Nichole tugged at the ribbons on her chemise.

"Stop dat, chile," the maid reprimanded. "Now turn around so's I can stuff you into dis corset and get you into dat fancy gown."

Hating to have the breath squeezed out of her again, yet knowing Miss Fender demanded she wear the wretched whalebone, Nichole complied, quite sure that man had invented the contraption out of spite to punish women.

"Dere now. Don't dat look nice." Chelsea beamed as she lowered the satin over Nichole's cinched torso and full petticoats. "Land' sakes. If you ain't a sight with all dem golden curls and dat milky skin." She secured the laces down the back. "And I knows just da necklace to show off dat purdy bosom of yours."

Wishing the woman wasn't quite so brazen in her appraisal, Nichole placed her hands on her almost invisible waist and inspected the bottom opening of the skirt that revealed a white ruffled underskirt.

Chelsea's squeal of outrage startled her, and she spun around, satin and ruffles swirling after her.

"Dey's gone! All your beautiful baubles is gone!"

"What?" What did she mean, *gone?* Then her gaze flew to her flowered jewelry box. A growing uneasiness took hold. Hallie had seen Gabriel upstairs. But why would he take her jewels? It didn't make sense. Once they were married, they'd belong to him anyway. All of her possessions would . . . not to mention herself. Afraid to approach the dressing table, she asked in a strained voice, "Is my locket there?"

Chelsea knew how Nichole cherished her mother's necklace. She was quiet for several seconds, then shook her head, causing the end of her checkered bandanna to sway. "No, chile. Dat's gone, too."

A cry escaped before Nichole could stop it. There had to be a reasonable explanation. She'd simply go see Gabriel and ask him if he'd taken her jewels. And if so, why. It was possible he'd meant to surprise her by having them cleaned, or polished, or the mountings checked. There was absolutely no reason to get into a lather.

But deep down, she wasn't so sure. She didn't know him very well, and it was very possible she'd made *another* horrific mistake, which was often her wont to do. She cringed at the notion. "Chelsea, have Jobe bring the carriage around. I'm going to pay a call on Mr. Bodine."

Chapter 2

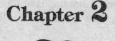

What do you mean, *he's gone?*"

"I's sorry, milady. But he ain't here," Gabriel's young Negro servant repeated, holding the door half closed. "The massa done ordered his clothes packed, had them loaded in a hired carriage, and left. And he ain't comin' back no time soon, neither, 'cause he tole us to close up the house."

Anger and dread took turns bouncing off Nichole's nerves. "Where did he go?"

"Don't know, your ladyship."

She felt like she was going to be sick. Dragging in a fortifying breath, she lifted her chin. "You said 'us.' Who else is here?"

"My mama."

"Where is she?"

When he didn't respond, she shoved open the door and advanced on him until they came nose to nose. "Where is your mother?"

He retreated a step. "I-in the massa's chamber, strippin' the bed."

Brushing past him, she stomped up the stairs, her anger so tangible she could feel it churn.

She collided with a thin maid, who was carrying an armful of sheets down the hall.

The woman jumped in surprise.

"Where's Gabriel going?" Nichole demanded.

"Who is you?"

"His betrothed. Now where has he gone?"

The maid's eyes flickered with uncertainty. "He tole me not to say, miss."

Nichole lifted a brow. "You can't imagine he meant that order to include me. His creditors, perhaps, even his acquaintances at the club, but certainly not *me.*" The outrage in her voice caused the servant to tremble.

Tightening her hold on the bundle, the maid inched back a step, shaking her head. "He said not to tell anyone, lady. I swears he did."

"Unless you want a taste of the strap, you'll tell me his destination this instant." She hated frightening the woman with such a blatant lie, but she was desperate.

The servant sucked in a horrified breath. "Cape Town! He's leavin' at dawn for Cape Town."

"What ship?"

She hesitated, trying to remember. "He tole the carriage driver to take his bags to the *Seacutter.*"

It was all Nichole could do to keep from stomping her foot. That cur! "Where is he now?"

"T-the Crimson Candle."

"Is that an inn?"

The maid did look uncomfortable now. "I-it's one of them places ladies ain't supposed to know about."

"A brothel?"

She gave a jerky nod.

"I see." And she did. She'd heard about men's lust, and

how it bothered them to go long periods without a woman's companionship. What better way for a man to spend the night before a lengthy journey?

Journey. She clenched her teeth as she made her way back to the carriage. Gabriel had stolen her jewels and was leaving her stranded.

She ignored Chelsea as she climbed inside the conveyance. She just couldn't believe Gabriel would do this to her. Not that she cared so much about the jewels—well, except for the pearl earbobs Nick had given her and the ruby bracelet from Jason. *No,* she thought. Those things meant a lot to her, but the locket meant everything. The night she was born, the midwife found the locket on Nichole's dead mother, and placed it around Nichole's neck. The Heathertons had kept it for her until her fifteenth birthday —the day they told her the truth. Inside the pearl-rimmed heart was the likeness of her real parents, Beau Kincaid and Mary Elizabeth Langford. It was the only reminder she'd ever have of them.

Gabriel wasn't going to get away with this. With an angry swipe of her hand, she rapped on the roof of the carriage. "Jobe. Take me to the Crimson Candle."

"Lord have mercy! What you doin', chile? You cain't!" Chelsea's jaw started wobbling.

"I'm going to find Gabriel. I have to. And I can't wait until tomorrow and chance missing him at the docks."

"But . . . but . . . not *dis* way!" She took a breath to calm herself. "Young un', I knows you has a good heart, and don't never get into mischief on purpose, but dis could get you in a whole passel of trouble. Besides," she said in a more level voice, "dey ain't gwine to let you in dere. Only payin' gents and *strumpets* pass through dem doors."

"I'll think of something," she vowed with conviction.

"Humph. Probably land you in da gaol, too." The maid sniffed, then crossed her arms over her large bosom and wedged herself into a corner to sulk.

Nichole explored her options. She should go to the

constable for help. She winced at the thought. After their last encounter, she wasn't sure that was such a good idea. She was sure he was still angry over her poking him in the eye with her parasol. He'd called out to her in greeting and she'd turned too sharply. Although, truth to tell, the minor incident wouldn't have been so bad if she hadn't tried to console him, the umbrella between them, and in doing so, caused him to fall off the boardwalk. He'd landed on his rear in front of the entire town.

After he'd recovered from the community's comical jibes, he hadn't been very amiable toward her.

No. She was sure he'd give her complaint only minor attention. Besides, American constables were more concerned with riots and violent crimes.

If only she could think of a gentleman who'd be willing to go into the brothel after Gabriel. But there weren't any. With the exception of Gabriel himself, her suitors and male friends amounted to none.

She considered asking Jobe, but were he caught stealing from a white man, the slave's punishment would be severe. There was no help for it. She'd simply have to do the deed herself.

Shoving aside the carriage curtain, she was assailed by a stream of late afternoon sunlight and a brisk March breeze that carried the scent of fish and rotting timber from the docks. She snuggled deeper into her velvet pelisse.

The wail of a child startled her, and she craned her neck out the window to see up ahead. Her heart plummeted when she saw that a small boy had tumbled from the bed of a parked wagon. She opened her mouth to tell Jobe to hurry to the youngster's aid, but at the same instant, two men on horseback reined to a halt in the middle of the road. A powerfully built man wearing buckskins leapt down. He picked up the child and brushed the hair out of the tyke's eyes, then bent his head and said something.

The child gave a wan smile, and the stranger dusted off the seat of the boy's breeches, then lifted him into the wagon.

He said something else and tousled the boy's tumble of curls before returning to his mount.

Nichole smiled as her carriage rolled past, wishing the stranger hadn't turned away. She hadn't seen the compassionate man's face. With all that had happened to her since coming to the colonies, it wasn't often she witnessed an act of genuine kindness.

When Jobe drew the team to a stop across from the Crimson Candle, her thoughts returned to her immediate problem, and her resolve slipped. Crowded among several two-story buildings stood a pair of wide double doors, their surfaces painted to resemble two giant red candles. Above the boardwalk, a yellow wood sign swung on hinges, the name CRIMSON CANDLE printed in bold scarlet letters.

"I wonder if there's a rear door?" Nichole mused aloud.

Chelsea drew in a scandalized breath. "No! Chile, don't you go thinkin' like dat. You is not gwine in dere, and dat's final." She slammed her palm against the carriage roof. "Jobe! You take us home dis minute."

"We're staying!" Nichole countered. She turned to her friend. "Chelsea, please. Don't put any more obstacles in my way. I need your help." She clutched the maid's hands. "You know how much that locket means to me. If Gabriel gets on that ship tomorrow, I'll never see it again. I'll have lost the only link to my real parents." *And my last chance at marriage.* At twenty-two and with no money—not to mention her reputation as an uncontrollable troublemaker—her prospects were sorely limited. "Chelsea, I've got to get my necklace back."

"Oh, chile, don't you think I know dat? But I's tryin' to look out for you." Her brown eyes softened, and she squeezed Nichole's hands. "You knows I'll help. I ain't been able to say no to you since da day you first arrived and broke Miss Fender's favorite vase." Her gaze drifted over Nichole's gown. "Still, dey ain't gonna let you inside in dem clothes. Dey'd take one look at dat fine gown and hustle you right out again."

"Well, what kind of clothes do the—er—ladies in there wear?"

The maid's eyes drifted to the window. "Dat kind." She gestured to a woman walking down the boardwalk away from the establishment.

"I see." Nichole studied the harlot's flashy attire, the red hairpiece and made-up face, then she rapped on the carriage ceiling. "Jobe, take me to Madame Armone's dressmaking shop."

Bragen didn't know whether to swear or hit something, although his companion's grinning face was a promising target.

"What are you going to do now?" Clay asked, his green eyes sparkling with amusement as he mounted up. "You can't start asking around. Someone might tip Bodine off again."

A muscle throbbed in Bragen's jaw as he swung up into the saddle. "Don't you think I know that? That's why I didn't mention him to that pinch-faced old lady, Miss Fender. I want to speak to Jason's sister. If she and Gabe are planning to marry soon, she'll know where he lives."

"In that case, why don't we find a room? I could use a bath and a change."

Resigned to another night's wait, and having been on the road too long, Bragen wasn't hard to convince. "I saw a decent inn on River Street."

"River Street it is."

After a refreshing soak and having donned clean clothes, Bragen and Clay wandered down to a tavern near the docks.

Clay sprawled in his chair, his fifth ale in front of him, his fuzzy gaze fixed on Bragen. "I don't know about you, old chum, but I want to do something more than stare across this wobbly table at your homely face the rest of the evening. Do you suppose they have any *entertainment* around here?"

Feeling rather jovial himself after a hot supper and several mugs, Bragen gave a lopsided smile. "What did you have in mind?" he teased, knowing full well what Clay meant. "Cards? The theater?"

"Mmm, yes, those do sound interesting, but I had something more *basic* in mind. What do you think?"

Bragen didn't have to give it much thought. "Sounds promising."

Clay chuckled and summoned the proprietor with a snap of his fingers.

The man rushed to their table, wiping his hands on a towel. "More ale, gov'nor?"

"I believe dessert is in order," Clay countered.

"Well, er, me wife did make a cobbler yesterday. Would ye care for some o' that?"

Clay's lips quirked. "I believe I'd prefer a *different* sort of dessert." He winked. "If you get my meaning."

The older man's eyes widened, then crinkled. "Aye, mate. I most surely do." He leaned closer, his voice a conspiratorial whisper. "And there's a right interestin' *dessert* house not far from here. It's called the Crimson Candle."

Nichole wrapped a carriage blanket around her bare shoulders to ward off the spring chill. But the closer she got to the docks, the colder she grew. She'd done a lot of foolish things in her life, but she was quite certain this one would go straight to the top of the list.

She fingered a dangling curl on the red wig covering her hair as she waited for Jobe to open the door, praying the hairpiece, along with the thick application of kohl and rouge, would be enough to disguise her.

"I's be waitin' right here for you, missy," Jobe assured her, his voice tinged with concern as he helped her down. "You be quick now, hear?"

Replacing the blanket, she rubbed her upper arms and peered around the gloomy alleyway behind the brothel. "I will," she said with confidence, but her thoughts fluttered like leaves in the wind. *I can't do this. It's a mistake. I know that as surely as I'm wearing this blasted red dress. Something awful is going to happen.*

Controlling her sudden burst of fear with superhuman effort, she lifted her chin. "Make sure you stay in the shadows until I return." She gave him a shaky smile. "I won't be long." On trembling legs, she turned away from the coachman and walked through the rear door of the Crimson Candle.

Bragen paid the shopkeeper for a box of cheroots, then wedged the box under his arm and staggered out onto the boardwalk toward the Crimson Candle, wondering why the walkway kept rolling beneath him.

Trying to focus on a yellow and red sign overhead, he smiled. Clay was already inside. Hell, he was probably upstairs—and Bragen would have been, too, if he hadn't seen the tobacco shop next door. But it had been a long time since he'd had a decent smoke. Just about as long since he'd had . . . He grinned.

He stumbled into a bench beside the brothel's double doors. He was taking care of all of his vices in one night. Ale, cheroots, and women.

Unable to hide his eagerness, he shoved open the door, catching up with his feet just as he came face to face with the large, buxom proprietress.

"Good evening, madam. I've come to . . . to . . . partake of some entertainment."

Her squinty pig eyes examined him with bold thoroughness. "With a gent as comely as yourself, there'll be no problem serving your purpose." She fixed on a spot just below his waist and smiled. "No problem atall." With a brassy wink, she took his box of cheroots and set them on a table by the door for him to retrieve on his way out, then flung a beringed hand toward a pair of ladies, each lounging on a separate settee in a dimly lit, scarlet-papered room. "'Tis a fine selection for you, milord."

Bragen was having a difficult time focusing, so he narrowed his lashes and peeked through the slits of his lids at the women garbed in tight satins. A big-busted blonde gave him an inviting smile, and he opened his mouth to announce his choice. But at that instant, a slim redhead moved out from behind her and crept toward the stairs. As she leaned forward to grip the banister, the neckline of her red dress dipped, giving him a full glimpse of one perfect breast. Desire shot through him. "I want her."

The matron glanced at the girl. "Oh, that's Tess—" she bit off the words, furrowing her brow in sudden confusion. Her gaze returned to the slim woman who was now halfway up the stairs. The proprietress watched for several seconds, frowning, then her eyes brightened with a dawning realization. She gave Bragen a sly grin. "That one comes at a high price, love. You sure you're willin' to pay the cost?"

Watching the gentle sway of the girl's hips as she climbed the stairs, Bragen felt the ache in his loins grow by bounds, and he knew he'd pay most any amount to settle himself between those slender thighs. "Name it."

The proprietress's thick lips spread into a beefy smile. "That'll be three crown, love. And you'll find our . . . *Tess* . . . in room four."

Chapter 3

Standing at the end of the lantern-lit upstairs hall, Nichole's nerves frayed. This was without a doubt the worst idea she'd ever had.

The rooms were numbered one through three on the right and six down to four on the left, with a fully stocked sideboard positioned between six and five. To find Gabriel, she knew she'd have to search behind each one of those closed doors.

The thought was unnerving at best. She placed a hand on her stomach to still a flutter of fear. Where was the Kincaid daring Jason had said she possessed so much of? She didn't feel in the least courageous . . . more like scared to death.

She couldn't do this. She took a step back. *Get hold of yourself, Nichole. You have to do it. Besides, it won't be so bad.*

Trying to control her shaking hands, she headed for the first door on her right. She was too frightened to reach for the latch. Eyeing the sideboard, she whirled around and raced to the liquor cabinet. With trembling hands, she filled a glass with cognac and swallowed it. Fire scorched her throat, and she gasped for breath. Her eyes watered. Good heavens. That stuff was awful.

Still, when the fire cooled, and her breathing returned to normal, her situation didn't appear quite so dreadful anymore. Perhaps a second glass would do the trick. She forced down another and did indeed feel more settled. Regaining her composure, she opened the first door.

Toilet water and body odor wafted from inside, but the room was empty.

More at ease, she crossed the hall to another door.

Inside, light from a bedside candle flickered over an entwined couple beneath the sheets. Shocked to her toes, Nichole blushed with mortification, but refused to leave until she saw the man's face. She bit her lower lip to keep from making a sound while she inspected what she could see of the gentleman. He was thin, with a beard and stringy brown hair, bearing no resemblance to the stocky, blond Gabriel.

Confident now that she felt the effects of the cognac, she moved to the next room and peeked inside.

A gray-haired man labored over a thin red-haired girl, his flabby bare rear bouncing up and down.

Nichole slapped a hand over her mouth to stifle a horrified gasp—or was it a giggle? *My word. What's the matter with me?* Closing the door, she clutched her stomach, her chest heaving, her face so hot from embarrassment, she thought she'd go up in flames.

She eyed the sideboard again, but decided against another drink. She feared she'd overdone it as it was.

Approaching the next chamber, she eased the latch down. That room, thank providence, was unoccupied. And there were only two left. Three and four.

Edging across to number three, she swayed and grabbed onto the wall. A wave of dizziness lightened her head.

"Mercy." She frowned, wondering at the potency of cognac. She hadn't had much experience with spirits, but she knew she'd never seen her brothers so unbalanced after only two drinks. She frowned. That was all she had had, wasn't it?

The image of Gabriel grabbing the wall after a snort made her giggle. She covered her mouth, and scolded herself for getting sidetracked. Besides, Gabriel was exactly who she wanted to see. Moving closer to room three, she placed her ear to the door. No sound came from within. Using caution, she eased open the door. Her fuzzy gaze focused on the bed.

Candlelight wavered over a beautiful brunette, who sat against the headboard of a brass bed, her arms wide, her fingers wrapped around the corner posts. Her head was thrown back, her eyes closed, while a naked, powerfully built man with dark, reddish brown hair kissed her breasts.

Nichole knew she should be embarrassed, should get out of there and leave the couple to their privacy, but she was too awed by the spectacle. Moral indignation tried to assert itself but managed only to roll sluggishly across her thoughts. The man's lazy, erotic movements held her attention far better. She was hypnotized by the graceful way his muscles flexed when he bent his head, by the way he slid his hand up and down the woman's thigh. Then, as if he had all the time in the world, he trailed his long fingers to the inside of her leg.

The woman groaned. "Oh, yes, Clay. Yes."

An answering throb resounded through Nichole's own body, startling her. Horrified, she shut the door. *How indecent,* she tried to tell herself, but in truth, it hadn't seemed that way at all—more like sinfully beautiful. The sensual images refused to leave her mind, as did the warm tingles that made her skin feel oversensitive.

Gathering her wits, and determined to remain unaffected, she moved on to room four, knowing this had to be where she'd find . . . ? Oh, yes. Gabriel.

She glared at the door and made an instant decision. She wouldn't give the thief a second's warning. Regaining her anger and her resolve, she grabbed the latch, twisted, then burst inside. She came to a skidding, staggering halt in the center of the room.

No one was there.

Disconcerted, she stared at the swaying, neatly made bed, at a sliver of moonlight slipping through a part in the heavy drapes, at the polished wood floors illuminated by the hall lantern. Where was he? *He has to be here.*

An arm caught her by the waist from behind.

"Sorry it took me so long, angel. But those stairs are damned difficult to climb when they keep moving."

Outraged, she spun around, taking him with her as she raised her fists for battle.

The hall light poured over her assailant's face and shoulders. He was the man she'd seen with the little boy. The kind, gentle man. She recognized his clothes. But up close, he was splendid, from the top of his silky black head to the width of his finely sculpted shoulders.

His midnight eyes were deep-set and fringed with long, thick lashes. They were hungry eyes, bottomless eyes, eyes that held secrets of passion and pain, eyes that made her body shiver. He was power, masculine beauty, and danger all rolled into one magnificent body.

She had trouble finding her tongue. "Listen, mister. You've made a mistake." *As much as she suddenly hated to admit it.*

He pulled her closer, trapping her hands between their chests, then kicked the door shut. The room plunged into darkness. His breath feathered over her ear. "The only mistake I made was not getting here sooner." He nibbled her neck, while one hand explored the curve of her bottom.

Warning bells resounded through her brain, and she tried to escape the touch of his palm on her rear. The action brought their lower bodies together.

He sucked in a sharp breath, then pressed her to his hard male flesh. The position was so intimate, she thought she'd swoon. "That's it, angel. Let me feel your heat."

Feel her *what?* "Please, mm—"

His mouth caught her words.

Only once in her twenty-two years had she been kissed with passion. The day Gabriel proposed, he'd done so. His lips had been limp, and a bit wet, but the experience hadn't been too bad—nothing like the rampaging sensations she felt now. This man's lips tasted so good. So hot, like the fiery cognac. He smelled of mint, and ale, and wood smoke— wonderfully male.

She sank closer.

Warmth moved in sluggish waves through her liquor-numbed veins. She softened and put aside her fear to explore the new sensations caused by his assault. It was so marvelous. She braced her palms on his chest, then raised up to more fully enjoy the taste of him. After all, who would ever know?

Vowing to call a halt in just a moment, she inched up onto her toes, then felt shock ricochet through her midsection when he eased his tongue between her lips. It was sinful, wicked, superb. She gave in to the impulse to explore the shape of his beautiful, pleasure-giving mouth. She touched his tongue with her own.

He gave a low, animal groan, and the kiss became explosive. Her thoughts whirled. Through a haze, she became aware of him freeing the ties at the front of her dress. Somewhere in the muddled recesses of her mind, she knew she had to stop him, but she didn't want to, not just yet.

She recalled his gentleness with the child and knew instinctively that he'd release her as soon as she asked. But right now, she wanted to savor the thrilling sensations. After all, how many times would she have the opportunity to experience something this exciting?

She parted her lips wider.

A shudder ran through him, and he deepened the kiss with drugging expertise.

The sensation was so mind-numbing, she was scarcely aware of him slipping the dress down her arms to gather at her waist, scarcely aware of the soft buckskin leather brushing her bare breasts.

Bare breasts? She gasped against his mouth and tried to get free.

He caught the nape of her neck with one hand, holding their lips locked together, while he worked the dress and petticoats over her hips, then let them slide to the floor at her feet.

Sweet heavens! She had to stop him. She pushed at his big chest, tried to squirm out of his powerful hold, tried to free her mouth.

Nothing worked.

Then she felt it—his hand sliding up her bare thigh, causing images of the couple across the hall to float through her fuzzy thoughts. Her skin started tingling. Her reason for struggling wavered.

Dazed by the wild, alien feelings, she was only half aware of being swept up into his strong arms and carried to the bed, of his mouth continuing its sensual assault as he moved. She felt the cool quilt at her back, his weight pressing down on top of her, and the heat of his mouth as he took hers again and again. His hot, male scent rushed her senses, embraced them, ravaged them.

Now, her mind screamed. *Get out of here now.* She jerked her head to the side, struggling for breath, her fear of not being able to control the situation mounting. She tried to push him to the side and wiggle out from under him. It was like trying to move a wall. "Please," she cried. "You mustn't—"

He devoured the rest of her words. He kissed her, long and deep, with intoxicating precision.

When he at last freed her to nibble her ear, she tried to speak, to form an objection, any protest, but only a soft sigh came out. She never dreamed anything could feel so good. This time, it was she who sought his mouth.

He took her offering with greed, then, without interrupting the fire-giving kiss, he shifted, giving himself access to her naked side. With infinite slowness, he drew his palm over the length of her ribs, down to her waist, and over the curve of her hip, massaging, caressing, learning her woman's shape.

Her whole body came to life. Anticipation shot through her, and she grew still, became anxious. Waited.

His lips touched her ear. "Is this what you want, angel?" He trailed his fingers over the tip of her breast.

Sensations exploded. "Oh, sweet mercy."

"Yes," he agreed, his breathing labored, ragged, his caress arousing.

She began to fight for mind-clearing air, her chest rising and falling in short pants.

"Those provocative sounds are charring me to cinders," he warned, as he gently rotated her crest between his thumb and finger.

What sounds? she wondered, but the thought slipped away when his mouth left her ear to nibble a path down her neck, over the swell of her breast. Moist, firm lips claimed an eager nipple.

Pleasure streaked through the center. Her body shook from a need she couldn't understand, couldn't stop.

His hands left her to strip off his shirt, but his lips and tongue continued their erotic assault, sampling first one crest, then the other, nursing, tugging, drawing every ounce of resistance from her body.

His naked chest brushed her stomach, then the peaks of her breasts, the soft hairs taunting her responsive flesh, as he moved up to again recapture her mouth.

It was then she realized he'd also lowered his breeches. Warm, hard male pressed against the inside of her thigh. Fear erupted. She clamped her legs together and pushed at his chest.

"Open for me, angel. I need to feel your fire." He edged gentle fingers between her legs and stroked her feminine curls, parted them.

This newest assault overwhelmed her. Flames erupted

beneath his hand. Her brain tried to form protests, but her body mindlessly opened for him, thrusted against his probing fingers. A moan tore from her throat when he gently explored her center. "Please, I can't stand any more."

His hand shook, and his voice came out in a ragged whisper. "Then hold on, angel. I'll give you everything you want."

Blindly, she gripped his strong shoulders.

He lifted her hips, then his mouth took hers. He thrust his tongue between her lips at the same instant he plunged deep inside her.

Her cry of pain shimmered over his tongue, then faded into a desperate whimper.

For the barest instant, he paused. "What's going on?"

"Please," she cried. She didn't want words. She needed him to move. She dug her nails into his tight flesh.

A low, soft hiss left him, and a shudder rippled along his big frame. As if the last of his control had slipped away, he drove fully into her depths, then began to ease in and out. He raised her hips higher, kissed her with fervor, impaled her, retreated, then plunged again.

Her fingers found his long, silky hair, then held on as fire raced to the middle of her body. The sensation was so overpowering, she became frightened and again tried to close her legs.

"Give in to it, angel," he urged. "Let it come." He withdrew, then thrust. He sank deeper.

It was too much. Pain and pleasure slammed together, spiraling her into a breath-stealing firestorm. Jolt after jolt tore through her, shook her, spun her, then flung her into a wall of liquid pleasure.

After what felt like an eternity, the searing hold snapped and at last released her.

Only then did she become aware of his hoarse cry, of the liquid heat flowing into her.

Several long seconds passed before he slumped and

moved to the side. He buried his face in the pillow, his palm on her stomach, his breathing harsh and heavy.

Realization of what had just happened crashed over her with the enormity of a landslide. She was too horrified to move. *What have I done? Dear God in heaven, what have I done?* Consumed with self-loathing, she knew she had to get out of there, right that instant. Without a second's thought, she sprang from the bed and groped for her clothes.

"What are you doing? Wait a minute, damn it. You owe me an explanation. You were a vir—"

"You got your money's worth," she spat, knowing he'd paid for a woman's services—*her services*—and too furious with herself to be rational. "Explanations are extra." Not giving him a chance to respond, she clutched the red gown to her chest and slammed out the door.

She dashed into a vacant room and yanked on the dress. Unable to reach the back ties, she left them—and ran out of the brothel and into the safety of Jobe's carriage. "Take me away from here," she cried, then curled into a ball on the seat and gave into strangling tears.

Bragen stared into the darkness, wondering what had just happened. Why had she run out? Bloody hell, he'd been about to give her more money. Their lovemaking had taken him to heights he'd never imagined.

Rising, he pulled up his buckskins and grabbed his shirt. He'd been so hot for her he hadn't even taken off all his clothes. And she'd been a damned virgin! The knowledge grated.

He shoved an arm into his sleeve. She must have just started in the profession tonight . . . and he was her first customer. If he had only known, he would have been more gentle.

Gentle hell. He wouldn't have taken her at all.

Although the urges of his body had been satisfied, he felt empty as he tied the laces on his shirt and staggered down the hall. When he reached the lower level, he scanned the large room but didn't see Tess. He did, however, see her employer.

"Madam," he greeted as he approached. "Did you see where Tess went?"

"Wasn't she in her room?"

"Yes. But after we . . ." He cleared his throat. "She left before I had a chance to talk to her."

The hefty woman's mouth curved into that sly smile again. "Sorry, love. I ain't seen her."

He again perused the dimly lit parlor room and saw the other two harlots in their sprawled positions on the settees. Visions of the innocent girl he'd just taken lounging in one of those lewd poses flashed through his mind. It sickened him.

Shoving his hand into the pocket of his breeches, he withdrew a large sum of money. "I want you to give this to Tess."

The woman's pig eyes almost bulged out of her face. "What?"

He thrust the cash into her hand. "I want her to have this. All of it." He pinned her with a hard look. "You've earned your funds for the night; this is for the girl only. And I will check to see that my orders have been followed." It was a lie, but hopefully a convincing one. But just to be sure, he added more inducement. "If I learn that Tess didn't receive this . . . well, the constable *is* a friend of mine."

The woman flushed. "But—but—"

"Is there a problem, madam?"

"No, but—"

"Is the money sufficient?"

"Oh, yes, but—"

He grabbed up his box of cheroots. "I'll say good night, then."

Nichole had changed and bathed, and now wore one of her own chemises, but she hadn't been able to sleep. All she'd done the rest of the night was pace, cry, and listen to Chelsea wail, making Nichole wish she'd never told her the truth about what happened in the brothel. But Nichole had been near hysteria by the time she reached home and sobbed out the whole sordid truth in the maid's arms.

Her only salvation had been that the noise hadn't awakened Miss Fender.

"Oh, chile, I's so sorry," Chelsea said for the tenth time. "I tried to tell you. But you wouldn't listen. Still, it's all my fault. I shoulda *made* you listen."

"You're not to blame." Nichole sniffed, determined to put this wretched night behind her. "My own foolishness caused this mess." *That and the cognac, and my impulsiveness, and my wretched curiosity, and my traitorous body's lack of control.* She dragged in air. "Now it's time to stop mewling over what's happened and get on with my life." She glanced at her maid's tear-stained face. "Help me dress. It'll be dawn soon, and I've got to stop Gabriel from boarding the *Seacutter.*"

Chelsea broke into renewed wails.

Loosing a disgusted sigh, Nichole walked over to the armoire and withdrew a pale lilac silk dress trimmed with pearls. Jason had given it to her for Christmas, and it was one of her favorites. Maybe wearing it would boost her spirits.

Within the hour, she'd sneaked out of the house without rousing Miss Fender and was ensconced in the carriage with Jobe at the whip and Chelsea at her side.

"Dem docks ain't no fittin' place for a lady," the maid grumbled again.

"Don't worry. I'll keep Jobe at my side. I've done enough foolish things to last a lifetime."

Chelsea touched her hand. "Maybe you should just let Mr. Bodine go."

"No. Gabriel's cost me more than I can bear. I won't let him get away with any more. No matter what I have to do, or where I have to go, or how far, I'll find him. And when I do,

I'll see that thieving bastard at the end of a hangman's noose." They were harsh words, but she felt them from the soul. If it hadn't been for his thievery, the events of last night would have never happened. He'd stolen her two most prized possessions, her locket, and inadvertently, her innocence. She *would* find him.

Dawn mist shrouded the waterfront, but the docks were alive with activity as captains and seamen rushed to finish loading and prepare their vessels for departure.

Jobe stopped the conveyance, then climbed down to help her out.

With the coachman at her side, she approached a seaman, who looked to be about fifty. "Sir?"

He turned, then straightened. "Yes, madam?"

"Do you know where I might find the *Seacutter*?"

His attention moved to Jobe's alert black face, then back again. "She has already sailed for London."

Panic seized her. "It couldn't have! It's not supposed to leave until dawn. And it's going to Cape Town, not London."

"It was supposed to leave then, yes. But I talked to her captain, John Grandview, last night. All his cargo was loaded and his passengers close at hand, so he left on the evening tide. He did not have call to wait. As for the ship's destination, I cannot say, but the captain would need to stop in London for supplies. Or it is possible London is the *Seacutter*'s destination, and the passengers wishing to continue on to Cape Town would board another vessel."

Her knees went weak, and Jobe braced her with a steadying arm. "You all right, missy?"

Dazed, she nodded, then clamping her teeth together, she spoke to the bearded man. Gabriel was not going to escape her. "When's the next ship leave for London?"

"That would be my ship—the *Graceful Lady*." He gestured proudly toward a three-masted British East Indiaman. "But she will not be sailing until first tide tomorrow. I am waiting for the rest of my cargo to arrive."

Seagulls soared with lazy grace overhead, but her decision was immediate. "I'd like to book passage. What's the price for one?" *And do I have enough savings left?*

Jobe drew in a sharp breath.

The captain stammered. "O-one?" He puffed out his chest. "Madam, I run a God-fearing, *honorable* ship. No unattached woman boards the *Graceful Lady* without a guardian or husband."

Of course. What had she expected, that her luck had changed and this would be simple? Then, the word *unattached* fluttered around in her head. "But I'm not unattached," she lied, hoping against hope that the enlightening statement would be enough to sway the captain. "I have a husband. He just doesn't plan to make the journey with me."

Jobe turned his back to her and began coughing, or was it choking?

The grizzled man shook his head. "I am sorry, madam. I cannot allow you on board without an escort." He touched the fold of his stocking cap. "Good day to you."

"Wait!"

The captain lifted a brow. "Yes?"

"When's the next ship, after yours, leave for London?"

"Not for a sennight."

Nichole tried not to groan. Seven whole days. Too furious to be cordial, she whirled around and climbed into the carriage. She'd find some way to get on the *Graceful Lady*.

When she reached Miss Fender's, she jumped down and slammed the carriage door so hard the vehicle shook on its hinges, then stomped inside.

"Where have you been?" her guardian's thin voice railed. "I've been looking everywhere for you. You have company."

I'd rather have the pox. Knowing it must be Mr. Alexander and a bit eager to hear news about Samantha and the boys, she checked her chignon for loose curls, then nodded. "Have you seen to refreshments?"

Miss Fender's flat chest rose in indignation. "I was in the

process of doing so. I assure you, Miss Heatherton, I know how to be a genteel hostess . . . unlike some I could name."

Nichole winced at the woman's reminder of her disappearance the last time Jason's friend came. Was that only yesterday? "I'll try to do better," she promised, then lifted the hem of her skirt and hurried toward the parlor.

Two men stood in front of the fireplace, with their backs to the room. They were examining the statue Jason had sent her.

At that instant, the one with overlong black hair turned toward her. Their eyes met.

Her whole body tensed, and for the first time in her life she wished she knew how to swoon.

This was the man from last night.

Chapter 4

Bragen was held motionless. Nichole Heatherton was without a doubt the loveliest creature he'd ever seen. She was so small, her head didn't reach his shoulder, yet every inch of her tiny body was created for a man's pleasure, from the generous swells of her breasts, to the minuscule waist he knew he could span with his hands.

Her thick curls glinted like minted gold pieces, while dense, amber lashes outlined perfect, almond-shaped eyes the color of a clear spring sky. But they were wary eyes. Anxious ones.

That bothered him.

Clay cleared his throat.

Bragen dragged his gaze away to watch his friend step toward the doll-like figure in pearls and lavender, his palm extended. "Miss Heatherton, I presume?" He lifted her slim hand to his lips. "I'm Clayton Cordell, your eternal slave."

The light banter was lost in the stillness of the room. Her

eyes fixed on his reddish hair, then grew wide. "Clay . . ." She blushed and lowered her gaze to the floor. "Er, it's a pleasure to meet you, sir."

"The pleasure is mine, without a doubt." Clay grinned, then turned toward Bragen. "And this tongue-tied fellow is my companion, Bragen Alexander, Viscount Bl—er—Blakely, a friend of your brother's."

Bragen gritted his teeth.

She watched him with wariness and seemed to hold her breath, as if waiting for him to say something.

He closed the distance between them and noticed the faint scent of lilac as he took her hand from Clay's. She was trembling. Bragen tightened his fingers over hers, then brushed his lips across the back of her hand. "If I'm as tongue-tied as my companion so readily claims, then it's solely because of your captivating presence." *Ah, hell, I hadn't meant to say that.*

She searched his eyes for a moment, looking for signs of mockery, then visibly relaxed. "If this is an example of your affliction, then I pray you never regain your tongue. My tender sensibilities couldn't withstand further flattery."

He chuckled and let her go.

"Would you care for some tea? I believe Miss Fender is seeing to it now." She motioned to a pair of gold, striped chairs flanking either side of the fireplace where a low fire burned. "Please, make yourselves comfortable." Lifting the hem of her skirt, she sat primly across from him.

She traced the edge of a pearly ruffle on the front of her gown. "How is Jason?"

"Fine. A bit browbeaten by his wife over his disagreement with you, at the moment, but otherwise well."

She smiled, and he caught a glimpse of small, straight white teeth. "I can imagine he was quite verbal about our difficulties," she conceded. "He likes to bluster a lot, and Samantha takes up for me because we're distantly related, and because we've been friends so long. Jason thinks she can sometimes be a little obstinate."

"About like a mule," Bragen mumbled.

Clay fingered the cuff of his gray frock coat. "I've never actually seen her myself, but if she's related to you, I can't help wondering if she's anywhere near as beautiful."

Nichole's hypnotic blue eyes crinkled. "Much more so, I fear."

Samantha was beautiful, Bragen acknowledged, but he preferred this woman's golden beauty to Jason's raven-haired wife.

"Ah, I see you have at last corralled Miss Heatherton," Miss Fender chimed, strolling into the parlor with a tray-bearing servant in her wake.

Both men rose out of respect.

As they greeted the matron and accepted refreshments, Nichole took the time to gather her composure. She'd been so relieved when Mr. Alexander hadn't recognized her, she'd nearly sunk to the floor. Thank heavens her disguise had worked so well—and for the inner control that had seen her through a score of unsettling situations.

Still, it was going to be awfully awkward trying to converse with the gentlemen while remembering how they looked without any clothes.

". . . don't you agree, Nichole?" Miss Fender asked.

Having no idea what the woman had said, but not wanting to admit her lack of attention, she gave a weak nod. "Yes, of course."

"You see, gentlemen. She *is* sincere in her wish to make amends for failing to be on hand to greet you yesterday."

"I am? Er, I mean, yes, of course I am."

Mr. Alexander's lips quirked.

Mr. Cordell coughed into his hand and turned away.

Nichole gave an inward groan. What had she just agreed to, for heaven's sake?

"Wonderful. Then we'll leave at once." Miss Fender rose. "Nichole, entertain the gentlemen while I freshen up and gather my shawl."

Baffled, she watched the rail-thin woman scurry from the

room. Her confused gaze drifted back to the two handsome men.

Mr. Alexander took pity on her. "I think a stroll through the French market is what we all need. In fact, it's been years since I've sampled French delicacies."

"Oh dear."

"Is something amiss?" Bragen watched her, trying to keep his grin in check. He knew she hadn't been paying attention to the conversation until Miss Fender spoke to her. Hell, his body was still warm from her sensual survey.

"I'm afraid Miss Fender has been misinformed about my culinary skills," she admitted. "You see, last year, while I was still in Williamsburg, Nick insisted I attend a French cooking school, probably in hopes of getting me out of his hair for a while. Unfortunately, Miss Fender was told about the school, but no one bothered to mention that I'd been dismissed—booted out—the day after I arrived."

Bragen bit the inside of his cheek to keep from smiling. "What happened?"

She fluttered a hand. "It was all rather silly. I'd been adding wood to the stove when Chef Duprée came rushing by with a pan of boiling sauce. In an effort to avoid a collision, I jumped out of the way and accidentally bumped into the man's worktable, sending marinated duck portions sloshing into a bowl of lemon pudding, and his antique *irreplaceable* recipe book into a vat of fermenting wine mash. By the time we fished them out, the pudding was spoiled, and the book was ruined." She shrugged. "I'm afraid I didn't get the chance to learn the art of cooking, French or otherwise."

"I see." He studied her angelic face, trying to figure a way to approach the subject of Gabe before Miss Fender returned. A possibility came to him. "I may have a solution to your dilemma."

Clay arched a brow and leaned forward. "This should be interesting."

Bragen countered his friend's mockery with a derisive smile, then spoke to Miss Heatherton. "Clay and I will cry off dinner, if you'll tell me where I can find Gabriel Bodine."

Clay's brows rose in surprise, then he tilted his head ever so slightly in a congratulatory salute.

Jason's sister stared at her hands, a golden curl teasing her smooth jaw. "Does this have something to do with Jason not approving of my hasty engagement? If so, there's no need to continue this conversation."

Bragen was startled by the determined note in her tone. It was apparent that nothing would sway her from marrying Bodine. The thought didn't set well. "It has nothing to do with your brother. Gabriel has some information I need. That's all."

She didn't look up. "And how valuable is this information?"

"Very." *My whole damned life depends on it.*

"Then, Mr. Alexander, I'll take you to him—under one condition."

The cold conviction in her voice made him uneasy. "And that is?"

"That you masquerade as my husband."

Clay sucked in a stunned breath, then the room went silent as death.

Her husband? The thought sent a stab of pain though Bragen that was so strong it closed his throat. If she'd asked him to masquerade as the pope, it would have been more acceptable. "Why?"

She tightened her fingers in the folds of her skirt. "Because my betrothed has run out on me."

Gabriel ran? Fury hit Bragen so hard it almost brought him to his feet. He held onto the arms of the chair to restrain himself. *That son of a bitch did it again.*

Clay muttered a curse.

"And in order to catch up to Gabriel," she continued, "I must board the next ship leaving for London, the *Graceful*

Lady. But when I spoke to the captain this morning, he refused me passage because of my unattached status. In a moment of desperation, I told him I was married and that my husband just didn't want to make the voyage with me. Now, in order to board, I have to produce a husband."

As much as Bragen was entertained by the idea of sharing a cabin with the bewitching woman, he didn't have time to play games. "I'm sorry, Miss Heatherton, but I can't help you."

Unruffled, she met his gaze head on. "Then, Mr. Alexander, I will simply have to find another way." She lifted a winged brow. "And you will have to learn Gabriel's destination from another source."

It was all he could do not to smirk. She didn't even know she'd given him the information, and perversely, he took great pleasure in reminding her. "You've already told me. He's on a ship to London."

She rose, not in the least concerned. "That's true. The ship is going to London . . . but Gabriel is not." She nodded at Clay, then directed her next remark to Bragen. "I'll make your excuses to Miss Fender."

Her iciness irritated the hell out of him. "Don't bother. I think I'll stay after all. The meal should prove amusing."

The corner of her lip twitched. "As you wish, but I'm afraid you're destined for disappointment." She traced the inside of her cheek with her tongue. "You see, I've come down with a blinding headache, so I won't be joining you. Or cooking." She sauntered toward the parlor door. "But if you should change your mind about my proposition, I'll be at the wharf in the morning, in time for departure—either as a stowaway, or as Lady Blakely." Her gaze slid to Clay. "Or, perhaps, Mrs. Clayton Cordell."

When the door closed behind her, Clay let out a long, awe-filled sigh. "She's magnificent."

"She's a termagant."

"But a very beautiful one." Clay wiggled his brows. "So,

which of us will give the lady our name?" He traced the arm of the chair with his finger. "And, of course, be forced to endure sharing intimate quarters with her for several weeks."

"Neither of us. Jason told me all about that little hellion. And, believe me, Clay, we don't even want to be on the same ship with her, much less in the same cabin." He stared at the statue on the mantel, reminded again of the saucy blonde who'd just left the room. "I'm afraid Miss Heatherton will have to find another way to accomplish her mission."

"What about Gabriel?"

"I'll follow him, just as I've been doing for the last three years. When we get to London, I'll find out where he went from there if that's not his destination."

"Wouldn't it be easier to take the girl up on her offer? And save time?"

"Probably. But, I'm sure she'd be more trouble than the information was worth."

"Do you truly think she'll try to sneak on board if we refuse her?"

"Perhaps. But it won't matter. You see, I intend to alert the ship's captain to the rising problem of stowaways in this area."

Darkness hadn't lifted from the waterfront when Nichole tearfully hugged Chelsea, then allowed Jobe to help her down from the carriage. It was much too early to board, but she had to get on that ship before Mr. Alexander discovered her presence and warned the captain.

As far as she could see, that was her only obstacle. She hadn't told Miss Fender about her jewels or Gabriel's thievery, so the note she left saying she and Gabriel had eloped and gone to London should keep the woman from sending someone after her.

A heaviness settled in her chest. She didn't know where she would go after she recovered her jewels, but she'd worry about that when the time came. Perhaps she'd sell a few of them and buy a small cottage somewhere and live out her days in modest, if lonely, comfort.

But first, she had to get on the ship. And she had to decide which man to claim as her husband. The choice wasn't hard to make. After losing her innocence to him, Bragen Alexander might as well be her husband.

Fully prepared to face the captain and announce herself as Lady Blakely, she directed Jobe to unload her trunk, then gathered her skirts and marched up the plank to the ship's deck.

In the gray light of dawn, seamen scurried in every direction, lugging barrels, ropes, and chains over their muscular shoulders. Salt, spring, wet hemp, and sweat drifted on the breeze that fluttered the edges of the rolled sails.

The captain stood at the head of the boarding ramp, bellowing orders, his features illuminated by several hanging lanterns. His blue coat with brass buttons was clean and pressed, his gray-black beard was well trimmed, his chin held at a lofty angle.

Nichole approached him with regal strides, her gaze cool and direct. "Well, captain. We meet again."

He glanced down at her, then stiffened with recognition. "Madam, I assure you, my rules have not changed since last eve. Unescorted women are not allowed on my ship."

"I'm well aware of that, sir. And so is my spouse. Believe me when I tell you that my husband, *the Viscount Blakely,* was infuriated that he had to take time from his business to escort me to London because of your regulations."

The captain eyed her with suspicion. "He was pleasant enough last night. He even forewarned me of the problems with stowaways in this area and suggested I stay alert."

Why, that low-life cur. She tightened her fingers on her satin reticule, wishing it was Bragen Alexander's neck. "In the presence of Mr. Cordell, I imagine he was quite pleasant. But I assure you, he was incensed. Because of you, he was forced to bring his business companion along to finalize their dealings without delay."

"But he never said anything about bringing his wife."

"Sir, my husband was so outraged over this foolishness, I'm surprised he recalled his own name, much less remembered to mention me."

"But he did not pay your fare."

"Are you certain? Have you checked with your purser?"

"Well . . ."

"I thought not." She tilted her head at a haughty angle. "Were I you, my good man, I'd make every effort to avoid Lord Blakely's presence—and temper—for the duration of this voyage." She sniffed. "Now, will you show me to my cabin? Or shall we wait and explain to my husband why I was forced to stand in this chilly, damp air . . . in my condition?"

His eyebrows flew up, and he swung toward the dock. "The viscount isn't with you?"

"He hasn't arrived yet, no. He and Mr. Cordell had to stop by the office to gather their documents." She sent him a tight smile. "Another inconvenience."

The captain grew paler.

Nichole sent a peek over her shoulder, but didn't see any sign of Mr. Alexander or his friend. Calmer now, she continued her charade by pulling her mouth down into an impatient frown.

With a slow expulsion of breath, the captain offered her his arm. "This way, madam."

"And how may I address you?" she inquired as she placed her hand on his arm.

"Captain Potter." He guided her down a short flight of stairs, then turned to lead her through a narrow, lantern-lit corridor that led into yet another hall.

"Tell me, Captain Potter, where have you placed Mr. Cordell?" She held her breath, awaiting his answer. If it was the same room, the game was up before it began. She'd have to find somewhere else to hide.

"In cabin six." He stopped in front of door number four and opened it, then entered first to light a candle.

She was both relieved and apprehensive as she stepped into the room—relieved that she'd made it, but concerned over the irony of the room number. Was fate trying to tell her something?

The scent of damp musk and lye soap wafted to her as she surveyed the sterile room that reminded her very much of the captain himself—functional. Two bunks, one on top of the other, were built into a wall in a shadowy corner, leaving extra floor space.

Three wooden chairs, a washbasin, dressing screen, and a plain pine desk sporting the candle, were all that adorned the smoothly scrubbed floors. Even the edge of the metal tub behind the screen, although scoured to a shine, was not in the least pretentious. It merely served its purpose. "Your cleanliness is to be commended," she said with sincerity, while trying to retain her haughty air. "I'm sure the viscount will be pleased with that, at least."

The captain gave the cabin a critical inspection, then nodded, his manner stilted and reserved—much like the room. "We will depart at first light. If there is anything you require, tell the cabin boy, Daniel. He should arrive soon with your trunk."

"I'm certain I have everything I need, thank you." Closing the door behind him, she sagged against it. She'd made it. Now all she had to do was get rid of her trunk and keep Mr. Alexander from finding her until they were at least a day out to sea—when it would be too late to take her back.

Bragen alighted from his carriage and scanned the dock for some sign of Nichole. When he didn't see her, he was disappointed. Had she given up on her plan to stow away? She had to have been bluffing. Besides, he'd warned Captain Potter last night to keep an eye out for "excess baggage."

"What are you grinning about?" Clay asked, motioning a young crewman to their luggage in the rear of the carriage.

"I guess the termagant has some sense after all. She's not here."

Searching the crowd of passengers and crewmen, Cordell shrugged. "Perhaps. But I wouldn't underestimate her. She seemed pretty determined to me."

"A flaw in your otherwise perfect character."

Clay laughed. "After you, O wise one."

Bragen examined the deck for signs of the girl, just in case. "I believe I'll stay topside until we sail. You never know *who* might pop up at the last minute."

Cordell's eyes danced with quiet mirth. "How about a spot near the bow? The view's always good from there."

"An excellent choice," Bragen agreed, strolling toward the front of the ship, ever watchful for Jason's hellion sister. Like Clay, Bragen, too, thought the girl had sounded too sincere to not at least make an attempt at boarding.

Still, a half-hour later, when the ship moved into the open waters, there'd been no sign of her.

Inexplicably, Bragen's disappointment resurfaced.

Chapter 5

Nichole's nerves were in tatters. The parade of footsteps in the outer companionway had sent her scurrying to her hiding place on the upper bunk too many times to count. Her chignon had been destroyed by the weight of the blanket she'd thrown over her head time and time again, and she'd torn the hem of her skirt. Well, enough was enough. She wouldn't hide anymore until she was certain someone was coming to *this* door.

She stared out the tiny porthole behind the desk. Shimmering gold danced across the ocean surface from the rising sun, flitting from one wave to the next in sparkling abandon. Gulls soared against the clear sky, their cheerful squawks welcoming the morning.

Again footsteps shuffled in the outer companionway.

Nichole swung around, poised for flight, then she caught herself up short. She would not hide until—

A heavy pounding rattled the door. "Your lordship? I brung your bags."

Panic seized her. When Mr. Alexander didn't answer, the cabin boy would surely bring the luggage inside.

Lifting her skirts, she hurried to the bunks, where she placed a foot on the bottom mattress, then hoisted herself onto the top. She snatched up the blanket and pulled it over her head, tucking her skirts beneath to make certain no part of her gown showed, then pressed herself flat against the wall.

The latch jiggled.

She held her breath, listening to the creak of hinges and heavy thuds hitting the floor. A moment later, the door closed with a quiet click.

Her breath slid out between her teeth, and she eased the blanket down to peek over the edge of the bunk.

A large brown carpetbag sat next to the door beside a trunk—her trunk.

Trying not to groan, she climbed down. She had to keep her presence undetected for at least a day, and she couldn't do that if Mr. Alexander saw her trunk.

With a tight hold on her rising fear, she eased open the door.

A young boy, who she assumed was the cabin boy, stepped out of the room next door—Mr. Cordell's room.

"Excuse me?" Nichole lowered her voice, not wanting it to carry in case Mr. Cordell was next door.

The boy turned. "Yes, mum?"

"I wonder if I might prevail upon you to take my trunk to the hold. I—um—won't have need of it for a few days."

He was surprised to see her standing in the doorway of the room he'd just left, but he didn't comment. He nodded. "Aye, mum. Right away."

Relieved, she opened the door wider, and motioned for him to come inside, but her anxious gaze never left the hall or stopped searching for signs of Mr. Alexander.

Although the boy didn't dawdle, it seemed to take forever before he left with her trunk on his shoulder and she was able to sag against the closed door. It took several seconds to settle the pounding in her chest.

The vessel shifted beneath her feet, and she felt a rocking motion as it slipped away from the dock. Her anxiety was replaced by a deep sense of relief. She'd done it. And no sign of her presence remained—except herself.

Now all she had to worry about was how unsettling it would be sleeping just above the man who'd taken her innocence. But there was no help for it. She had nowhere else to go . . . except, of course, the cargo hold, or Mr. Cordell's cabin, both of which were only slightly more disagreeable than her current location.

Too, she was taking a great chance that Mr. Alexander wouldn't prefer the top bed. But logic belied that possibility. With his immense height, it would be a difficult feat. Headroom was almost nonexistent above the upper bunk.

Her stomach gave an uncomfortable twist, reminding her that in her haste that morning, she'd forgotten to eat. Well, there wasn't anything she could do about it now. She'd have to wait until her cabin mate retired for the night, then sneak out of the room and go in search of the galley. She couldn't chance traipsing about in daylight, not until they were far enough from land. She'd just have to wait . . . and pray the captain didn't inquire as to her whereabouts.

"What do you think's wrong with Potter?" Bragen asked as he struck a flint to his cheroot, his gaze drifting over the airy gentlemen's parlor.

Clay leaned into a cushioned corner of the long sofa they shared and braced an arm across the back. "I don't know. But I swear he's doing his best to avoid us."

"You know, I get the impression he's anxious about something."

"Maybe he's just a busy man," Clay concluded graciously, even if his tone was filled with humor rather than sincerity.

"You could be right. But I still think I'll have a word—"

"I say, ol' chaps, how 'bout another go?" Their fellow passenger, Prichard Haviland, interrupted Bragen, his voice a nasal wheeze as he stopped in front of the sofa. His round stomach protruded over his stick-thin legs like a ripe melon, straining the buttons on his silver breeches and matching waistcoat. His snowy cravat wilted beneath a substantial second chin. "Hate to go back to the cabin, you know. Can't tolerate the wife. Garbles all the time. Always wanting a body to do this and that. Never satisfied. Snooty ol' sow, if I do say so. Drives a man to the cups, you know." He shook his head, causing his powdered wig to slip. A pair of sausage curls bounced against one meaty jowl, as he swung a thick, beringed hand toward a vacant table. "Well, gents?"

Bragen shared an amused look with Clay, then glanced at a younger version of Prichard waiting by one of the chairs—the man's son, Rupert—and their fourth needed for the game of whist.

Smiling, Bragen nodded. He'd had the misfortune to sit next to the man's wife, Wilhelmina Haviland, at dinner, and his sympathies were with Prichard. "Let's get supper over with first, then we'll ask Potter for a bottle of brandy and play all night if you wish." Bragen was irritated over the captain's stringent control of liquor aboard ship, and he wasn't all that enthused over another game, but what else did they have to do? Stare at the walls of an empty cabin?

Prichard's pudgy face beamed. "Jolly good, ol' chaps. Jolly good indeed!"

Nichole picked up the timepiece she'd found in Bragen's bag, then set it down. Nearly midnight! Where in heavens was he? She was starving to death, and the wretch hadn't been anywhere near his room. Not even to freshen up before supper, which she knew had passed hours ago. She had smelled the delicious aromas and listened to the parade of people pass the door.

She paced to the tiny porthole and peered out over the moonlit water, wondering if something might have happened to the men on their way to the docks. Startled by the thought, her gaze swung to the entrance.

Why, any number of things could have gone wrong. Illness, an accident, heavens, they could have even been set upon by thieves. For all she knew, they could be in Charleston—while she was hiding out like a criminal.

Well, she decided, there was only one way to find out. She started for the door.

Male laughter and thudding footsteps rumbled from the other side, then stopped—right outside the door.

"Oh, mercy." She raced to the candle and blew it out, then scrambled up onto the top bed. She flung the woolen blanket over her head and scooted to the wall.

The latch clicked.

Air lodged in her throat, and she prayed that Bragen wouldn't notice the scent of candle wax in the room.

She heard firm footsteps, then the scrape of a flint. A soft yellow glow filtered through a small tear in the blanket.

"Did you see the expression on young Haviland's face when his father wagered Wilhelmina's diamond earbobs?" Mr. Cordell remarked with a chuckle. "Ol' Prichard's got more nerve than I gave him credit for. What are you going to do with them anyway?"

Mr. Alexander's smooth voice sent shivers along her flesh. "One of them's yours. We were partners, remember?"

"I'll take the jade snuff box. Believe me, neither of us has use for one earbob."

"Done."

She heard the clink of glasses, then a sloshing sound as they were being filled. A chair creaked.

"Where'd you get the rum?" Mr. Cordell asked. "I thought Potter kept his precious liquor under lock and key."

Nichole knew. She'd seen the bottle in Mr. Alexander's bag.

"This is my private stock. Have a seat, Clay. Relax."

"I've been sitting so long, my ass is numb."

Nichole flushed with mortification.

"Speaking of asses," Mr. Alexander said, a smile evident in his warm tone. "I think I know what I'll do with the earbobs."

A rumble of laughter erupted from the other man. "I'm not about to touch that remark."

Bragen Alexander gave a returning chuckle. "I wasn't speaking literally. I was thinking of my companion at the Crimson Candle."

"Oh, *that* kind of ass."

Nichole knew she was going to die of humiliation. There was no way she'd survive this conversation.

"Yes, that kind. The girl who entertained me was exceptional. When we reach London, I think I'll post them to her as a token of my appreciation."

"Isn't that a bit extravagant?"

"Perhaps," Mr. Alexander conceded. He was quiet for several seconds, then spoke in a low tone. "But believe me, Clay. She was worth it."

Shame almost choked Nichole. How could the man speak of such intimacies with another? He was a cur, and a rakehell, and a—a— She couldn't think of enough vile names to call him.

"My companion wasn't bad, either," Mr. Cordell returned, "but I damned sure don't plan to send her my snuff box."

Both men laughed, then Nichole heard the sound of a glass being set down. "Well, ol' chum," Mr. Cordell said. "I'm off to bed. It's been a long day."

Finally.

After the door closed, she listened to Mr. Alexander undress. Heat rushed to her cheeks at the knowledge of their close proximity, and she wished she were anywhere else but here—and that she didn't have the sudden urge to peek over the edge of the cover.

An eternity later, she heard a creaking noise and assumed

he'd at last gone to bed. Then she noticed light penetrated the hole in the blanket. Of all the rotten luck. He'd forgotten to extinguish the candle.

Inching her head out from beneath the cover, she raised up. Her breath caught. He hadn't forgotten. He was at the desk, leaning back in the chair, a drink in one hand and a volume of Keats in the other. *And he's wearing next to nothing.*

Her first impulse was to bury her head again, but her second—the desire to study him at her leisure in full light—won out.

Candlelight wavered over his raven-black hair, some silken strands slipping free of the leather strip that had held them secure at the nape of his neck. One long, glistening lock brushed his angular cheek and lightly shadowed jaw. He brushed it away and bent his head toward the book in his lap. A wave fell onto his high forehead. It was a smooth forehead, an intelligent one, marred only by the thickness of his straight eyebrows.

The gaping front of his wine-colored dressing robe revealed the smooth width of his chest and sprinkling of dark hairs that trailed down over his tight stomach.

Her own fluttered, and she redirected her gaze.

His legs were crossed and lazily propped on the desk, their long, muscular length clearly visible where the robe parted.

A reticent memory of how those powerful limbs had felt against her own rose to taunt her. She closed her eyes and eased her head down. She didn't want to think about that night, not ever again.

For a long time she lay there, listening to pages turn, to his occasional chuckle or mumbled curse, then the sounds drifted into the distance, grew softer. . . .

A groan snatched her from sleep.

Her eyes flew open, but met only darkness and a tiny beam of moonlight seeping through a porthole. It took her brain a minute to associate the small window with her whereabouts. When she did, she felt like groaning herself.

"Nooo."

A tortured cry came out of the dark.

"Damn you, *no!*" he cried, his anguished plea rising from the cot below.

She slumped in relief. He was asleep—and dreaming. Calmer now, she listened.

"Not you . . . ah, God, Meela, not you."

She'd never heard such heart-wrenching torment in a man's voice. He sounded so hurt, so devastated. The urge to go to him and soothe his pain away was almost more than she could stand.

She didn't dare, of course. But, she couldn't help wondering what this Meela had done to cause Mr. Alexander such suffering.

The answer wasn't to come this night, though. The ropes on the lower cot scraped, as if he'd turned over, then all went silent except for the deep, even rhythm of his breathing. It was a warm sound, but a strangely sad one.

She gave thought to going to look for food, but the pangs had subsided, and she was too exhausted to attempt it. Tomorrow would be soon enough.

"Have you ever had the feeling that someone was watching you when you were alone?" Bragen asked Clay as they strolled into the empty galley the next morning.

"Not that I can recall. Why? Have you?"

Bragen nodded. "Ever since last night."

"Did you search the room?"

"What's to search? You can see every inch of it. But I did check the clothes locker this morning."

Clay straddled a wooden bench edging the table, then swung his other leg over. "Interesting."

"I wish I could brush it off, but the sensation was too real." Bragen filled each of their cups from a china tea service centered on the table.

"Perhaps it's—"

A scuffle sounded from the doorway.

"Prichard Haviland!" Wilhelmina Haviland's high-pitched voice ricocheted off the walls. "If you have gambled away the earbobs Mother gave me, I'll have you nailed to a cross and burned."

"Here, now," Prichard retaliated. "Didn't even see the bloody things, you know. Probably fake anyway, knowin' that old hen."

An outraged gasp reverberated from Wilhelmina's enormous chest. She whirled around to face her husband, her towering hairpiece swaying on her head with the movement. "How dare you speak so of my dear, departed Mama!"

"Now, Mother," Rupert cooed from behind. "Father was only jesting." He sent an anxious look over the woman's broad shoulder to Bragen. "And I'm certain you'll find the earbobs somewhere in your trunks."

"Humph," she snorted, then swung her large girth toward the table. She stopped, then had the grace to look chagrined when she saw they were not alone. Regaining herself, she lifted her layers of chins. "Good morning, gentlemen. I trust the voyage has agreed with you thus far."

Bragen and Clay rose and greeted the Havilands.

Another couple and three more gentlemen joined them, and Bragen tried his best to recall their names but couldn't. The captain's seat, he noted, was vacant.

Clay gestured toward the empty chair at the head of the bench. "What do you think?"

"I think he's avoiding us, and I intend to find out why." He started to rise, but at that instant, Captain Potter walked through the door.

The seaman surveyed the room, then his gaze came to rest on Bragen. He stiffened and started to turn, but stopped; then he lifted his bearded jaw and took a deep breath. Ramrod straight, he marched to his chair and sat down. He glowered at Bragen. "Good morning." He made it sound like an accusation.

"Yes, it is," Bragen returned, wondering what had the man so edgy.

The captain waited.

So did Bragen.

The older man's beard twitched, then he curled his fist on the scarred tabletop. "I refuse to apologize for inconveniencing you. And I refuse to skitter around my own ship trying to avoid you. If you are going to loose your temper on me, then do it now and be done with it."

Bragen didn't know what he'd expected the man to say, but it hadn't been that. He sent Clay a baffled look.

Clay shrugged, his expression stating that he had no idea what the man was talking about.

"I—" Bragen cleared his throat. "I beg your pardon?"

Instead of answering directly, Potter addressed everyone present. "When I took to the sea, I did so with my good parents' blessing—and with God's guidance. And I swore to both I would run a decent, God-fearing ship. I do not allow my men—or my guests—to imbibe too much or use foul language, nor do I allow women aboard without escort." He sent Bragen a damning glare. "If those rules cause problems for you, I am sorry. But I will not change them."

Feeling as if everyone was waiting for him to respond, Bragen shifted. What brought all this on? "Captain Potter, I find no fault with your regulations. In fact, I find them admirable."

The older man's beard drooped with relief. "Then you have no objection? You are not angry?"

"Of course not."

"Wonderful!" He lifted a hand and snapped his fingers toward a boy waiting by the door. "Daniel. Have cook serve breakfast."

"What the hell was that about?" Clay asked while he stirred sugar into his tea.

"Damned if I know."

A pair of aproned crewmen came hurrying into the room, bearing trays piled with plates of scones, ham, berries, melons, and poached eggs.

Intermittent comments about the delicious meal scattered around the table as they ate, but Bragen's thoughts were on the captain's odd declaration. It was as if Potter's statement had been directed at him. Puzzled, he bit into a piece of melon.

"So, tell me, Lord Blakely, how does your wife fare?"

Bragen's head shot up. "What?"

"I was wondering how she fared. I did not see her at dinner yesterday, nor supper last night. In fact, I have not seen her since I led her to your cabin yesterday morn. I pray she is—"

Bragen choked on the melon.

Clay burst out laughing.

Chapter 6

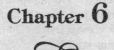

"I'm going to turn her over my knee," Bragen vowed to Clay as he paced the otherwise vacant gentlemen's parlor.

"I'm doing my best not to say I told you so."

"Damn her! We're too far out to sea to send her back." Bragen kicked a chair in angry frustration. "I have no choice but to move in with you, Clay."

"No."

"What?"

"As much as I enjoy your companionship, I enjoy my privacy more. Besides, everyone on board thinks you're married, so there's no compromise involved. And just think of how miserable you could make the little imp by staying."

Bragen rubbed the nape of his neck. The woman had certainly muddled his already chaotic life. "I wonder how long she plans to remain hidden."

"My guess is, she'll reveal herself today. As you said, we're far enough out to sea that there's no threat of her being returned to Charleston."

"Of course that's what she's been waiting for. I should have guessed, and I should have listened to Jason. He warned me about her. I should have taken her threat to stow away seriously and had Potter search the whole miserable ship before we departed." He jammed his hands into his pockets, his anger rising to a slow simmer. "Someone needs to teach that sneaky vixen a lesson."

"So, what's stopping you?"

Bragen stared at him in surprise, then curved his mouth into a slow, wicked smile. "Absolutely nothing." Straightening to his full height, Bragen gestured toward the door. "Come on, Clay. I have an urgent desire to return to my cabin."

Carrying a full tray of food left over from breakfast, Bragen opened the door to his room.

They both scanned the cabin, and fixed on a smooth white arm visible on the top bunk. She was still asleep.

Bragen set the tray down, then silently walked past his friend—and slammed the door. He turned just in time to see the arm disappear.

Unable to hide a smile, Bragen snagged a chair and sat down. "I don't know about you, Clay, but I'm starved."

Clay tilted his head, but didn't respond.

"Mmm. Doesn't this ham smell good? And I can't wait to taste that hickory-cured sugar."

They both heard a small, muffled groan.

"I just hope there's enough of it to last until we reach London. We're already a day behind, and the current doesn't look like it's going to let up. Hell, we can still see the shoreline," he fabricated.

Dead silence.

Clay rolled his eyes, and his mouth split into a huge grin as he caught onto Bragen's game.

"I guess we won't make it much farther today, either," Bragen continued. "I heard one of the crewmen say a coming storm was responsible for the current's landward pull. The way things are going, we might remain in this spot for several days. Are you sure you won't have one of these berries? They're delicious."

"No, thank you," his friend managed through a laughter-tightened throat.

Bragen sucked noisily on a gooseberry. "Did you hear what happened this morning?"

His companion sprawled out in the chair, blinking rapidly, trying to hold back tears of mirth. "No."

"Captain Potter found a stowaway down in the hold."

"Really?"

"The first mate found a woman—a runaway bond-servant—hiding behind a row of water barrels."

"What did they do?"

Bragen clasped his hands behind his head, his smile evil. "They gave her a turn at the lash, then *since we were so close to shore,* they threw her overboard."

A stifled gasp whispered from the top bunk.

Clay gnawed his lip to keep from laughing. "I've never heard of setting the lash to a woman before. I'm surprised she survived."

"No one knows if she did. She passed out after the first blow and hadn't regained consciousness when they dumped her over the side."

"That's barbaric."

"I know. And at first, I thought it might have been Jason's sister, but I'm sure glad it wasn't. She was so small and delicate, she couldn't have withstood the cat-o'-nine-tails."

"Don't the authorities object to such cruel treatment?"

"No. They endorse it. Stowaways are a real problem in this area. In fact, it was the constable who suggested harsher punishment."

They both watched the upper bunk, but saw no movement.

"Surely they could have found a gentler way to deal with women."

"They did. Women are given only five lashes. Men get twenty." He saw the woolen blanket give a slight quiver, and the game didn't seem so funny anymore. She was frightened. Damn it, now why did she have to make him feel like a cad? He came to his feet. "Come on, Clay. Let's see if we can find the Havilands for a game."

Clay rose. "What about your meal?"

"I've lost my appetite." He strode toward the door.

"What about the tray? Aren't you going to set it in the hall for the cabin boy to pick up?"

Bragen knew Clay wanted him to admit he was leaving the food for the girl, but he'd be damned if he would. "No. I'll nibble on it later."

Clay arched a brow but didn't speak when he strode out with Bragen.

As they walked down the corridor, Clay asked, "How long are you going to make her think we're just off the Carolina shore?"

"Long enough to teach her some discipline."

"And after that? What are you going to do with her?"

"Damned if I know. But I do know the minute we reach London, I'm putting her on the first ship returning to the colonies. But until her game is brought out into the open, and except for giving her a few minutes to take care of nature's business, I plan to spend a lot of time in my cabin."

The instant the door closed, Nichole gave into a hysterical sob. *What have I gotten myself into?* Just the thought of being beaten was bad enough, but the idea of being thrown overboard was horrifying. She couldn't swim.

She curled into a ball on her side, and pulled the blanket closer. The temperature in the cabin had grown considerably cooler. It must be because of that storm Mr. Alexander spoke about.

Her stomach gave a loud growl.

She raised up and peered over the edge of the bunk, wondering if she should chance eating a small portion of the food left on the tray.

Her hunger overcoming all else, she climbed down and made for the desk. Careful not to disturb the looks of the tray, she ate small bits from each entree and cleaned up every crumb she dropped from a scone.

When she was at last appeased, she went in search of the chamber pot.

After taking care of the most urgent needs of her body, she concentrated on the not-so-urgent ones. She found Bragen's brush in his portmanteau and dragged it through her tangled hair. Unable to restyle the wayward locks into a chignon by herself, she left the mass falling clear to her waist, then moved to the water pitcher.

After washing, she emptied the bowl and the chamber pot out the porthole.

If only she could go to the hold for some clean clothes. But did she dare risk it? She thought of the fate of the other stowaway and shivered.

A man's footsteps carried down the companionway, and she recognized the firm, long-legged gait of Mr. Alexander.

"My word," she hissed, scrambling up into the bed and under the woolen blanket. Another chill swept her as he opened the door, and she wondered if she was coming down with something—or was just fearful of getting caught.

Bragen walked deeper into the room, trying not to smile. The plates on the tray weren't empty, but their contents had been substantially reduced.

His gaze slid to the chamber pot under the bed. It was shoved farther back toward the wall. And the bowl by the water pitcher was wet. She'd accomplished a lot in the time he'd allotted her.

Placing the tray outside the door, he picked up his book from the desk, settled into the chair, and began to read. It was going to be a long day.

The entire morning passed without a peep from the upper

bunk, and Bragen congratulated her on her stamina. He'd have been climbing the walls by now.

A knock on the door startled him.

"I brought a deck of cards," Clay announced, striding into the room. He nodded toward the bed, then sent Bragen a questioning look.

Bragen shook his head in answer to the silent query, then he cleared off the desk. "Why don't we make the game interesting with a wager?"

"How much?"

"Not for money. I had something else in mind."

"What's that?"

Bragen winked. "Confidences."

"I'm not sure I understand," Clay said, his tone carrying a ring of truth.

"It's simple. Whoever loses tells one of their innermost secrets—or confidences, if you will."

"Intriguing."

Bragen scowled at him. The man didn't have to look so damned pleased.

With that silly grin in place, Clay gestured to the cards. "Shall I deal?"

"By all means."

Clay trounced Bragen—because Bragen *let* him—then smirked. "All right, Lord—er—Blakely, let's hear it."

Bragen's eyes crinkled with humor. "Let me think. . . . Ah, yes, I have it." He fingered one of the cards as he stared up at the bed, knowing his next statement would shock the brat's tender sensibilities. "One of my greatest 'confidences' is what happened the night I had my first woman."

They both heard the soft whoosh of an indrawn breath.

It was all Bragen could do not to burst out laughing. "I"—he cleared his throat—"was eleven—"

"Eleven," Clay sputtered, but regained himself. "Eleven, you say?"

All right, so he was stretching his age a bit. He'd actually been fifteen. "I believe so. I could have been ten, but I think

I was eleven. Anyway, my parents had gone to a ball, and I was left with my governess, the widow Montclair, a pretty woman, thirty and five. Even though I was taller than she was, she always made a show of tucking me in at night, and giving me a kiss on the forehead. That night, she discovered a better place to kiss. Several, in fact."

"You don't say," Clay said with unfeigned interest. "Then what happened?"

Not certain he should go further with this, he peered at the bunk. "Do you want all the sordid details, or just the outcome?" Bragen didn't want to subject the girl to too much, any more than Clay did, but Bragen also knew Clay was dying to hear the details . . . because they were true. Bragen had mentioned his relationship with the woman one night when he'd been well into his cups.

"Only the outcome," Clay responded with the slightest hint of disappointment.

"Then let's just say that she enlightened me to many, many aspects of the human body, and when she left, I slept like the dead—in total, blissful exhaustion. She taught me things that went beyond the imagination. I fell head over heels in love with her, and after that night, we had clandestine meetings on several occasions—and continued to do so until I was shipped off to school in Italy."

"What ever happened to her?"

"While I was away, she discovered my brother. My father discovered *them* and dismissed her." He pushed the cards toward Clay. "Another game?"

"No. I think one of those a day is enough."

"Then how about dinner?" Bragen suggested. "I'll find Daniel and have him bring our trays to the cabin."

"I'll go, then afterward, we can see who's about in the parlor."

When they'd finished eating, both leaving a healthy portion untouched that neither mentioned, they headed for the gentlemen's parlor.

"Good afternoon," Captain Potter greeted them on deck.

"I am glad to see you both recovered from that upset at breakfast." He directed his gaze at Bragen. "For a few minutes there, I feared you would expire from strangulation."

Clay's lips twitched.

Bragen scowled. "As you can see, I managed to survive."

"Yes, thankfully." The man glanced around. "Is your wife not about?"

"No. She—er—she's never fared well in sea travel."

The captain appeared genuinely sorry. "The poor lady. I imagine it is even more difficult in her present condition."

Bragen froze.

Clay swore under his breath.

"Condition?" Bragen managed between stiff lips.

Unaware of the tension he'd caused, the seaman continued. "Mmm, yes. I know from experience, women are awfully fragile and unpredictable when with child. Why, my missus—"

"Excuse me," Bragen snapped, then whirled around and walked off, his blood rolling to a boil. So that's what this urgent trip was all about!

Clay caught up to him. "Maybe she told him that as part of her charade."

"And maybe she didn't. After all, she and Gabriel *were* to be married soon. Hell, no wonder she's so desperate to find him."

"What are you going to do?"

"Turn her over to the captain. I'll be damned if I'll share a cabin with Gabriel's whore." Bragen knew he wasn't being fair or rational, but he just couldn't help it.

Nichole shoved the platter away, her hunger at last appeased. The hours between breakfast and dinner had seemed like days.

She eyed the plates, and decided to keep some of the food for tomorrow. At least she could nibble between meals and silence her stomach. She couldn't count the times over the last two days she'd feared her belly's noise would give her away.

Removing a neck scarf from Bragen's bag, she wrapped a fluffy biscuit, two juicy pieces of fried chicken, and a few berries. Satisfied, she placed the bundle into her skirt pocket.

She thought about taking a book to bed, but wedged into a far corner like the bunk was, very little light reached it, and she wouldn't be able to see well enough to read.

"I can't take any more of this," she muttered to the empty room. "If I don't get out of here, and do *something,* I know I'll go mad." Even the walls of the cabin had shrunk. *And if I wear this wretched dress one more day, the blasted thing will probably start growing on me.*

Since she'd already washed, she decided to chance a trip to the hold for a change of clothes at least. Not wasting a second of her freedom, she grabbed a lighted candle, then checked the hall. Finding it empty, she raced along the corridor. At the end, where the steps led above, she turned right and descended to the bowels of the ship.

The hold smelled of tobacco, indigo, wet wood, damp wool, mold, and animal waste. Trunks and crates of squawking chickens were piled in every available space from floor to ceiling. Rats skittered across aging planks, disappearing behind the stacks of water barrels and cargo.

She shuddered and picked her way toward a towering mound of trunks, praying hers was within easy reach.

A low, dangerous growl reverberated through the dim chamber, and she froze in place. Warily, she moved the candle from side to side, trying to find the source of the sound.

Light wavered over a stout, steel animal cage.

"Oh!"

Inside the cage, a scarred black dog was crouched down on its front legs. The animal's ears were lowered, its fangs bared, and its growl had turned into a ferocious snarl.

Chills swept over her flesh, and she backed up another pace, the candle wavering with her nervous tremors.

Fortunately the distance she placed between herself and the beast must have pleased it, because the dog didn't make any more threatening sounds. Instead, it sat down on its hindquarters and watched her.

He must be protecting something, she decided, something close to his cage. Lifting the candle, she peered through the darkness. He was surrounded by trunks, and the cage itself sat on top of one.

Spying her own, she gave a small groan. It wasn't the one under him but it was much too close to the animal, whose head could fit through the bars.

"We've got a problem, boy. You don't want me over there, but I need to get to my clothes."

The dog cocked its head as if listening.

"If I give you some food, will you let me fetch a clean gown?" Withdrawing the bundle from her pocket, she broke off half of the large biscuit, then eased forward a step and held out her hand.

The animal made a half growling, half whining sound.

The poor thing was starved. Disgust at the dog's owner rose. Were the scars attributable to him as well? No wonder the poor thing snarled. It was undoubtedly terrified of being beaten.

More confident now, yet wary, she set the candle on a barrel and edged nearer the cage, then tossed the biscuit inside.

The starving animal attacked it with relish.

Filled with pity, she pitched the other tidbits into the cage. She'd get more after breakfast tomorrow. The animal needed food now.

She hurried over to her trunk and pulled out the first gown she could reach, then retreated.

Keeping her eyes on the dog, she tore off her soiled dress and dragged on the other one, a frothy peach silk creation that laced up the front. But the neckline was low, and since she wore no petticoats, the skirt clung to her hips with brazen accuracy.

Wishing she could wear at least her undergarments without their bulk revealing her hiding place, but knowing she couldn't, she picked up her discarded gown and spread it over a crate near the candle and sat down.

She just wasn't ready to return to that miserable cabin.

"You know, dog, if my locket wasn't so important to me, I wouldn't be here. I would've let Gabriel go and never given him a second thought."

The animal, having finished its meal, scrunched down on its belly, its head resting on its paws, its black eyes fixed on her.

Well, at least he wasn't snarling. "Anyway, we were going to be married before the end of the month, but he stole my jewels and ran away."

The dog yawned.

She sent him a reproachful glare. "The least you could do is pretend you're interested. After all, you're the first one I've talked to in days."

He licked his nose.

"Now, where was I? Oh, yes. Gabriel. Did you know he was the only man in Charleston who would court me? It's true."

The dog growled and perked its ears.

She smiled. "No. Don't blame him. It's my reputation, you see. I tend to get into a lot of scrapes. And I guess I'm not a very appealing person. People always have trouble believing me—and loving me. Even the parents who raised me."

She knew it was silly talking to an animal, but it felt good. She'd never been able to talk to anyone about her difficulties. Not even her brothers—and Samantha had been too busy with the twins. "My mother, my *real* one, might have loved me. I don't know. She died the night I was born. And my father wasn't even around. That wasn't his fault, though. He didn't know about me, and he died the same night. And my uncle, Harvey Langford, who most certainly didn't want me, ordered the midwife to get rid of me. I think she was supposed to drown me or something, but she gave me to the Heathertons instead."

Crossing her legs at the ankles, she stared at the toes of her slippers. "They may have tried to love me. I don't know. But I don't think they were ever meant to have children. I felt like an unwanted ornament, an object Mother Heatherton used to make herself equal to the other women in her circle. She was the only one who hadn't had a child, you see, and belonging was very important to her. Father Heatherton never cared about me one way or another."

She twirled her finger in the material of her skirt. "I didn't see them very often, and the governess I had, Miss Mundy, was a tyrant who made it a daily ritual to rap my knuckles or switch my bottom. By the time I reached adolescence, she'd graduated to using her fists and a strap."

Leaning against the barrel, she folded her hands over her middle. "To be fair, I guess I deserved most of the punishment. You see, there's a flaw in my make-up—I can't stay out of trouble, no matter how hard I try. When my brothers found me, and I went to live in Williamsburg, I'd hoped things would change and I'd find someone who truly cared. For a while, I thought I'd succeeded, but I made Nick angry one day, and he sent me away. Jason, my other brother, did, too. You see my quandary? Gabriel was my last hope, and he left me. Now I have no one."

"Consider yourself fortunate."

Nichole gasped and whipped around to see Bragen Alexander's tall, powerful frame braced against the edge of the door, one foot insolently crossed over the other. Any excuse she might have wanted to make for her presence aboard ship died on her lips when she saw his fierce scowl.

He wasn't going to listen to a word she had to say. *He was going to murder her.*

Chapter 7

Bragen, I can explain!" Nichole blurted.

"I'm sure you can." His gaze moved over her. The first time he'd seen her, he thought she was beautiful. But the adjective fell short when it came to describing the striking figure that stood before him at that moment. She was so much more.

A wealth of golden curls rippled over one shoulder like a waterfall of shimmering topaz gems, covering a firm breast and teasing the front of her waist. Her small hands were clutched nervously in the folds of the frothy pink skirt that clung to her slender curves. Those hypnotic eyes were round and clouded with fear, her soft lips parted in a soundless gasp. She was frightened . . . and exquisite.

Although he'd been angry when he left Clay, after listening to part of her conversation with the dog, most of the steam had been taken out of him. Bodine had promised her marriage, gotten her pregnant, then ran out on her. Her presence aboard the ship wasn't a prank. She was desperate. Her child's name and her own reputation depended on her locating and marrying that son of a bitch.

The thought of this lovely woman married to Gabe made the sarcasm in his voice more pronounced. "I wonder if our chance meeting can be attributed to destiny?"

"Or a curse," she mumbled, her hands trembling, but she held her head at a defiant angle.

He admired her spirit, and in a gesture meant to reassure, and perhaps offer friendship, he held out his palm. "Won't you join me in my cabin? I believe we have some matters to discuss."

"Yes, I imagine we do." Her back straight, she ignored his outstretched hand and walked to the door.

Her slight grated, but he understood her reasoning. She was holding onto her control by a thread. She undoubtedly thought he would turn her over to the captain and have her put to the lash. Visions of her slender, bare back marred by bloody gashes knotted his stomach, and he crossed to a partially open trunk he assumed was hers and pulled out a petticoat she would need.

When they reached the cabin, he motioned her to a chair. "Would you care for some refreshment before you explain your presence on this ship?"

"No." She anxiously eyed her lacy petticoat draped over his arm and blushed. "What are you doing with that?"

"I'm sure when we leave the cabin you don't want to be seen in polite company without one. Now, you were about to explain."

"There is no explanation. I told you I would stow away if necessary, and I did."

"Gabriel's not worth it," he stated quietly, tossing the undergarment over the top of the dressing screen.

"Oh, but he is."

"Nichole . . . May I call you that?" He smiled with wry amusement. "After all, we have been sharing the same cabin for some time now."

Her startled gaze flew to his, then she looked away, her cheeks flushed. "Call me whatever you like."

The retort might have infuriated him at one time, but after hearing her discussion with the hound and knowing of her "problem," instead of anger, he felt pleased by her control.

Still, maybe he could reach her with reason. "Nichole, even if you find Gabriel, there's no guarantee he'll marry you. Chasing after him isn't the answer. You'll gain nothing."

"Yes I will."

"I honestly understand your feelings, but this whole trip is pointless."

She cocked her head to the side, clearly stating that he didn't understand anything. But she didn't argue.

"Chasing him isn't the answer," Bragen reiterated. "I doubt even knowing about the babe you carry would make a difference to him. There's nothing you can do to make him give you something he doesn't want to give, whether it's his name or protection."

She was startled by his knowledge, confused, then oddly thoughtful. "You wouldn't want to make a wager on that, would you?"

"What do you mean?"

"Just what I said." She wet her lips and chose her words carefully. "I'll wager anything you name that when I find Gabriel, he'll give me exactly what I want."

It was a tempting bet, but he refused to take advantage of her. "You're that sure?"

"Oh yes," she said emphatically.

Bragen examined the obstinate tilt of her chin, the determined blaze in her eyes, but there was a wariness there, too, an uncertainty he knew she was trying to hide. "Give it up, angel. Go back home."

"I have no home—and I won't have until after I've found Gabriel."

"Jesus, how you must love that bastard."

A delicate brow lifted, but she didn't comment. She didn't have to. Her feelings were transparent by the way her eyes darkened at the mere mention of him.

Bragen studied her, then came to a decision that both annoyed and intrigued him. If he returned her to Charleston, she'd just find another way to reach Gabe. Too, he wasn't wholly certain that Gabe didn't want her. There was a strong possibility he left only to avoid Bragen. Every time Bragen got close to confronting Bodine, he'd vanish. Apparently that was the case this time, too, and it made Nichole's situation Bragen's fault. It was only fair for him to try to right the wrong, no matter how much it galled him. Besides, she had something Bragen wanted.

"All right, Nichole. Since you won't listen to reason, I concede. I'll see that you find your precious Gabriel—and after I've talked to him, I'm sure he'll explain why he left so hastily." *If the bastard is still breathing.* "Too, our alliance has its benefits. You have what I want—Gabe's true destination—and I have what you want—a way to remain aboard this ship."

"You mean you aren't going to—"

"Tell the captain? No. I'll let him continue to believe you're my wife."

Tears of gratitude sparkled in her eyes. "You're doing this because of my . . . er . . . feelings for Gabriel, aren't you?"

No! he wanted to shout. *I'm doing it because I'm to blame for him running out on you.* Bragen didn't meet her eyes. "Something like that."

"You won't be sorry. I promise."

"Oh, but I will," he vowed. Hell, he already was. Six weeks in the same room with a beautiful woman who was in love with another man would be pure torture, and more so because that man was Gabriel Bodine.

She peered around the cabin. "What are we to do about the sleeping arrangements?"

"Since you've chosen the top bunk, I don't see any reason to change, unless, of course, you prefer the botton.."

"No. No, the top's fine."

"Then it's settled. Now, what would you like first? A bath or a stroll?" He was sure each held an appeal after all this time.

"Both."

He chuckled. "All right. We'll walk to the galley and ask cook to heat the water, then take a turn around the deck. By the time we get back, your bath should be ready."

She watched him with wary eyes. "Why are you being so nice to me?"

He drew her to her feet, then urged her toward the dressing screen and her petticoat. "Let's just say I feel like we're kindred spirits." *After all, we both want Bodine badly.* He couldn't tell her that, though. In an effort to protect her lover, she might try to warn him.

After they saw the cook and cabin boy about retrieving her trunk, Bragen escorted her along the starboard side of the ship. Several unlit lanterns hung from a rope stretched down the entire length.

"You know, the only time I was ever on a ship, my chaperone made me stay below most of the time. I guess she feared I'd get into trouble, and the easiest way to prevent mishap was to keep me under foot. I never walked on the deck at night. This is rather an exciting adventure for me."

Compassion moved through him, and he wondered why Nichole's family was bent on destroying her spirit. He sensed a kindness about her that didn't correspond with the thoughtless deeds her brother had spoken about. Something was wrong, but whether on Jason's side or Nichole's, Bragen didn't know.

Taking her arm, he pointed out various crewmen and explained their tasks. "That man with the ledger, standing by the water barrel, is the yeoman. He's tabulating the daily use of water. He keeps all the records concerning cargo, water, supplies, and food stores." He gestured to another man. "The fellow at the wheel is the first mate. He's the second in command, and his job is to carry out the captain's instructions, assist when necessary, or even take over the command should the captain become ill or die."

"What's that one doing?" she asked with interest.

"Repairing sails. Strong ocean winds make his job a full-time chore."

They rounded the bow of the ship and started down the leeward side. The lanterns swung as a gust of wind caught the ocean spray. Nichole gasped, then smiled and raised her face. "That breeze feels wonderful."

He stared down at her smooth ivory features framed by a cascade of mint-gold curls that shimmered like new coins beneath the wavering light. Her silvery blue eyes were bright with pleasure behind long, amber lashes, her lips parted and full as she reverently breathed in the moist sea air.

She's Gabe's betrothed, he reminded himself. He turned away and spotted Clay talking to Captain Potter. Touching her as little as possible, he ushered her in that direction and greeted the men. "Good evening."

Clay started in surprise. His gaze darted from Nichole to Bragen.

Ignoring the silent query, Bragen addressed the seaman. "Captain. I believe you've met my wife, Lady Blakely." Bragen swiftly suppressed the pleasure he felt at claiming her as his.

Clay lifted a brow.

Potter gushed. "Oh, yes. Of course." He nodded respectfully. "Lord Blakely told me how hard it is for you to endure sea travel, your ladyship. But I trust you are feeling better."

Understanding brightened her eyes and they crinkled with silent laughter. "Oh, yes. Now that my darling husband has coerced me from the confines of the cabin, I feel much, much better. Thank you." She grinned. "It's amazing what fresh air will do for a body. Why, I feel as if I haven't been ill at all."

"It hasn't marred your lovely appearance any." Cordell found his tongue.

"It has not, for certain," the captain agreed. "And I do hope you will join us for supper."

She licked her lips. "I'm looking forward to it."

Bragen applauded her performance. She was a delight. No wonder she'd gotten by the captain the morning they boarded. She had more courage than most men, and her poise and control—not to mention her acting abilities—were amazing.

Suddenly, his mischievous side wanted to test her limits, to see if he couldn't give her composure a jolt. He slipped an arm around her waist and pulled her close to his side. He nuzzled her ear, but spoke loud enough for the others to hear. "I think your bath water's ready by now, sweetheart. Come on, I'll help you out of that gown."

Clay sputtered and coughed into his hand.

Nichole stiffened for just an instant, then relaxed and turned, completely at ease. But her eyes sparkled with retribution. She traced her teeth with her tongue. "No thank you, *darling.*" She paused, then placed a hand on her stomach. "I haven't forgotten what happened the last time you . . . helped."

The captain sucked in a breath.

A flush crept up Bragen's neck. Furious, and not quite certain why, he gripped her arm. "Whether I *help* or not, you don't want the water to get cold." He nodded to the others. "If you'll excuse us, gentlemen." He marched her toward the cabin, vowing he wouldn't underestimate the vixen again. She'd bested him twice. That was enough.

"You're hurting my arm."

"Be thankful I don't break it."

"You started it," she huffed as he dragged her into the room and slammed the door.

"And I'll finish it." He swung her around. His gaze landing on the tantalizing mounds of flesh rising above her bodice. Desire speared through him, and it angered him even more. With punishing intent, he jerked her against his chest and crushed her lips with his own. He tried to tell himself the kiss was to punish her—*not* because it was something he'd wanted to do since he set eyes on her.

She squirmed, trying to drag her mouth away.

Her resistance angered him even more. He tightened his grip and rasped against her mouth, "If I'm going to be accused of fathering your bastard child, then I'm at least entitled to some of the pleasure."

She sucked in a breath. "Stop. Oh, Bragen, please stop!"

The genuine fear in her voice brought him to his senses, and he shoved her from him so fast she almost fell. "Don't play me for a fool again," he warned. He knew he was being irrational, but too many thoughts were running through his head: catching Bodine, his own unexpected desire for Nichole, the lost hours from a night so long ago—ones he desperately needed to remember—and the fact that Nichole was the *second* woman to carry Gabe's child.

Overwhelmed by anger and frustration, Bragen spun on his heels and stormed out of the room.

Nichole was a mass of nerves by the time he returned to escort her to dinner. In the hours since his departure, she had tried to understand his volatile behavior, but only managed to become distracted with thoughts of how good she'd felt pressed against his hard length. The man had taken her innocence, for heaven's sake. She shouldn't be having *feelings* for him. But she couldn't stop the sensations, nor could she understand what had set him off earlier. It was apparent, though, that he hadn't liked being accused of a deed he hadn't done. She'd remember that in the future.

Contemplating his actions as they walked to the galley, she stopped just outside the door. "Bragen. There's something you need to know."

His hand stilled on the latch, but he didn't look at her.

"I'm not with child. When I tried to get on the ship in Charleston, the captain was uncertain about letting me come aboard before you arrived. I invented my 'condition' so I could escape to the cabin before you exposed my ruse. Then on deck this morning, I knew you were trying to taunt me, so I retaliated. I didn't mean to anger you. Truly, I didn't."

Disbelief flickered in his eyes. "Your 'condition' doesn't matter to me one way or the other—as long as I'm not involved."

Nichole wanted to kick him. He thought she was chasing Gabriel because she was pregnant with her betrothed's child. Nothing she could say would convince him otherwise. Why did everyone doubt the truth of her words? She was sick to death of distrust, and it angered her to know that he was like all the rest—her parents, her brothers, Miss Fender, and, of course, her hateful relatives, the Wentworths.

"But," he continued, "I suppose I should apologize for my temper. It's always given me a devil of a time."

It just doesn't matter, she thought tiredly. Nothing did anymore—nothing but retrieving her jewels. "Shall we go in? I'm famished."

He opened the door and swung his hand toward the galley. "After you."

Four men and two couples sat with Captain Potter and Mr. Cordell, and they all looked up as she approached the long bench table.

The men rose. "Lady Blakely," the captain said, "may I introduce your shipmates?" He gestured to a heavy-set older couple on his right. "This is Mr. and Mrs. Prichard Haviland, and that fellow standing next to Prichard is their son, Master Rupert.

"Beside Mr. Cordell, whom you, of course, know, is Mr. McNall, a tobacco grower from the Carolinas."

The attractive man dipped his blond head, his hazel eyes alight with appreciation.

She became wary when she recalled seeing him somewhere before, only she couldn't remember where.

"The two next to Master Rupert are George and Joshua Pitt, owners of the Pitt Brothers' Exhibition, a renowned animal show, I believe."

The two well-dressed gentlemen, one with a narrow, pointed face, and the other whose large teeth protruded, greeted her with indifference. She thought of the dog in the cargo hold. Were these the owners? She hoped not. There was a cruel air about them.

"And the pair next to Mr. McNall," the captain continued, "are Mr. Wilson, a London practitioner, and his lovely daughter, Abigail."

"How do you do," Nichole acknowledged the entire group as she took her place between Bragen and Mr. Cordell, but her gaze kept returning to Miss Wilson. She looked tall, though it was hard to tell with her seated, and she was fashionably slender, with bright gold eyes and red hair. But there was a sophistication about her that was almost haughty, and the pale green gown she wore was a Paris creation of which Nichole had seen sketches at the dressmaker's. The extreme cost of the gown made her wonder just how much London physicians earned.

Her thoughts were distracted when dinner arrived. The meal of smoked salmon, potatoes, honeyed carrots, and cheese passed in near silence, which she didn't mind in the least since she was so intent on her food.

When they were almost finished, Mr. McNall interrupted the quiet. "You know, Lady Blakely, all during dinner I've been trying to place you. You look familiar. Are you from the Carolinas?"

Nichole's gaze flew to his, and in that instant, she knew where she'd seen him before. He was an aquaintance of Gabriel's *and* he'd been with the constable that day she'd knocked him off the boardwalk.

Bragen sensed her distress and reached for her hand. "I'm sure you're mistaken, Mr. McNall. We're not from your area at all. We merely boarded in Charleston on our journey from Charlotte to London."

The captain was puzzled, and she knew he was remembering her statement about Bragen stopping by his office on his way to the docks.

Bragen, too, saw the seaman's response and gave her hand a reassuring squeeze, but he didn't take his eyes off McNall.

Mr. McNall gave her a close inspection, much too close for her comfort, then drew his brows into a thoughtful frown. "Is it possible our paths have crossed somewhere else, then?"

"No!" Nichole groaned inwardly at the outburst. What was the matter with her?

Bragen tightened his fingers around hers in warning.

Mr. McNall shrugged. "I assure you, Lady Blakely, I never forget a face. But no matter. Before the voyage ends, I'm certain I'll recall where we met."

That was what Nichole feared. Once he placed her, he'd know she wasn't married to anyone . . . unless she could convince him she and Bragen had eloped.

And that wasn't going to be easy.

Chapter 8

"If Mr. McNall remembers where he knows me from—*and who I am*—what will Captain Potter do?" Nichole asked Bragen as they entered the cabin.

"Who is McNall?"

"An acquaintance of Gabriel's. They were together the evening before Gabriel disappeared, playing cards at the club. I remember Gabriel telling me about the game the next morning and reminding me to send Ian McNall an invitation to the wedding. He'll know you and I aren't married."

"We'll tell Potter we obtained a special license and married the night before we boarded. I'm a peer of the realm. He won't call me a liar."

"But what if, out of a sense of duty and *honor*, he demands proof? Then what?"

Bragen wished he could ease her distress, but he honestly didn't know what the righteous captain would do. "Let's pray he doesn't. Since we've been sharing the same quarters,

I imagine he'll conclude that I've compromised you beyond redemption. Too, the earlier mention of your 'condition' isn't going to help matters."

She dropped down into a chair, and he tried not to smile at the way her lower lip thrust into a pout. "Just when I thought I could walk freely about, now I'm going to have to remain out of sight as much as possible . . . and avoid that wretched tobacco grower at all cost."

"How long ago were you introduced?"

"We were never introduced. Because of my penchant for mishaps, Gabriel didn't like to take me out in public, but I did see Mr. McNall once." She told him about that day on the boardwalk several weeks ago.

"Anyway," she continued, "Mr. McNall most assuredly heard the constable curse my name. Everyone for miles did. Once Mr. McNall recalls the incident, he'll know who I am . . . and that I was betrothed to Gabriel the day before we left."

Just the mention of Bodine's name caused Bragen's stomach to churn. "Maybe you should come down with another bout of seasickness."

"There must be another way. I've been confined to this wretched cabin so long I'm starting to think of it as part of my wardrobe."

"I can be of assistance there."

"How?"

"McNall spends a lot of time in the gentlemen's parlor. Myself or even Clay could keep him entertained for a few hours each day, allowing you some freedom."

Her silvery eyes flashed with gratitude. "That's very kind of you. But how am I to know when he's engaged?"

Bragen sat down at the desk. "One of us would get word to you, then escort you on your outings."

She folded her hands in her lap. "You really are a nice man."

She wouldn't say that, Bragen thought, if she could read his mind, which, at the moment, was fantasizing about what lay beneath her clothing. "I'm not as nice as you think," he admitted, coming to his feet. "Listen, why don't we take a stroll around deck. I saw McNall heading below when we left the galley. He's probably in the parlor now."

"Far be it from me to miss a single opportunity for freedom." She rose and extended her arm. "Ready, milord?"

Bragen had second thoughts about touching her, but he didn't want to appear discourteous. He opened the door, then with extreme care, he laced her delicate arm through his. Her lilac scent enveloped him, and he tried not to let the arousing fragrance affect him.

Fortunately, the brisk sea air helped. But his gaze lingered on her flawless features, illuminated by lantern light.

As she stared out across the moonlit water, a breeze feathered a long strand of hair across the front of her throat, draping the slender column like a gold necklace. Her breasts strained against the soft fabric of her peach gown when she leaned over to watch the waves slap at the hull. The action pushed the smooth mounds upward, and for one heart-stopping instant, he feared she might overflow the bodice. He gripped the rail to steady himself.

"I love the ocean," she said in a soft tone. "It's so serene. So humbling."

She could have been describing herself. Her gentleness and beauty were enough to bring a man to his knees. "But it's also dangerous." *Just like she is to my piece of mind.* "And that peaceful beauty can change, without warning, into a deadly storm.

"Have you ever been in a storm at sea?" she asked.

"Several."

Nichole traced a finger along the polished wood. "I haven't. The voyage from London to the colonies was the only other time I'd been on a ship, and we had fair weather the entire journey."

"You were fortunate." He studied her delicate profile.

"How did you attend a French cooking school if not by ship?"

Her cheek dimpled. "Chef Duprée journeyed to Canada with other French settlers and opened his school in Nova Scotia."

"That must have been a long carriage ride from Vir—"

"Well, good day to you again," a man's voice rang out from behind them.

Nichole stiffened.

Bragen tried not to swear as he forced himself to turn. "Mr. McNall."

The planter's gaze was fixed on Nichole's slender back. "I went to the parlor for a game after supper, but no one was about." He eyed Bragen. "I was in hopes you'd like to try your hand . . . and give me a chance to recoup some of my losses."

Anything to get him away from Nichole. "With pleasure. I'll meet you there in ten minutes."

Nichole still didn't turn. Instead, she leaned farther over the rail, pretending extreme interest in something below.

"Ten minutes, then." With a curt dip of his head, the planter ambled off.

Nichole's shoulders sagged when McNall left, and Bragen's resentment grew. "If that peacock gives you any trouble," he only half teased, "I'll toss him overboard."

She grinned. "I've considered that, myself."

She probably had, too. "Come on," he urged. "I'll take you back to the cabin."

"Must I? It's so lovely out here. Couldn't I stay while you keep Mr. McNall entertained?"

"Nichole, it isn't a good idea for you to wander around alone, especially at night. Let me see if I can find Clay."

"I'm not a complete dolt, Bragen. For heaven's sake, Potter's crewmen are perfect gentlemen, and I certainly can't get lost without falling overboard, which I assure you I have no intention of doing. I'll be just fine. Now run along before McNall returns, and stop coddling me as if I were a child. In case you haven't noticed, I'm a woman fully grown."

Oh, he'd noticed, all right. "As you wish," he conceded. "But avoid Potter's 'perfect gentlemen' crew as much as possible. Just to humor me, hmmm?"

Her beautiful face brightened with eagerness. "Yes, yes, of course. I'll stay out of everyone's way."

He fought the urge to touch her dimpled cheek. "I'll try to keep McNall below for a couple hours." He hesitated, unsure about leaving her, then, damning the protective feelings he didn't understand, he turned and walked away.

Nichole watched his long-legged stride as he crossed the deck. Memories of the night at the brothel warmed her insides. But the warmth turned to a chill when she thought of the possible consequences. What if her lie to the captain about being with child wasn't a lie at all? What kind of future would she have? What would her brothers say? Dear God, how could she ever face them? Refusing to think along those perilous lines, and praying with all her might that she'd come through this unscathed, she headed for the galley in search of scraps for the dog.

With a platter the cook had given her, and a flickering candle, she descended the dark staircase and set the candleholder down several feet from the cage. "Good evening. I've brought you something."

The black dog sprang to its feet and snarled, his wary eyes alert.

"Ah, I see you're still anxious. Very well, I'll keep my distance." She placed the plate on the floor, then piece by piece, tossed the tidbits to him.

The hungry animal devoured them without pause.

"You poor thing. Your owner should be horsewhipped for the way he's treating you."

The dog licked his mouth, then sat down, watching her, his floppy ears perked forward in attention, exposing jagged, scar-covered nicks and tears on the furry outer edges.

Nichole knelt. "You know, since I don't know your name, maybe I should give you one of my own. What do you think?"

The dog merely stared.

"I'll take your silence for a yes." She scrutinized him for several seconds. "How does the name George strike you? He was a mighty king."

The animal curled its lip.

"No good, huh? All right, what about Hercules? He was very strong and the son of a powerful Greek god."

The dog yawned.

Nichole rolled her eyes. "How about someone smart, like Socrates?"

The critter shook its head, flapping its ears back and forth.

"Well, for heaven's sake. What name *do* you want?"

He just blinked his black eyes and watched her.

His inky coat might have been shiny at one time, but it was now dull and matted, marred by numerous old wounds. He must have been in a score of fights, and she could tell, more often than not, he'd been the victor. Her eyes widened. That's it!

She eased closer to the cage. "How does the name Victor suit you?"

Those jagged ears shot upward, and his tail gave one long swipe to the side.

"Thank providence. One that suits you." She smiled. "All right. Victor it is, and, in case you've forgotten, my name is Nichole, and I'd like very much to be your friend. But I'm afraid I can't do that if you keep snarling at me all the time." She inched forward. "And since I've taken it upon myself to bring you treats, I'd prefer you didn't bite me should I get too close to your pen. Is that understood?"

The dog lifted its head, sniffing her scent.

"I hope you're doing that so you'll recognize me the next time I come in—not taking note for a future meal."

She wormed her way nearer.

The animal retreated as far as the metal bars would allow.

"All right, Victor. I won't pressure you any more. But I'll see you again tomorrow."

Pleased with her progress, however slight, she gathered the candle and plate, then went topside, reminding herself to save some of her breakfast for Victor. After setting the objects on a crate, she scanned the moonlit deck. Moist salt air feathered her cheek as she spied the cabin boy, Daniel, sitting beneath a swaying lantern, braiding rope.

"Evenin', milady," the boy greeted as she approached. "Did ye need somethin'?"

"Just conversation." Victor hadn't been much company.

Daniel nodded and motioned to a stack of rope. "Have a seat. I can't stop workin', but I can talk while I'm at it."

She sat on the cushiony pile and straightened her skirt around her. "How long have you been a crewman?"

"Since I was ten. My sire was Potter's first mate, and after me mum died, Papa brung me aboard."

Nichole scanned the deck. "Which one is your father?"

"None. He was washed overboard in a storm near Madagascar last year." He could have been commenting on the weather for all the emotion that showed on his youthful face. Except for the eyes. She could see the pain there.

"Do you think there's a chance he survived?"

Daniel's gaze fluttered away and returned to his work. "No, mum. I don't."

The finality in his voice tore at her heart, and her own problems seemed insignificant. "How old are you?"

"Twelve."

So young to be orphaned. "Do you like the sea?"

He glanced up, his eyes bright blue behind a rim of dark lashes. "I love the sea. And someday, I'm gonna buy me own ship, twice as big as this one, and black as night."

She smiled at his enthusiasm. "Why black?"

" 'Cause it's gonna be a pirate ship. And it's gonna have a black flag with a white skull and crossed bones."

She swallowed to keep from chuckling. "I see. And when do you plan to do this?"

"Soon as I'm grown. Probably when I'm fourteen, or so."
He sent her a sideways glance. "Say, ye wanna learn how to
knot a rope?"

It was an offer of friendship she couldn't refuse. "I'd like
that very much."

"I'm afraid you don't have time, Lady *Blakely.*"

Nichole's nerves jumped. McNall!

"You'll have to excuse us, boy," the planter decreed. "I
need a private word with her ladyship." He extended his
broad, calloused hand toward Nichole.

Something in his tone frightened her, and she didn't dare
refuse. Avoiding his hand, she shakily came to her feet.
"Whatever do we have to talk about, sir?"

His hazel eyes squinted with mockery. "Oh, several
things. Constables, boardwalks, recent marriages . . .
charades." He offered his arm. "Besides, I'd rather talk to a
beautiful woman than the captain any day."

The veiled threat couldn't have been clearer were it
surrounded by glass. He'd recognized her, and he was going
to use the knowledge to his benefit. Nichole pulled in a
calming breath, reminding herself of the many scrapes she'd
gotten out of with level-headed thinking. "How can I resist
such . . . flattery?"

His hand clamped onto hers, then he led her over to the
opposite railing.

The instant McNall stopped, she pulled free of his hold
and folded her arms. "I thought you were playing cards."

"I was. But when it dawned on me who you were, I left the
game on the pretext of retrieving more cash from my cabin.
With your watchdog, Alexander, about, I knew it was the
only way I'd be able to see you alone . . . Miss Heatherton."

"So you know who I am."

His chuckle was brittle. "Did you truly think I'd forget?
Not hardly." He slanted her a sly look. "And since your
betrothed and I were together less than forty-eight hours
before this ship departed, and he spoke at length about your
coming nuptials, I know for a fact that you're not married to

87

anyone. The question is, though, what should I do with the information?"

She knew what she'd like for him to do with it. "You're mistaken, sir. Gabriel and I dissolved our engagement some time ago, leaving me free to marry Bragen by special license."

"I'd have to see proof of that—as would the oh-so-righteous captain, I'm sure."

"What do you want from me?"

"Just a little cooperation for my silence."

"Meaning?"

"A favor now and then."

That's what she feared. "What kind of favor?"

He trailed his fingers up her spine. "I'll let you know. Later." He leaned so close his lips almost touched her ear. "Meet me in the cargo hold after your lover falls asleep. Say midnight?" His thick fingers caressed her waist. "We'll discuss it then."

Fear skipped through her. "But—"

He dug his fingertips into her side and squeezed, sending her a silent, painful warning. "Just be there."

Chapter 9

"You're going to do *what?*"

"I said, I've got to meet Mr. McNall in the cargo hold at midnight."

"Absolutely not."

Nichole arched a calm brow. "It's not your decision to make."

Bragen paced the cabin, which grew smaller by the second. "I think you've been confined too long," he concluded, irritation evident in his voice. "You've lost your senses. You must have to even consider that I'd allow that whoreson to blackmail you."

Sitting at the desk, she swirled her fingers on the smooth surface. "What's the alternative? Public flogging?"

He tried not to wince. "Nichole, Captain Potter wouldn't flog us. I'm certain he wouldn't be happy with our situation, but—"

"What about the stowaway he set to the lash and threw overboard?"

Did she have to bring that up? Bragen couldn't meet her eyes. "There was no stowaway. I'm afraid that was a tale I fabricated when I learned of your presence in my cabin. I wanted to teach you a lesson."

Her pretty blue eyes narrowed. "I see. So am I also to assume there was no landward pull to the tide?"

He did wince this time. "Right."

"And the coming storm?"

"That's always a possibility, but if there's one threatening, I'm not aware of it."

"I see." She braced her elbows on the desk. "Well. Since there's no longer a threat of the cat-o'-nine-tails, there's no reason to worry over the captain's punishment, now is there?"

Bragen wished that was all there was to it. "I'm afraid there is. Captain Potter could very well demand we correct our situation."

She cocked her head to one side, and he knew she didn't understand what he meant.

"What could he possibly do?"

"Force us to wed."

"He wouldn't."

"Yes, he would." And that was something Bragen would avoid at all cost.

"How could he do that?" Nichole demanded. "Hold a pistol to our heads, and shoot us if we refused?"

He admired her spirit, but it was wholly useless in this instance. "No. But there are other means to gain our acquiescence, least of which might include imprisonment and starvation."

She gave his words careful thought, then rose. "In that case, we have no choice. I must keep my appointment with Mr. McNall." She glanced at the clock. "And it's nearly midnight now."

Bragen shoved his hands into his pockets. "I'll go."

"No. You'd just get us into more trouble. Besides. Mr.

McNall probably doesn't expect me to tell you about his treachery. And I think you're worrying overmuch. Why don't we wait until I know what he wants before we become concerned?"

Bragen was afraid he already knew. He was across the cabin in a heartbeat, gripping her arms. "You are not leaving this room."

She shoved out of his hold, her stance rigid, defiant, her eyes alight with battle. "Lord Blakely, need I remind you that you have no control over my actions whatsoever? I will do as I please. Now, kindly step aside and allow me to pass."

He preferred to shake her senseless. But she spoke the truth. He didn't have the right to tell her what to do. But full surrender was out of the question. "All right, *Miss Heatherton,* you've got ten minutes." There wasn't much McNall could do in that space of time. "If you're not back by then, I'm coming after you." He cocked an eyebrow. "And if that happens, the captain will learn of our situation before the stroke of one, because I will do my best to break every tooth in Ian McNall's mouth."

She eyed him with wariness, then decided that was a compromise she could live with. She nodded. "Ten minutes it is."

Soft lantern light glowed from the stairs as Nichole approached the cargo hold. Tightening her fingers in the folds of her skirt, she took a fortifying breath, then lifted the hem and descended the steps.

Mr. McNall looked up from his watch, then slipped it into his fob pocket. "Right on time, I see." He stood on the opposite side of the room from the dog's cage.

Victor gave a welcoming bark.

The tobacco grower sent the animal a sharp glare, then motioned her forward. "Come. Sit with me." He gestured to an upended crate holding the candle. Next to it stood a pair of smaller boxes to be used as chairs.

"Just tell me what you want."

Gloating, he sidled up in front of her. "I merely wish to enjoy your company for a while."

"I don't have time. Bragen was tossing in his sleep when I left, and I must return at once." She hoped that sounded believable.

"Then we'd better get to the business at hand." McNall smiled and lifted a finger to trace the low neckline of her bodice.

She gasped in outrage, and sprang back, a hand splayed over her bosom. "How dare you!"

Victor growled.

McNall glowered at the dog, then back to her. "I dare anything I like. But, for now, I'll adhere to your wishes. As you will to mine." He straightened the cuff of his ruffled sleeve. "I find I'm in need of a stout drink, but our dear captain has locked the brandy away in his quarters. I want you to get a bottle for me and bring it to my cabin, number eleven, before dawn."

His demand set her teeth on edge, but she was relieved that the petition was minor enough. "How do you expect me to get into the captain's quarters?"

He looked satanic and foreboding in the dim light. "That, my dear, I will leave up to you. Who knows, you might use that tempting body to gain your purpose. But, no matter. I want the bottle before dawn. And I don't have to remind you of the consequences should you fail, now do I?"

Nichole tried to control her jumping nerves. *All right,* she told herself, *his request isn't that bad.* She just hoped that pilfering a bottle of liquor from the captain's store would pacify McNall for the rest of the journey. "Very well, sir. You'll have your brandy, but I warn you, this is the end of it."

"And just how do you plan to stop it, missy? By confessing to the captain?" He gave her a nasty smile. "Go ahead."

Furious, she whirled around and stormed up the steps.

That self-serving, blackmailing, low-life *cur!* She would put an end to his debauchery if she had to shove him overboard.

Just as she reached her cabin, the door jerked open, and she met Bragen's hostile brown gaze. "It's about damned time," he hissed, hauling her inside. He slammed the door and inspected her for injury . . . or did he? He appeared awfully interested in the condition of her clothing, almost as if he were looking for suspicious wrinkles or tears. Apparently satisfied, he met her eyes. "All right, out with it. What does McNall want?"

Somehow, Bragen was more frightening that the planter. "Brandy."

That took some of the steam out of him. "What?"

She rubbed her upper arms and sat down. "He wants me to steal a bottle of brandy from Captain Potter's room and bring it to his cabin—by dawn."

Bragen was thoughtful for several seconds. "That's not as bad as the demand I feared he would make."

Deciding not to mention McNall's advances, she agreed. "I was surprised, too."

"But I don't see how it can be accomplished," Bragen continued, "especially in so short a time."

"If we worked together, it might be possible. You could divert the captain while I snatched the bottle."

"Have you lost your mind? Do you have any idea what would happen to you if you were caught? Christ, woman. A beating would be welcome compared to being locked in the brig for a month."

Nichole crossed her arms over her stomach. "What choice do we have? I'll tell you what . . . none at all. And if you won't help me, then I'll do it alone."

He ground his teeth together. "No. Damn it, Nicole. Listen to me. If you give in to McNall's demands, we're just going to get in deeper. He'll expect more and more. And eventually, he's going to want something you can't or won't give. I think we should go to the captain and explain the situation. He's a reasonable fellow. I'm sure he'll understand."

She shook her head. She'd been in enough scrapes to know differently. "It won't happen. Nothing concerning me ever works out for the better. He'd most likely keelhaul us. I'm not exaggerating when I tell you I'm well and truly cursed. So, either you help me . . . or I'll attempt the deed alone."

"I won't help you," he countered with dogged determination. "I'll get Clay, and *we'll* get the blasted brandy."

She softened at his backhanded way of protecting her. "I don't want him—or anyone else—involved in this." It was the truth. And, if it came to getting caught, she'd explain to the captain that Bragen had no part in any of it. The punishment would rest solely on her head. "I've got to go." She rose and headed for the door.

"I should have listened to my common sense when it warned me not to get involved with you. And I know I'm going to live to regret this." He caught her arm. "Come on, minx. I'll get the brandy while you divert the captain."

Warmed, and concerned, she followed him out the door.

The ship was dark and silent as they made their way to the other side of the vessel and tiptoed down the short corridor toward the captain's quarters. She hadn't yet figured what ruse she would use to get the man out of his room, but she knew she'd come up with something when the time was at hand. Thinking on her feet had always been one of her best assets.

Bragen stopped in front of a cabin. "This is it," he whispered, then touched her arm. "You get him out of the cabin, but, if anything goes wrong, I want you to swear to me that you'll tell the captain you knew nothing about my intentions. Is that clear?"

"Stop talking, or we will get caught," she returned, not giving him her oath. Bragen was not going to take the blame.

Looking around for a place to hide his big frame, she almost groaned aloud. There wasn't a single nook or cranny to stuff him in. She'd have to get the captain completely out of the hall. "Hide at the top of the stairs behind one of the barrels. I'll lure the captain up to the deck."

Bragen hesitated, then gave her arm a light squeeze before sprinting toward the steps.

As soon as he was out of sight, she raised her hand and knocked.

A grumbling sound came from inside, then the door swung open to reveal the sleepy-eyed captain dressed in a long gown and nightcap. He blinked and stared. "What is it?"

"Captain, come quick," she blurted. "I—I think one of your men fell overboard."

"*What?* Who?"

"Hurry!" She backed toward the stairs with feigned urgency.

Snagging a robe from a peg near the door, he flung it around his thick shoulders and raced past her, the tail of his nightcap bouncing against the back of his head.

When they reached the deck, she pointed to a spot by the rail. "There. He was standing right there." Out of the corner of her eye, she saw Bragen dart below. Satisfied, she continued to ramble. "I had come up for a breath of air because I couldn't sleep, and I saw him there. Then I heard a noise and turned away. When I looked back, he was gone. He must have fallen over."

The captain swung his head from side to side, scanning the few crewmen on deck. "What did he look like?"

"I don't know," she wailed. Warming to the game, she rushed to the rail and leaned over. "He was medium build, with shaggy hair and loose clothing." The description, she knew, applied to just about every sailor on board.

"Blast it, woman. What color was his hair? Did he have a mustache? Beard? What?"

She faced him, just in time to see Bragen emerge from the steps, a conspicuous bulge beneath his shirt. He nodded, then raced toward the stairs that led to their cabin. Shifting her gaze, she focused on a crewman standing by a coil of rope, scratching his head and watching the captain. "Him!" she cried. "He was the one I saw. Oh, thank heavens." She rushed to the befuddled sailor. "I was so worried. I thought you'd fallen overboard."

"But—"

She hugged him. "You're safe. Sweet providence, you're safe."

His face showed his embarrassment. "Why, thank ye, lady. But—"

"Oh, I'm so ashamed," she moaned. "I've gotten the poor captain out of bed, and caused a horrible ruckus." She whirled back to Potter. "Oh, sir, can you ever forgive me?"

"There, there, madam, it was an honest mistake. But in the future—"

She placed a hand to her head. "Oh, dear, I'm feeling quite dizzy. All this excitement has been such a strain." She swayed.

Concerned, the captain placed an arm around her shoulder. "There, there, lass. Let me take you below."

Leaning into him, she allowed him to return her to the cabin. When the door closed behind her, Nichole sagged against it, then winked at Bragen. "We did it."

His eyes were filled with admiration . . . and warmth. Her pulse quickened. Every time he looked at her like that, she was reminded of the night they . . .

"You are truly amazing," he said with gentle praise, then caught himself. "But it's not quite over. There's still the matter of delivering the brandy."

"That won't be difficult. Mr. McNall's room is only around the next corner." She held out her hand for the bottle.

"Three minutes," Bragen warned as he opened his shirt and withdrew the brandy. "Not a second more."

"What is this love affair you have with your timepiece?"

"Just call it one of my idiosyncrasies." Even though the

words were said in light banter, she sensed he was worried about her being alone with McNall.

She gave him a reassuring smile, hiding her own misgivings as she took the liquor from him. "I'll be back before you know I've gone."

He didn't look convinced. In fact, he was wavering with indecision again.

She had to get out of there before he changed his mind and demanded they forget the whole thing and go to the captain.

McNall opened the door on the first rap. His eyes went to the liquor in her hand, then to her bodice, and at last, her face. "Remarkable." He pulled her inside and closed the door.

She thrust the brandy at him. "Take it and be happy, because it's the last you'll get from me." She turned to leave.

"Not so fast, woman." He caught her arm. "There's another topic we need to discuss."

Her blood iced over as she swung back around. "We have nothing further to say to each other."

"Oh, but we do." His eyes fixed on her breasts. "There's the matter of what I have planned for tomorrow night."

Chapter 10

W-what about tomorrow night?" Nichole demanded.

McNall took a swig from the bottle and set it on the desk, then watched her for several long seconds, his blond head bent, catching waxy glints from the candle, and his hazel eyes bright with malice. "Oh, I think you have a pretty good idea." Straightening, he walked toward her.

She backed up, right into the door.

He stepped closer and placed his palms on either side of her head. With a boldness that frightened her, he thrust his lower body against hers, pinning her hips to the wood. "You know what I want."

Nervous tremors ran along her flesh, and she wedged one of her hands between his body and hers, pushing at his chest. "Move."

He dipped his head and nibbled her neck. "Not just yet."

Revulsion gripped her, then anger. She lifted her free hand and grabbed his hair, jerking his head up. "I said, move." She twisted brutally.

"Ow!" He lunged backward, and wrenched free of her hold. "You damned viper. I wasn't going to rape you, for God's sake."

"You could have fooled me."

He scowled at her. "With that attitude, missy, my meeting with the captain is growing closer by the minute." He plopped down in a chair. "And, if you want to ensure that doesn't happen, you'll do what I tell you."

For just a heartbeat, she felt like telling him to go straight to the devil. She'd rather suffer the captain's wrath than put up with *his* lecherous advances. But she wasn't the only one to consider. Bragen would suffer, too. "And just what might that be?"

He eyed her grumpily. "I've lost a great deal of money to your lover over the last couple days, and I wish to recoup it."

"You want me to steal money from Bragen?"

"Nothing so dastardly. I just want you to keep him from coming to the gentlemen's parlor tomorrow night. With him out of the way, I should be able to win most of it back."

Nichole felt a measure of relief. "How can I keep him in the cabin?"

McNall's eyes traveled over her curves. "I'm sure you'll think of a way."

The lewd innuendo made her sick, and she refused to give it credit by responding. Instead, she lifted her chin and left the room.

There would be no problem at all, she decided as she walked back to her quarters, if she could tell Bragen. But she couldn't. If he knew McNall continued to blackmail her, Bragen would end McNall's game by going to Potter—or by beating the planter into a lump. And, since McNall's petty requests weren't *that* damaging, she saw no need of either. Besides, she now knew she could handle McNall. His immediate compliance when she put off his advances bore out the truth of that, something she hoped wasn't just because she'd caught him off guard. She would keep the man satisfied by playing this last game, but she wouldn't tell Bragen. One frustrating male was enough to contend with.

"What the hell went on in there?" Bragen demanded.

Startled, Nichole jerked her head up to see him coming down the hall toward her. "Nothing, I—"

"You've been gone *five* minutes."

He'd really been counting? "Nothing happened. Mr. McNall was just pleased to get the brandy, and k-kept talking. I couldn't be rude and walk out in the middle of a conversation."

Bragen's jaw hardened, then he spun around and stalked back down the hall. "Of course not. You wouldn't want to offend his tender sensibilities. That would be just *too* discourteous."

Nichole sighed. Yes, one male was definitely enough to contend with.

Inside their quarters, Bragen started pulling the ties free on his shirt.

"What are you doing?"

He sent her a startled look, then glanced down at his hands as if he hadn't realized his actions. He shrugged, then turned away and continued working on the laces. "I'm getting undressed. It's late, and I want to go to bed." He whipped the buckskin shirt off over his head.

Nichole watched in frozen fascination. Candlelight danced over every muscled inch of his back. Memories of how that flesh had felt beneath her hands flashed through her. Warmth rushed through her, and she stared at the way his smooth skin rippled while he unbuttoned his breeches.

Unbuttoned his breeches. She whirled around, and her gaze swept to the dressing screen that was secured to the floor near the bunks. She darted behind it. "W-when you're finished," she called out, "extinguish the light, will you?"

"Isn't it a bit late for modesty? You've seen me undress."

"I have not. I—I kept my head covered."

A low chuckle was followed by the thud of boots and a

soft whoosh of cloth; then the room plunged into darkness. The bed ropes gave a soft creak before all went silent. "You can come out now, angel. I'm in bed . . . and decently covered."

Decent? Ha. The man didn't know the meaning of the word.

Bragen didn't sleep well. Memories of that night three years ago had plagued his dreams. Images he didn't understand wavered in and out of his mind—a flash of silver, a strangled cry, and rivers of blood. But none of them made sense. Then visions of Nichole had drifted into his dreams.

Gazing at her now as she slept with such peace, he relaxed in the desk chair and studied her. She was so beautiful it hurt to look at her, and he hadn't realized what transparent nightclothes she wore, or how full her breasts were, or how the firm mounds tipped upward beneath the thin material to proudly flaunt pouting, rose-colored nipples. The fabric stretched across those tight peaks, emphasizing the sensual contours.

The cover had been shoved down to the top of her thighs, leaving most of her exposed, her smooth, peach-colored skin visible beneath the sheer fabric. With reluctant interest, he inspected the narrow curve of her waist, her flat stomach, and the gentle flare of her hips. They were the perfect size for a man to settle between with arousing pleasure.

He shifted to ease his growing discomfort and concentrated on her sleeping face, surrounded by a wealth of shiny gold curls. It was an exquisite face with its porcelain texture, small, uptilted nose, and kissable mouth. It was an impish face, a heart-stopping one.

Closing his eyes, he rested his head on the chair back. All these lustful musings were for naught. He wouldn't follow through on his urges. If her tale of not being pregnant were true, she might very well be a virgin, a fact that didn't endear her to him. Too, however temporarily, she was engaged to Gabriel Bodine.

A sadness filled him when he remembered how he and Gabe had been inseparable in their youth in London. They'd grown up only a mile apart, on bordering estates in a lush green valley. They attended the same schools, fished in the same pond, then explored the American colonies together, tried their hand at trapping . . . and lived with the Shawnee.

He missed the friendship they'd once shared, the witty conversations, the laughter and warmth. But it had all ended with a vicious argument, the day Bragen had asked Meela to marry him.

Gabe's words haunted him, and he swallowed to ease the pain tightening his chest. *Alexander, please. Don't do this. Don't let her come between us.*

"Bragen? Is something wrong?" Nichole's soft voice floated across the cabin.

His eyes snapped open. "What?" She'd been so quiet he hadn't heard her get out of bed. Or, more likely, he'd been too deep into his thoughts to notice.

Standing behind the wobbly dressing screen, Nichole watched him. "I asked if something was wrong with you," she repeated.

He shoved his fingers through his hair, gathering himself. "No." He rose. "I'm going topside. Get dressed, then I'll escort you to breakfast."

She watched him close the door, then unlaced her nightgown and slipped it off. Over and over again, she pictured how he'd looked when she'd first awakened. He'd been sitting in the chair with his head back and eyes closed.

The soft leather of his buckskins had stretched across his broad shoulders, the unlaced front swooping down to midchest, exposing his strong throat and a forest of silky black hairs. He was magnificent—yet his torment had wiped all thoughts from her head but one. He was in pain, terrible, terrible pain.

She draped her nightdress over the top of the screen, then

located a sea-green taffeta gown and slipped it on. She didn't want to cause him any more distress by keeping him waiting.

With rapid strokes, she brushed the tangles from her hair, then attempted to coil it into a bun. The wayward strands refused to be confined, so she left it down.

Setting the brush aside, she retrieved a light shawl from the trunk, then made for the door. Her hand stilled on the latch, and a feeling of doom settled over her. How on earth was she going to keep Bragen away from the gaming room that evening? After all the trouble she'd caused him last night with McNall, Bragen probably desired her company today about as much as he did the pox.

Shaking her head, she opened the door. It wasn't going to be easy . . . but she'd think of something.

Chapter 11

Nichole kept to herself most of the day, trying again and again to figure a way to keep Bragen in their cabin that evening. But by the time supper was over and they'd returned to their quarters, she still hadn't come up with a plan.

He sat at the desk, writing figures on a piece of parchment. His dark head was bent forward and candlelight danced over his shiny hair, offering brief glimpses of blue-black highlights. He'd just changed into the first silk shirt she'd seen him wear, and she knew he'd soon leave for the gentlemen's parlor.

Unless she stopped him.

She darted a peek around the room for some means of assistance or, at the very least, to spark an idea. Her attention came to rest on the lower bunk. His bed. She stared at it for several seconds. A notion took hold, and a feeling of anticipation replaced her dread.

There might be a way to detain him, after all.

Rising, she walked to the center of the cabin and lifted her hand as if to speak. "Bragen, I—" She swayed, then closed her eyes and folded to the floor.

"Nichole!" he bellowed. Then his hand was on her throat. "What's wrong? Can you hear me?" He smoothed the hair from her brow. "Damn it, wake up. What's the matter?"

The distress in his voice almost caused her to end the game, but she kept her eyes closed.

He slid an arm behind her shoulders and another under her knees, then carried her to the bed. He disappeared for a few seconds.

Then, out of nowhere, a cold rag draped her forehead. It was so unexpected, she gasped.

"Nichole? Are you all right?"

She gave a low, drawn-out moan, and opened her eyes. She blinked several times, giving credibility to her supposedly dazed state. "Bragen?" She glanced in bewilderment at the bed she was lying on. "How did I get here?"

"You collapsed right in front of me. Don't you remember?"

She rolled her head from side to side, feigning exhaustion. "No. The last thing I recall, I was sitting in a chair, then I got up to get a drink of water."

Worry furrowed his smooth brow. "Have you ever fainted before?"

"No. Never." At least, that was the truth.

He removed the damp rag and drew it along her cheek and throat. "Are you feeling ill?"

What she felt was warm. His hands were magic. "Yes," she lied. "I do feel a bit ill. My head keeps spinning, and my stomach hurts."

"Where?" He placed his palm on her lower abdomen. "Here?"

The heat from his hand sent shivers racing through her. "Y-yes."

He massaged the area, his long fingers much too close to a

very eager part of her body. Her pulse picked up speed. Visions of the night they'd shared swarmed her.

She sucked in a scandalized breath.

"Does that hurt?" He halted the movement of his hand.

It felt wonderful. "Y-yes. It hurts."

"I'll get the physician."

She grabbed his wrist. "No. Wait! I'm sure it'll be all right in a while. Please, don't leave me." She sent him a pleading look that had worked wonders on her brothers.

Bragen wavered. "Nichole, something could be wrong. I'd feel much better if the physician checked you." He squeezed her fingers. "I won't be gone long."

She held onto him. "No. I'm sure it'll pass. And I'd feel like such a fool. Please. Just stay with me. If I'm not better in a few hours, then you can go."

Not waiting for an answer, she brought his hand to a spot just above her low bodice, and pressed his palm to her bare flesh, hoping to distract him. "Besides, if I were gravely ill, would my heart beat with such vigor?"

A tremor ran through him, and he knelt by the bed. "No. I don't suppose it would." He stared at his tanned fingers splayed across her white skin. One long, slender digit rested a pulse-beat away from the tip of her breast.

His eyes remained fixed for several seconds; then traveled back to hers. A muscle throbbed in his jaw as he searched her face, her cheeks . . . her lips. "I think," he said so softly the words came out in a husky whisper, "I'd better go."

She dug her nails into the back of his hand. "Please, Bragen, just this once, don't make me argue. I swear to you, if I feel a genuine need for the physician, I'll tell you at once."

He hesitated, then at last gave a resigned sigh. "All right, angel. But you've given your word. Remember that." With reluctance, he withdrew his hand and rose. "Get some rest. I'll be right over here if you need anything."

Nichole closed her eyes and willed the flutters in her belly to cease. That hungry look he'd given her had made her recall every devastating detail of his fierce lovemaking, the way he'd kissed her with such drugging passion, how he'd touched her, then brought her such breath-stealing pleasure. Her body throbbed with a wave of need.

A moan escaped her dry lips.

"Nichole?"

Her eyes shot open, and she held up a hand. "No. I'm fine. Just stay where you are." If he came near her again, she'd melt all over him.

"Maybe I should ask Mr. Wilson for some laudanum to ease your pain."

"I told you. I'll be fine after a while. Stop worrying."

"At least let me give you some bourbon."

"No. Don't bother the captain with——"

"It won't be a bother."

It would to her. She didn't want him anywhere near Potter—or for Bragen to chance crossing paths with the physician. "Can I just have some water?"

He filled a goblet from the pitcher, then knelt beside her and brought the glass to her lips. "I think bourbon would make you feel better."

After her experience with the taste of the cognac that evening at the Crimson Candle, she had her doubts about any kind of alcohol making her feel better. She took a sip of water, then turned onto her side, holding her stomach in a show of discomfort. She felt the roll of the ship beneath her cheek, listened to the creak of wood.

Bragen rubbed her back. "I wish I could take the pain away for you."

Why did he have to be so kind and make her feel like such a wretch for duping him? "You wouldn't like it," she murmured, pretending to doze off.

The hand on her back continued to soothe and comfort and arouse. She felt hot and tense and lethargic, all at the same time.

"You should get out of that tight dress. You'll rest easier."

"I don't think I can," Nichole countered in truth. Her

arms and legs felt as if they were tied to anvils. Her blood felt thick.

She heard air hiss through his clenched teeth, then his uneven voice. "I'll help you."

He pulled her to her feet. "Be still while I free your laces."

She felt his fingers working on the ties at the front of her gown, but she couldn't stay focused. The scent of his male flesh held all her attention. He smelled like the sun and the wind and the sea. Unable to stop herself, she nuzzled his chest with her forehead. His shirt felt cool against her hot skin.

Bragen's hands stopped. "Nichole . . ."

"Hmmm?" She loved the sound of her name on his lips. It was so sensual. She ran her palm up his corded arm. His skin rippled.

"Nichole, you should be in bed. . . ."

She smiled at the way his husky voice reverberated inside his chest. It rumbled through every sensitive spot in her body. She lifted her face to his. He was so beautiful, she wanted to pour herself all over him. She focused on his mouth, remembering how it felt against her own. Her lips parted.

She heard his quick intake of breath, then a muttered curse. His breathing became harsh, heavy. "You're ill. You don't know what you're—"

She pressed her mouth to his, and moaned at the streak of desire that shook her. His lips were firm, yet soft, so exciting. She wanted to taste more of him. She pressed her tongue between his lips.

A shudder ran through him, and he deepened the kiss, exploring her mouth with urgent, masculine thoroughness.

She opened for him, anxious for the sweet warmth of his tongue. It was silky smooth, and so hot. . . .

He pulled her close, his hands restless as he shaped her to fit his hard contours.

The kiss went on and on, drowning her in its moist sweetness. She felt his fingers brush her shoulders, then, without breaking contact between their lips, he slid her gown down her arms. He ran his palms over her exposed flesh, then her back, her sides.

Her whole body started tingling. Her senses spun.

He cupped the back of her neck with his fingers while his thumbs traced her jawline. His kiss gentled, became taunting, playful, then he eased away.

Her gown slipped to her waist. Cool air touched her naked breasts. It was an incredibly erotic feeling. She lifted her gaze to his face.

His dark eyes feasted on her chest as he explored her full shape and tight pink centers. "There aren't enough words to describe what your beauty does to me," he rasped as he raised a finger to touch her.

She shivered. The ravenous look on his face told her how fierce his thoughts were, how much he wanted her. He covered her breast with his palm, tested her weight, the firmness of her nipple.

She had never known what power his hands could have. She gripped the sides of his shirt, pressing into his palm. "Sweet heavens."

Without warning, he relinquished his arousing hold and pulled her into the circle of his arms. He just held her for a moment, his heart thudding against hers, giving her time to come to her senses—or was it him? His lips brushed her ear. "I can't do this to you, angel. Not when you don't have your senses about you."

"Yes, you can."

"No." He brushed a finger over her lips. "No." With a regretful sigh, he stepped back, then removed the last stitch of her clothing and swooped her up into his arms. He held her for several seconds, his breathing harsh, then he lowered her to the bed. He kissed her one final time, before he rose to stare down at her.

She felt herself grow hot under his bold scrutiny, and she could sense the indecision pulling at him. He reached out a trembling hand, paused, then drew the blanket up to her chin. "Close your eyes, angel. If you keep looking at me like that, I may do something we'll both regret."

The threat behind those gentle words both frightened and excited her, and she lowered her lashes before she made a fool of herself. "Good night, Bragen."

He gave a harsh chuckle. "Believe me, Nichole, there isn't going to be anything good about it."

Bragen felt like hell the next morning. It had taken him half the night to cool down. Only his constant reminder that she was engaged to Gabriel Bodine had stopped him from taking what she had offered.

Damn his principles anyway.

"We missed you at the game last night," Clay commented as Bragen entered the galley.

"I was busy," Bragen snarled, plopping down on the bench across from him.

A reddish brow rose in question. "Problems?"

"Since I set foot on this ship. No, make that since I set eyes on Nichole Heatherton."

The corner of Clay's mouth twitched. "What's she done now?"

"It's not what she did. It's what *I* almost did. The little vixen fell ill last night, and I stayed with her."

"What happened?"

Bragen braced his elbows on the table. "She tried to seduce me."

Clay was silent for several heartbeats. "Did she succeed?"

Bragen glared at his friend. "Since when have you known me to bed another man's woman?"

"Never."

"That hasn't changed. She belongs to Gabe, or at least, *thinks* she does, and I'm sure she'll be appalled by her behavior this morning. I know I'm appalled by mine—by how far I let it go before I called a halt."

"You said she was ill?"

"Her stomach."

"Is she better this morning?"

"I haven't talked to her yet. She's asleep. I just came to get a tray to take back in case she's hungry when she awakens."

Clay chuckled. "You know, I'm beginning to wish I'd offered the lady my name and cabin for this voyage. She sounds delightful."

"I wish you had, too," Bragen grumbled, not meaning it. Cordell was a gentleman, but when it came to women, his male urges often overshadowed his morals. The man had been a pirate far too long. "And, Clay, *delightful* isn't the word I would have used to describe her. *Exasperating* is more like it."

Nichole's head felt like someone had stuffed it with mud. Her mouth was dry. Too much sleep always made her feel this way, but all her discomfort wasn't enough to erase the memory of her scandalous behavior the previous night. Good heavens, she hadn't really kissed Bragen, had she?

A moan slipped through her parted lips. Yes, she had. What the man must think of her. Of course, it was all his fault. If he hadn't awakened her body to sexual desire that night at the brothel, she wouldn't have trouble controlling the urges now.

No. She took it back. That night wasn't his fault. It was Gabriel's. *And he will pay for it.*

"Well, I see you're awake." Bragen carried a tray to the desk and set it down. "How are you feeling?"

Compared to what? She sat up and brushed her tangled hair out of her eyes. "I'm not sure."

His indrawn breath startled her, and she looked up in confusion.

His face had gone pale, and his dark eyes were fastened to her chest.

She glanced down—and her own breath stopped. The blanket was gathered at her waist, and a beam of sunlight from the porthole accentuated her totally naked breasts. "Good heavens!" She snatched the blanket up to her neck.

He gave her a tilted smile that said her display of modesty came too late. "Want some tea?"

Too flushed to speak, she nodded. While he poured, she wrapped the blanket around her, then held out her hands for the blood-starting brew.

"Hungry?"

Remembering her supposed illness, she shook her head, causing wisps of hair to tickle her cheek. "My stomach feels like a battleground. It must have been something I ate yesterday." She took a sip of tea to soothe the lie. "It's not so bad this morning, but I'm sorry you had to miss your game last night."

"There'll be other nights." He poured himself a cup, then sat down. "I've ordered water for your bath. As soon as you're dressed, I'll take you on deck. The fresh air might help."

His thoughtfulness made her feel worse. "Thank you. I'd like that."

They sat for several minutes in companionable silence, then a knock sounded at the door.

Making certain she was fully covered, Nichole watched as two crewmen came inside to fill the tub.

When they left, Bragen followed them out. "I'll be back in half an hour."

She didn't waste a minute of the time allotted to her, and was bathed, dressed, and ready by the time Bragen returned.

"Ah, a punctual woman at last," he praised as he looped her arm through his and escorted her topside.

Although the sun was bright, the spring breeze was crisp and cool as it blew across the ocean waters and pitched the ship over frothy waves. Nichole steadied her feet on the rolling deck and clutched Bragen's arm.

"Lord Blakely?" a sultry voice drifted on the wind.

Bragen turned, dragging Nichole with him.

The physician's daughter stood nearby, her red hair tousled by the wind.

"Good morning, Miss Wilson," Bragen greeted.

The redhead had eyes only for him. She devoured his rugged features and broad shoulders. "My papa asked me to find you." She flicked a glance at Nichole. "You wouldn't mind if I borrowed him for a few moments, would you, Lady Blakely?" She sent Bragen a coy smile. "I believe Papa wants to discuss business."

Nichole minded very much, but what could she say? She had no hold on Bragen. "Of course I don't mind." She eyed her supposed husband. "Run along now, dear. See what the good doctor wants."

Bragen arched a dark brow, but didn't comment. Instead, he followed Miss Wilson's rotating hips toward the stairs.

"Well, well, aren't you the gracious one. But, then, of course, he *is* only your lover."

The snide remark chilled her blood. She turned to face the tormentor. "I've often been noted for amicable behavior, Mr. McNall. As you well know."

"Ah, yes. Quite so. By the by, the game last night was quite profitable—thanks to you." He stepped closer, so close their chests almost touched. "However did you manage to keep him in the cabin, I wonder?" His eyes flicked to the flesh rising above her bodice. "Then again, perhaps I already know."

The man made her skin crawl. "If you'll excuse me." She stepped back and pulled her shawl closer. "I'm getting chilled. I believe I'll go below." She started to leave, but he caught her arm.

"An excellent idea. I'll escort you." He guided her down the stairs, but rather than turning up the hall that led to her room, he hauled her toward his.

She dug in her heels. "My cabin is the other way."

He tightened his hold. "We're going to mine . . . for a chat."

"No." She tried to pull free.

His grip became brutal. "Yes." Marching her forward, he shoved her inside his room and slammed the door behind him.

113

She kept as much distance between them as the cabin would allow. "W-what do you want?"

His hot gaze raked her from head to foot, then stopped at her breasts. "You know what I want."

Fear spurred her into motion. She raced around to the other side of the desk, placing it between them. "Stay away from me or I'll scream."

"Go ahead. No one can hear you." He moved toward her, his thick body crowding her into a corner. "Besides, why should Alexander have all the pleasure?"

Terror skipped up her spine. "It's not what you think. Bragen and I never—"

In a lightning-fast move, he caught her by the throat and ground his mouth down on hers in a cruel, painful assault. He thrust against her, slamming her into the wall, trapping her.

Horrified, she pounded at any part of him she could reach. It didn't stop him. If anything, his attack became more vicious. He forced his tongue between her lips, violating her mouth. He dug his fingertips into her breasts and squeezed.

Pain streaked through her, and she cried out.

He bit her lip to stop her protest, his calloused fingers sadistic in their invasion.

The taste of her own blood pushed bile up the back of her throat. She kicked and twisted.

He caught her around the legs with one of his and tripped her. They both tumbled to the floor. He landed on top of her, his weight causing bright dots to explode behind her eyes.

She jerked her head to the side. "No! Let me go!" She bucked in fright, but it only aroused him more. "Damn you, *stop.*"

"Shut up!" He grabbed her by the hair and slammed her head into the floor. "We both know you want this as much as I do."

"Doesn't look that way to me."

McNall leapt to his feet, his eyes fastened on the doorway where Bragen stood. "Back off, Alexander. Unless, of course, you want me to have a word with the captain about your arrangement with Miss Heatherton."

Nichole clutched her torn gown to her breasts, her heart pounding. Bragen wouldn't leave her, would he?

Bragen's gaze darted over her, stopping for a moment at her bleeding mouth, then moved to her torn gown. His eyes narrowed dangerously. But when he spoke, his voice was deadly soft. "Nichole, go back to the cabin. Mr. McNall and I have a few matters to discuss."

Not needing a second prompting, she bolted for the door. But just as it closed behind her, she heard a horrendous crash, followed by groans and grunts and flesh hitting flesh. She hesitated, her fear for Bragen warring with her fear of being seen in her present state.

He can take care of himself, a voice urged. *Get out of here.* Praying Bragen would be safe, she raced down the hall.

Her nerves in shreds, she washed and changed, then awaited Bragen's return. But she hadn't been able to do anything about the puffy cut on her lip or the darkening bruises surrounding her throat and breasts. She was just reaching for a bodice tucker to conceal the marks when the door burst open.

"Are you all right?" Bragen asked in a tight voice.

She nodded.

"Come on, then. We're going to the captain."

Nichole drew in a steadying breath. She knew he didn't mean it. He was just angry. "Bragen, come in and sit down." She inspected him and found only a slight red mark on one cheek, and discoloration around his knuckles.

"Sit down, hell!" he bellowed. "Why didn't you tell me that bastard was still blackmailing you?"

"How did you know—"

"I beat it out of him. Everything. Even to your *supposed* illness last night." His jaw clenched. "Damn it, Nichole, I told you that would happen."

"That's no reason to tell the captain," she pointed out with as much calm as she could muster. "I'm sure Mr. McNall would think twice before crossing you again."

"He won't have to." Bragen's chest rose and fell with rage, his eyes nearly black as he stared at her puffy lip—at the darkening bruises. "We're getting this out in the open right now. And damn the consequences."

"Be reasonable. Mr. McNall will be locked up for attacking me. Even if he does tell the captain, Potter probably won't believe him. And, if he did, well, we could always point out that Mr. McNall was making up tales to be vengeful."

"It won't be that easy, Nichole. After such an accusation, Potter will want proof."

"Maybe he won't."

"And maybe he will. But it doesn't matter either way. I'm sick of the subterfuge." Without giving her a chance to argue, Bragen caught her arm and hauled her out the door. "We're going to the captain now."

Chapter 12

Ian McNall did *what?*" Captain Potter's voice boomed across the deck.

Several crewmen and guests turned to stare.

Nichole rubbed her aching arm—the one Bragen hadn't let go of until now—and groaned inwardly. Couldn't he have waited until they were in the privacy of the captain's quarters? She lowered her gaze, too embarrassed to meet the eyes of the onlookers.

"You heard me," Bragen proceeded. "That bastard black-mailed Nichole and tried to rape her." His tone turned dangerous. "And if you won't do anything about it, I will."

The captain started sputtering. "Do anything about it? Sir, I assure you, this kind of behavior will not be tolerated on my ship." He motioned to a pair of crewmen. "See that Ian McNall is locked in the brig for the duration of this voyage." The captain again spoke to Bragen. "He will remain there until I can turn him over to the authorities in London."

"I appreciate that, Captain. But there's more." Bragen sent her a determined glance, then went on. "Nichole and I aren't married."

The captain started sputtering again, but Bragen continued. "I agreed to pose as the girl's husband to get her aboard the ship."

Nichole refused to let Bragen take the blame. "That's not true. It wasn't Bragen's fault. He didn't even know I was here until a day after we set sail. I'm the guilty one and fully prepared to take the consequences. Mr. Alexander is innocent of any wrongdoing."

Bragen stared at her in wonder.

What did he think? That she'd allow him to suffer on her behalf?

"If that is so," the captain huffed, "then why did he not report you as a stowaway?"

She defended him. "Because he's too much of a gentleman to cause a lady distress."

Bragen arched a brow.

Clay, who had walked up behind Bragen, coughed into his hand. Or was it laughed?

The captain snorted. "Well, *miss,* that chivalrous act just cost him his freedom."

"What are you saying?" Nichole demanded. There was no way she'd let Potter lock Bragen in the brig for simply being kind.

"I mean, Miss Heatherton, that Lord Blakely's bachelor days are over. You will be married before sunset."

"No," Bragen snapped. "Do whatever you like to me, but we're not being forced into an unwanted marriage."

Nichole winced. Did he have to make it sound like a hanging?

Clay looked thoughtful.

The captain puffed up his chest. "You, sir, are under my

command on this ship. And you will be married—or be set adrift. The choice is yours."

"Then you'd better break out the oars, Captain, because I'll take my chances on the ocean."

"Not just you, sir. You *and* the lady." Giving a mock salute, Potter turned and strode away.

Bragen's fists drew into knots, and he started after the captain.

"Bragen, wait." Clay stepped in front of him. "We need to talk."

"No."

Cordell's eyes narrowed. "I'm not going to watch you suffer over something that can be easily rectified. So, either hear me out, or I'll marry the damned woman myself to appease the captain." He sent Nichole an apologetic smile. "Excuse the expression, Miss Heatherton. No offense intended."

Nichole was too numb to feel anything. Set adrift? Good heavens. You'd think they'd committed murder.

"And just what is this miraculous solution?" Bragen asked in a harsh voice.

Clay scanned the people still watching them. "I'd rather discuss it in private."

"Fine." Bragen whirled around and strode toward the stairs.

Battling feelings of dread, Nichole followed.

"I'm waiting," Bragen announced once they'd entered the cabin. He slouched in the chair behind the desk. The insolent fury in his mannerism was unmistakable.

It was easy to tell that Mr. Cordell was fast losing his patience. He placed both palms flat on the desk, then leaned toward Bragen. "You jackass, just because you marry the girl doesn't mean you'll have to *stay* married to her. Damn it, man. Use your head. You can get the marriage annulled in London."

"By going to the magistrate, Clay?"

Cordell let out a long sigh, then shook his head. "I'll marry her."

"No."

Shocked by the fury in that single word, Nichole stared at Bragen.

Clay shoved away from the desk. "Then get an annulment when we return to the colonies."

"I thought of that," Bragen grated. "And the answer is still no."

"Why the hell not?"

The chair slammed to the floor. "Look at her, Clay. Damn it, *really* look at her. Could you stay in the same cabin with her for a month, knowing you were married—and fully within your rights to bed her—without doing so?" He rose and paced behind the chair. "It would take only one slip, and the marriage couldn't be annulled."

Nichole blushed to her soles, but held onto her composure *and* common sense. "Do you plan to rape me, Bragen?"

He snorted. "Of course not."

"Then you have nothing to worry about."

He glared at her. "That's not the way I saw it last night."

The man did have a cruel streak. "True. But, that won't happen again, I assure you."

Cordell cleared his throat. "If the situation became too unbearable, Bragen, I could relent and allow you to share my cabin, much as I would detest it."

Bragen's gaze fastened to his friend's. "Marriage isn't for me, Clay. And you know why."

"I know nothing of the sort, but you can take comfort in the fact that it won't be a real marriage."

Bragen looked as if he wanted to throttle him. He glared for several seconds.

Clay stared right back.

Pulling in a harsh breath, Bragen threw up his hands. *"All right.* But, I guarantee, friend, I'll hold you responsible if anything goes wrong. And it will. No matter how hard we try to prevent it."

Clay had the good sense to keep his mouth shut.

Bragen was dead right, and they all knew it. But what choice did they have? Certain death on a raft on the ocean?

After the men left to speak with the captain, Nichole collapsed into the chair. How had her life gotten so complicated? A pang of homesickness swept her. She longed for the simple days before she learned about her birth, the days when no one paid much attention to her actions.

With her heart heavy, she rose. Whether she liked it or not, she needed to dress for her wedding to Bragen Alexander.

A tiny smile pulled at her lips. What irony. The man who took her innocence would soon be her husband. "Husband." She tested the word and, inexplicably, she was suddenly filled with new hope.

Shortly after supper, Bragen and Nichole were pronounced man and wife by the staid Captain Potter. The passengers and crew standing on deck watching the ceremony weren't sure what to do after a forced wedding, so most remained silent. Too, the stiff kiss Bragen gave her declared just how much he disapproved.

Nichole wasn't of the same mind. After giving the situation several hours' thought, she rather liked the idea of being married to Bragen. Very much, in fact. He was everything she wanted in a man: kind, gentle, sensitive. Their wedding was a solution to all her problems . . . after she retrieved her jewels.

She harbored no girlish ideals, though. The marriage would end the minute an annulment could be obtained. The black look on Bragen's face gave truth to that. Unless, of course, she could change his mind.

"A bride isn't supposed to frown on her wedding day," Clay whispered in her ear. They were standing around a small table on which the cook had placed a special cake for the festivities. Another table, laden with a caldron of punch and tin cups, stood nearby.

"The groom isn't, either," Nichole pointed out. "And I have a feeling he's going to make the rest of this journey quite miserable for both of us."

"Give him time, beautiful. He just balks at being forced."

"Why did he say marriage wasn't for him? That's rather an unusual statement, isn't it?"

"Bragen's an unusual man."

She wasn't going to let him off that easy. "He said you knew why he felt that way."

Clay directed his gaze to where Bragen leaned on the rail. He was staring out across the ocean, his features hard and brooding. "It's not my place to talk about Bragen's problem. If he wants you to know, he'll tell you."

Nichole didn't know what to say. Until that instant, she never knew Bragen had a problem.

"I say, ol' chap. Fine ceremony, don't you think?" Prichard Haviland boomed as he joined them, his waistcoat buttons straining with the jiggle of his belly. "Could have bowled me over, you know. Had no idea the lady was a stowaway. Jolly good end to it, though, don't you know?" He winked a puffy eye at Nichole. "Lord Blakely got him a fine miss."

"Prichard Haviland." His wife's voice shrilled. Her fleshy face was red with indignation, noticeable even from clear across the deck. "Get over here this instant!"

Mr. Haviland harrumphed. "Ol' sow. Thinks you're tainted. Don't want us associatin' with you. Might dirty her lily-white reputation." He shook his head in disgust. "Oughta tell folks 'bout *our* rendezvous before the marriage bed. Wilhelmina wouldn't be so righteous then, you know." He ambled off, mumbling something about their son not really being born prematurely.

Clay's mouth twitched.

Nichole was torn between outrage and laughter. Wilhelmina and Prichard? It was hard to imagine them in the throes of premarital lust.

Strains of music drifted across the deck, and Nichole

turned to see one of the seamen gliding a bow over the strings of a violin. Another man accompanied him with a flute.

Miss Wilson and her father, along with the Havilands, moved to the center of the cleared deck and formed two lines. They began to advance and retreat to the steps of a contredanse.

Clay held out his hand. "Would you like to give it a go?" He dipped his head toward Bragen, who still stood at the rail looking angry. *"Someone* should dance with the bride."

She'd rather dance with her husband, but that wasn't an option. Husband . . . yes, she liked the sound of that.

"Well?" Clay urged.

She sank into a curtsy. "I'd like that very much."

They joined the others, swaying to and fro in time with the enchanting rhythm. She was snubbed by Mrs. Haviland and regarded with contempt by Miss Wilson, but she ignored them and concentrated only on her partner. Clay was an exceptional dancer.

Nichole was laughing when the dance ended. But her laughter turned into a screech when her arm was gripped from behind.

"Stop making a spectacle of yourself," Bragen ordered.

Clay tactfully retreated.

Nichole had been ignored, embarrassed, and shunned. That was enough for one day. She wrenched her arm free. "Just because we're married, Lord Blakely, it doesn't give you the right to manhandle me—or order me about—so refrain from doing so."

His mouth spread into a slow, wicked smile. "Oh, but it does give me the right, angel. For that . . . and much more."

That "much more" meant beatings, she was quite sure. The law did not interfere when a man chose to punish his wife, no matter how severely. However, Nichole, quite frankly, was allergic to pain and would avoid it at all costs. "I was dancing with Clay only because you wouldn't show me the courtesy. If you hadn't been so stubborn, I wouldn't have made a 'spectacle' of myself. Therefore, it's your fault."

A fleeting look of surprise brightened his eyes, then grudging humor. "Then, by all means, let me rectify my mistake." He motioned for the music to begin again, then led her to the center of the deck.

The other dancers joined them with reluctance. Mrs. Haviland did so under protest, being urged by her husband. Miss Wilson, escorted by her father, merely held her nose at a disdainful tilt.

"Ignore them," Bragen murmured when they glided past each other in step to the dance. "They're snobbish fools."

She took pleasure in that. He might be angry with her for this miserable situation, but he didn't like others shunning her. Yes, he was a kind man—and a heart-stoppingly handsome one in his finery. But, no matter how he dressed, he couldn't conceal the power in those taut muscles or the commanding aura that caused even the burliest man to step aside. There was just something about him that drew women and put wariness in other men. Or was it fear? Bragen was extremely big, after all—and he was a marvelous dancer, even better than Clay.

"What did Mr. Wilson want with you earlier?" she asked in an effort to make conversation and draw Bragen out of his dark mood.

"He didn't want anything. His daughter did." He gave her an amused look. "Which I refused."

An emotion she recognized as jealousy rolled through her, but she managed a smile. "I do admire your principles, Mr. Alexander."

He chuckled and twirled her back into line. It was a warm sound that seeped into her heart. Did the man know how gorgeous he was when he did that?

When the dance ended, he took her to the table, then cut a piece of cake. "I don't want to be accused of another impropriety," he remarked as he handed her the plate.

"Your wedding cake, madam." His eyes narrowed. "But this is the last concession I'll make this day."

Knowing he referred to what would normally take place later that night, she blushed. "Your protest has been duly noted throughout the day, milord. Truth to tell, even this small courtesy was more than I expected."

The corner of his mouth twitched, and a flash of admiration touched his eyes. "I'm glad to know we understand each other."

We don't understand each other at all, she wanted to *shout. You're too pigheaded to consider we might have a wonderful life together*. Being Bragen's wife would be exciting and beautiful—or could be if he didn't liken marriage to a trip to the gallows.

The dismal thought sapped the strength out of her, and she felt a wave of unexpected fatigue. It had been a long day, one she wouldn't soon forget—nor could she forget the genuine warmth in Bragen's voice when he pledged to love her until death. "If you'll excuse me," she said, handing him her plate, "I'm going to retire."

"It's not even gone dusk."

Too irritated with him to be cordial, she set her hands on her hips. "I'm not asking you to join me."

A muscle throbbed in his jaw. "I don't have a choice. This *is* our wedding night, after all. How would it look if I didn't retire with my bride?"

"I don't give a fig how it looks," she hissed. "But, if it'll make you feel better, you can buy yourself some time by hinting that I wanted to prepare myself for our nuptial bed." Furious, and not even sure why, she whirled around and stalked off.

Bragen stared after her, unable to move. Just the thought of her preparing herself to receive him in her bed had constricted every muscle in his body. Damn the minx. She knew just where to hit to hurt the most.

"For the sake of her reputation, don't you think you

should follow her?" Clay asked as he approached. "Or do you want everyone on board to think she doesn't suit you?"

"I don't give a damn what the others think. And I'm damn sure not going to join her in that cabin. Where that vixen's concerned, my control deserts me."

Bragen wished he'd kept his mouth shut. He knew Clay was wondering at his odd behavior. Since Bragen had found Meela in bed with Bodine, he'd avoided any involvement with women. The pain of Meela and Gabe's betrayal had almost killed him.

Clay had stuck with him, encouraging him to confront Bodine and learn the truth about that night, using his far-reaching influence to locate Gabe, and reassuring Bragen over and over again that not all women were treacherous.

Bragen couldn't allow himself to believe that. He wouldn't survive the pain a second time. But there was no denying he *was* becoming involved with Nichole.

And it had to stop.

Chapter 13

By the time Bragen entered the cabin, Nichole was asleep. Looking at her in the bed was more temptation than he could handle, so he didn't light a taper. He just wanted to get his clothes off and climb into his bunk without waking her. As much as he tried, he couldn't get her softly spoken vows—or his own—out of his head. They were married before God and man. She belonged to him. The thought both pleased and scared him.

"Bragen? Is that you?"

Not now. His senses were too alive. "Go back to sleep, Nichole."

"I haven't been asleep. I've been waiting for you."

His pulse took a giant leap. "What?"

"I wanted to talk to you."

Well, he damn sure didn't want to talk—or anything else. "Can't it wait?"

"No."

Her musical voice coming out of the dark was driving him crazy. He lit the candle and glared at her. "All right. What's so important that it can't wait until morning?"

She sat up and tossed a long lock of hair over her shoulder. "I want to know why you're so opposed to marriage."

That took him back a notch. But after the way he'd been acting all day, he couldn't blame her for wondering. He watched her earnest face in the flickering light. The soft swells of her breasts were visible above the low bodice of a ruffled chemise. "Where the hell's your nightgown?"

"It's still wet." She gestured to the dressing screen where the garment hung limply over the top edge. "I washed it this afternoon—and you're avoiding the question."

"I'm not avoiding it. I don't plan to answer it. My views on marriage are none of your concern." He hoped his harsh retort would make her angry enough to end the conversation. The sight of her in that skimpy chemise was playing hell with his restraint.

But instead of reacting as he'd expected, her features softened with concern. "Someone must have hurt you badly."

It staggered him that she could read him so accurately. "Go to sleep, Nichole."

"Was it Meela?"

The pain was so unexpected, he couldn't speak. How did she know about Meela? It didn't matter. That was one subject he definitely wouldn't discuss. "Nichole, go to slee—"

"Did she call off the wedding?"

"No. Now, go to sleep."

"Did she favor another man over you?"

"Yes, damn it! *After* we were married."

"Oh, Bragen. I'm so sorry. I didn't know. . . ."

Her sympathy was the last thing he wanted. "Now you do." He blew out the candle. "And for the last time, *go to sleep."* Making short work of his clothing, he disrobed, then climbed into his bunk.

The silence in the cabin was surprising. It was so unlike her to let him have the last word. He rolled over and pulled the cover up to his ear, feeling quite satisfied. He must have rendered her speechless—for once.

"I'm not like her, Bragen." Nichole's voice drifted downward. "I just wanted you to know that."

This from the woman who was engaged to Gabriel Bodine, the man he'd found in bed with his wife? "You're more like her than you know."

Nichole left the cabin before Bragen awakened the next morning. She didn't want to talk to him yet, not after what she'd learned last night. She had hoped that Bragen's loathing of marriage was fear of commitment. Now she knew it wasn't. He had been hurt, and he wouldn't open himself up to that kind of pain again. Oh, how he must have suffered under the scandal of divorce.

Bragen wouldn't give their marriage a chance. If anything was to work between them, she'd have to do it herself. And, if she wasn't so certain they were right for each other, she wouldn't even attempt the feat. But they were. *They were.*

A new determination lightened her step as she headed for the galley. After gathering scraps from the cook, she went to see Victor.

She had no doubt the dog was glad to see her, unlike ill-tempered others she could name, and she felt ashamed that she'd forgotten about him during the chaos yesterday afternoon. "How are you today, boy?" She greeted him, stepping into the musky room.

His tail wagged.

She smiled, then slowly, so as not to frighten him, she set the candle she carried onto a trunk and inched closer to the cage. When Victor didn't retreat, her smile widened. "You're not afraid of me anymore, are you?"

The dog lifted his nose toward the plate in her hand and sniffed.

Warmed by his wary acceptance, she unlocked the barred door. "I'm sure you'd rather have the entire meal at once, rather than piece by piece." She set the plate on the cage floor, then, leaving the door ajar, she retreated to a nearby crate and sat down.

Victor dove into the food with relish.

When he'd finished, she gave her knee a light pat. "Would you like to come out of that cramped space for a while?" Since she'd closed the main door to the hold, she didn't worry that he'd escape and cause a stir. She whistled to him.

In hesitant steps, the animal leapt down and padded toward her.

"Good boy," she crooned, holding out her hand.

Victor shied at first, then flicked his tongue over her fingertips.

It was all she could do not to throw her arms around the sweet dog and hug him. But she didn't want to scare him. Using great caution, she leaned forward and scratched a spot behind his ear.

Seeing she meant no harm, he licked the inside of her arm.

"You may not be a ravishing beauty outside," she murmured, "but inside, you are stunning."

Victor edged closer, starved for attention.

Using care not to startle him, she slipped her other arm around his neck, then nuzzled her cheek to his hairy jaw. "I wish you belonged to me."

He licked her ear as if to say he wished it, too.

"Here, now. What's this? What have ye done to me Chow-Chow?" a man's angry voice boomed from the stairway.

Victor crouched and growled.

His dog? Nichole jumped up and placed herself between the animal and the man she recognized as one of the Pitt Brothers—the thin-faced one. "I haven't done anything to your dog, except feed it and show it attention, something you've neglected to do."

Victor edged around the side of her skirt and gave a sharp, fierce bark.

Nichole placed a calming hand on the animal's head.

Mr. Pitt glared, but he didn't advance. "You've ruined him, that's what you've done. The best killin' dog I've ever had, and you've turned him into a simpering lick-finger."

Shock held her immobile. "Killing dog? Are you telling me this poor animal has been forced to fight other dogs?"

"He did before you got your dainty little hands on him. In order to win, he had to be mean and vicious. Now, the jackal's useless. *And you're gonna pay for it.*"

She edged back a step. "What do you mean?"

"I mean, Lady Blakely, that your new husband is gonna hand over a hefty sum for me prize dog."

Nichole was torn between relief that her life wasn't threatened and concern over how Bragen would react. "Mr. Pitt, there's no need to tell my husband. I'll give you the money myself, just as soon as I can."

His eyes squinted. "And when might that be?"

"Shortly after we get to London." It wasn't exactly the truth, but she'd send a letter of explanation when she and Bragen boarded the ship to Cape Town. As soon as she recovered her jewels from Gabriel, she'd pay Mr. Pitt.

The thin man snorted. "Just where are ye gonna get two hundred crown?"

"Two hundred crown!" She doubted all her jewels together were worth that amount. "That's outrageous."

"I told ye, lady, that's me best dog. I'm gonna lose a lot of cash because of what ye done."

She'd like to see him lose a lot of teeth, and she opened her mouth to tell him so, but she changed her mind. She would not allow that detestable man to subject Victor to any more cruelty. "Fine. I'll pay your price, the moment I'm able."

"That ain't good enough." He shook his head of stringy, brown hair. "Better your man pay me now and be done with it." With a smug smile, he swung around and sprinted up the stairs.

"Oh, dear," Nichole groaned as she knelt beside Victor. "I fear we're in a pack of trouble."

Bragen was so furious he didn't see Clay coming down the hall until he collided with him.

"Whoa, what the hell?" Clay blurted. "What's wrong with you? Don't tell me your first night married to Nichole was that difficult."

"No. But this morning's been hell. The vixen just cost me two hundred crown for a mangy dog that's about as appealing to the eye as raw liver."

"You don't say?"

Bragen's temper went up another notch. "Stop grinning, you jackass. I may very well hang for murdering the minx." Although the words were said in half jest, the second they were out, Bragen paled.

Clay sucked in a sharp breath.

They stared at each other, then Bragen shoved past his friend and stormed toward the upper deck.

"Bragen, wait!" Clay called after him.

Ignoring him, Bragen climbed the stairs, fighting his demons. When he reached the deck, he stood by the railing, gripping the teakwood, allowing the sea and wind to calm the riotous emotions surging through him at every turn. Damn his tongue! Damn his temper!

He took several deep breaths and buried his head in his hands. For three long years, he'd kept his emotions under tight control. But after one night married to Nichole, his rigid composure had dissolved like sugar in hot tea. One lousy night. He gave a harsh snort. He'd never make it through the next month.

Forcing himself under control, he dragged in several more

lungfuls of sea air. When he felt he'd gotten himself in hand again, he headed for the cargo hold. He still had Nichole and the dog to deal with.

No one was there.

Bragen eyed the empty animal cage, then the stairs. She wouldn't take the dog to their cabin. She wouldn't. "The hell she wouldn't!"

When he opened the cabin door, the sight that met his eyes froze him in place. The dog sat in the brass tub, covered in soap suds, while Nichole, soaked to the skin, attempted to wash its tail. The front of her gown was molded to her round breasts.

She glanced up, suds clinging to her lashes. Her eyes widened, and she cleared her throat. "I can explain if you'll give me the chance."

The dog growled.

She muzzled the animal with her hands. "No, Victor. It's all right. He's our friend."

"I wouldn't wager anything of value on that, Miss Heatherton."

She arched a golden brow. "It's Mrs. Alexander, if you'll recall."

Oh, he recalled, all right, too damned well. He kicked the door shut. "I believe you said you had an explanation"—he flung his hand toward the wet dog—"for this?"

Nichole brushed a lock of hair away from her cheek. The action caused her to leave a trail of suds along her jaw. "There isn't much of one. Just accept the fact that I'll pay you for Victor as soon as I get the money."

That was the least of his worries. "And just where do you plan to keep . . . Victor?"

"He can sleep with me."

Bragen spoke slowly, enunciating each word so there'd be no mistake. "That animal is not staying in my cabin."

"It's half mine. Victor can stay in my part."

"No."

"Bragen, be reasonable. You can't expect the poor thing to remain in that cargo hold."

"The hell I can't!"

"Stop shouting. You'll frighten him."

He was surprised to see the animal backed against the side of the tub, shivering. A spark of sympathy stirred, and Bragen lowered his tone. "Nichole, would you just try to consider my side of this? I've given up my privacy for you, my freedom, and a good deal of money. Now you're asking me to share my quarters with a smelly dog who doesn't even like me?" He crossed his arms. "And you think *I'm* being unreasonable?"

"He won't smell," she defended. "Not when his bath's finished."

She rose and moved between them. "And I'll help you make friends."

With her standing so close, and that damned dress clinging to her curves, he couldn't think of anything but kissing her senseless.

He fought the urge, denied it, and cursed his lustful reactions. But none of his silent objections meant a thing. Without realizing he'd even moved, he found himself hauling her against him, bending his head to take her impudent mouth.

The dog gave a sharp, vicious bark.

Startled, Bragen jerked back. He stared at Nichole's surprised face, then at the animal. Frustration warred with feelings of satisfaction. Victor might be an asset after all—might keep things from getting out of hand. Smiling, Bragen released her and stepped back.

She scowled at the dog.

Bragen's grin deepened. "You know, I think you're right. Victor should stay."

"You would." She picked up the soapy brush, then scrubbed the animal's coat with fervor, all the while mumbling something about him being a traitor.

Bragen couldn't contain a chuckle as he lumbered to the desk and sat down. He watched her try to untangle the dog's thick, matted fur without much success. Still, as with everything else he'd seen her do, she persevered.

He wondered at this unique woman who was supposed to be such a hellion, at least according to her brother. Bragen's thoughts drifted back to his last visit with Jason Kincaid.

Bragen and Clay had lost Gabe's trail in Yorktown and hadn't known where to go from there. The ever-enterprising Cordell had taken advantage of their setback by looking over ships in Chesapeake Bay that were for sale. He'd purchased one to add to his fleet and hired a crew to restore it.

Since Bragen was familiar with the area, he had set out to earn some extra cash by guiding a party into Shawnee territory and to question folks about Bodine.

After a hard journey, Bragen had spent a few days at Jason's place, and during the course of their conversations had learned about Nichole, about her many antics—and about her engagement to Gabe.

But the hellion Jason described and the gentle woman in front of him were at odds. She wasn't a malicious person. He'd stake his life on that. "Nichole? Did you burn down Jason's stables?"

"No." She looked up from her task. "How did you meet my brother, anyway? In his letter he just mentioned you were a friend."

She was good at changing the subject. "We went to school together in Florence, and our paths have crossed a few times in the colonies."

She returned her attention to the dog.

"He thinks you did it, Nichole."

"I know."

The sadness in her reply touched a soft spot inside him. "Why?"

Lifting a sudsy hand to her cheek, she brushed her hair

back. Rivulets of water ran down her arm and disappeared inside her ruffled sleeve. "Because I was the only one near the stables when he smelled the smoke."

"What were you doing?"

"Trying to save the horses."

"Do you know how the fire started?"

She resumed scrubbing the dog. "Yes. It was my nephew Damon, one of Jason's twins. He'd ridden his father's prize mare that afternoon and had taken the animal into a creek Jason had forbidden him to ride in. When the mare cut her leg on a rock, Damon brought her back to the stables, and since their groom had gone to Petersburg to pick up another mare, Damon was going to tend the animal's wound himself. But supper was ready, and he couldn't tarry without making his father suspicious. After everyone retired that night, he took a poultice and a lantern out to the stall."

She stared at the top of Victor's head. "I was reading when I heard the back door close, so I went to investigate. I walked in just as the horse kicked the lantern over. Damon panicked and ran, so I was the only one there when Jason came out."

"Did you tell him about Damon?"

"No. That's something Damon needs to admit on his own. But I did tell him I didn't start the fire." She wiped a tear from the corner of her eye. "He didn't believe me."

Bragen sensed the pain behind her soft words. Her brother had hurt her. That strange feeling of protectiveness rose again, and he felt anger toward Jason, then himself. Damn it, he wasn't going to let her get under his skin. "By not telling Jason the truth, you *were* lying to him."

"You're right, of course. I'm a liar, and a cheat, and heaven only knows what else. If I were you, I'd avoid my villainous presence at all cost." She tightened her fingers in Victor's fur.

The animal whimpered.

Nichole gentled her touch, but not her words. "Go away, Bragen."

He'd wounded her with the truth, and he wished he could take it back. She'd been through a lot with Gabriel's disappearance, McNall's blackmail, and their forced marriage. But in all honesty, her anger was just what they needed right now.

It would make the voyage easier for both of them.

Chapter 14

For most of her life, Nichole had blamed others for distrusting her, never once considering that she herself might be the cause. The thought didn't set well at all. And the fact that Bragen had pointed it out didn't endear him to her, either.

The dog sneezed.

Fearing he'd been in the water too long, she helped him from the tub and picked up a towel.

"You know, Victor," she murmured as she dried the shivering animal, "Bragen is a good man." She leaned down to look him in the eye. "Which reminds me, we have to come to an understanding. I'm married to Bragen, and if he wants to kiss me, well, then you shouldn't interfere."

The dog cocked his head to the side, listening, one scarred ear dangling.

She ruffled that ear with the cloth. "Perhaps I can explain

it better this way: you see, Bragen doesn't want to be married to me."

Victor woofed in disagreement.

Nichole smiled. "No, he's not at fault. He was forced into this situation and is trying to make the best of it. The problem is, Bragen and I have different opinions about this situation. You see, I happen to want this marriage very much. Now do you understand why you mustn't snarl when he tries to . . . well, you know?"

The animal blinked and flicked his tongue over the point of her chin as if he understood.

She laughed and gave him a hug. "Good boy." When she finished drying him, she took a brush to his shiny coat and was amazed to see how fluffy and silky his fur was. Why, except for the scars on his face and ears, Victor was beautiful.

After righting the room and settling the dog on her cot, she left to find the cabin boy. She needed her own bath.

Two hours later, when her ablutions were complete, she pulled on a pale yellow silk dress and took Victor for a walk, using a ribbon for a collar and leash.

Pride swelled in her chest when they walked up on deck and a ray of sunlight touched his inky coat. The fur shone like polished onyx, and he smelled wonderful.

"What *is* that horrid creature?" Miss Wilson's thin voice insisted as she walked across the deck toward Nichole. Her red hair swung in the wind, while her wide hips rotated with the roll of the ocean.

"That creature is a man-eating, killer dog."

The woman's lips drew into a narrow line, and she stopped several feet short, her slanted cat eyes studying Victor. "Why hasn't he eaten you, I wonder?"

"He prefers redheads."

Victor gave a rumbling growl, as if to give credibility to Nichole's outrageous comment.

Miss Wilson retreated a step, splaying a long-fingered

hand across her bulging bosom. "Why isn't that beast in a cage where he belongs?"

"He doesn't need to be restrained," Bragen's warm voice answered from behind Nichole. "He's simply protecting his mistress from anything he considers a threat."

Nichole warmed at Bragen's defense.

The redhead lifted her chin and sniffed. "I see that disgusting animal isn't her *only* protector." With a flip of her hair, she whirled around and strode regally away.

Bragen didn't take his eyes off the woman until she trudged down the stairwell. Then he returned his attention to Nichole and gave her a wry smile. "I came to find you because I wanted to apologize for my harsh statement earlier."

"There's no need to apologize for speaking the truth."

"There is if you hurt someone." He drew her arm through his. "And I plan to make it up to you. Come on, let's go below. I have something I want to show you. By the way, Victor looks great."

Basking in his praise, Nichole followed him below.

The something he wanted to show her turned out to be a beautifully carved chessboard with bronze and silver chessmen that he'd set up on the desk.

"Where did you get that?"

"From Clay. He spends a lot of time aboard ships, so he always keeps it with him. It helps alleviate boredom during long journeys. Bragen motioned to the board. "Care for a game?"

"Only if you can teach me how to play."

"With pleasure."

Victor curled on the lower bunk and lay down as she and Bragen sat across the desk from each other.

It took several games before she caught onto the basics, but she knew it would be a long, long time before she'd be able to give Bragen competition. "You're good at this."

"I'm sure my brother would disagree. He's trounced me more times than I care to remember."

"What's his name?"

"Christian. And my sister is Fiona."

"I would like to have been raised with my brothers. I never had anyone to argue with or cry with or laugh with. I felt cheated because I never experienced the love siblings share, or enjoyed fond memories like my friend, Morgan Frazier, had of his brother."

"Morgan Frazier?"

"You know him?"

Bragen chuckled. "I should. He's Clay's half-brother."

"But Morgan said his brother was a—*Clay's a pirate?*"

"Not in the true sense of the word. But his father was."

"Have you known Clay and Morgan long?"

He straightened the chess pieces. "Most of my life. I was born and raised just outside of London, and they were neighbors. So was Gabe." He set the last castle into place. "Morgan was younger than Gabe and I, so we wouldn't see much of him until Clay would come home from his latest sea voyage; then Morgan would tag along. How did you meet Gabe?"

She was still reeling from the fact that Clay and Morgan were brothers. "I met Gabriel when Miss Fender gave a soirée and invited every eligible gentleman in Charleston who hadn't heard about my knack for trouble." She moved her bishop and took Bragen's pawn. "He was one of the three who showed up. Why are you trying to find him?"

"I told you. He has some information I need."

"Concerning what?"

"A personal matter."

"Oh." She watched his queen take her knight, dying to know what that *matter* was. "I didn't want to marry him, you know."

Bragen's head shot up. "What?"

"I've got to talk to him, but it's not because I have feelings for him. I never did. And after that, I'm going away." *Unless you want me.*

"Where?"

141

"To the colonies. I want to be near my brothers, but I plan to buy a cottage a good distance from other people. It's the only way I can stay out of trouble."

A frown creased his brow as his rook captured her queen. "You don't plan to marry?"

"You mean *again?* No."

"Then why is it so important for you to see Bodine?" He slid his queen across the board and took the pawn guarding her king.

She smiled. "A personal matter."

Bragen arched a brow, then lifted his timepiece from his pocket. "We should end this game soon. They'll be serving supper in half an hour."

"Apparently, the game will end sooner than I planned." She eyed her few remaining chessmen. "I imagine I should concede so I can change for supper."

His gaze drifted to the swell of white flesh above her bodice. "You look good just the way you are."

So did he. With his eyes all smoky and warm like that, he turned her bones to soft wax. She rose. "I need to at least brush my hair." And get rid of the silly flutters in her belly. She found her brush in the trunk and tried to drag it through her tangles. Her eyes stung from the pain.

Bragen muttered something under his breath and took the brush. "Let me." He nudged her shoulder. "Turn around."

She hesitantly gave him her back.

He stroked the length of her curls with his hand. "Your hair feels like velvet."

Out of the corner of her eye, she saw Victor watching them from the bunk, but he didn't snarl. Her talk must have done some good after all. She closed her eyes and enjoyed the feel of bristles gliding through the strands, followed by the heat of Bragen's palm. Again. Again. Her body began to tingle.

He loosened the ribbon holding her hair back, and pulled it away. The satin fluttered to the floor in a shimmering yellow pool. He continued to brush, his fingers gliding over her ears, her forehead, her throat.

His hands stilled, but he remained close. "I'm done, angel."

She was done, too. Completely done in. Unable to stop the impulse, she turned to him. Their lips were so close she shivered.

Their eyes met and held. His darkened with desire, then he lowered his head.

Her lashes fell shut as his warm lips moved over hers, exploring her with gentleness. He traced her lips with the tip of his tongue, then eased it between her teeth.

Sweet heavens, how long had she waited for him to kiss her like this?

A loud pounding rattled the door. "Bragen? Are you in there?"

With a curse, Bragen released her. "What the hell do you want, Cordell?"

There was a long silence, then Clay's voice rumbled through the door. "I was going to walk with you and Nichole to supper. But I guess this is a bad time."

Bragen laced his fingers through his hair. "No. Your timing's perfect. Listen, go on ahead. We'll be there in a few minutes."

When Clay's footsteps receded, Bragen turned around. His gaze fastened on her, then drifted to the dog, who sat quietly on the bunk. For several seconds, he didn't move, but she sensed his building rage. He hadn't been able to control what was happening between them, and it infuriated him. And she knew that irrationally, he blamed the dog for not interrupting.

With a cold insolence that chilled her, Bragen smiled. It was an evil smile, one laced with anger, and when he spoke, he said each word clearly, making sure there was no mistake. "Get rid of the dog."

* * *

"You want me to what?" Clay asked, his tone incredulous.

"Keep Victor with you," Nichole repeated, hoping Clay wasn't going to be difficult about this. "Bragen's angry and won't let me keep him in our cabin." She sent Cordell a pleading look. "You're the only person I can trust. He's skittish because those men that owned him mistreated him so."

When she saw Clay's eyes soften, she pressed on. "They starved him, neglected him, and forced him to fight wild, vicious animals so they could win money. He's a good dog, Clay. I promise you. And he won't give you any trouble at all—but if he should, well then, I'll find somewhere else for him. I swear I will."

Clay wavered.

Encouraged, she continued her attack. "I'll even walk him and feed him, so you won't have to. He'll be great company. Honestly."

Eyeing the animal, Cordell sank down onto one knee. He held out his hand to Victor. "Come here, boy."

Victor growled and edged closer to Nichole.

"He's just a little nervous. Here, I'll help you make friends." She approached Clay, then knelt beside him. "Put your hand on my head, like you were going to pet me."

"Nichole, I don't think—"

"It's all right. He won't hurt you. Come here, Victor. Meet Mr. Cordell. He's a very nice man."

Victor took tentative steps, his eyes never leaving the man beside her. When he reached Nichole, she rubbed behind his ears. "Good boy." Then she spoke to Clay. "Continue to stroke my head while you raise your other hand, very slowly, to pet Victor's."

He did as she instructed.

The dog flinched, but because Nichole still had her hand on him, he didn't move.

"See, Victor, Mr. Cordell won't hurt you. He's my friend—and yours, too." She implored Clay with her eyes. "Well?"

"He can stay. Until we reach London. After that, you'll have to find other accommodations." He glanced at her sharply. "Where are we going from London, anyway?"

Because of his compassion for Victor—or perhaps because he was Morgan's brother—she considered giving him the information, but she just couldn't chance it. "I want to tell you, Clay. But I just can't. Not yet."

"Why?"

"Let's just say that finding Gabriel means more to me than anything else at the moment."

Giving Victor a final pat, she headed for the door, but stopped once it was open. "Thank you, Clay—for myself and for Victor."

Clay turned a melting smile on her. "I didn't do it for the dog."

Not sure what to think of that remark, she wrapped her shawl around her and headed for the rocking deck. She was surprised to see a beautiful clear sky instead of black storm clouds as she'd expected.

A gust of wind whooshed behind her, and she turned around. In the distance, thick gray clouds clung to the horizon. A storm wasn't far off. It was a depressing thought at best.

"Did you get rid of the dog?" Bragen's voice sliced through the wind.

"I found him a place to stay, if that's what you mean."

He stood beside her, his hands planted on his lean hips, his head bent toward her, causing a shimmering lock of midnight-black hair to slip from its queue. The fringe on his buckskin shirt danced in the breeze. "Where'd you put him?"

"Your concern's a bit late."

He shrugged. "I'm asking only because there's a storm brewing and things will get pretty hectic when it hits."

"When will that be?" She'd never been in a storm at sea, and from what Bragen had told her, she was quite certain she didn't want to be in one now.

"Tomorrow, most likely. But the crew have everything under control. Even now, they're battening down the ship."

She wasn't sure what that meant, but it sounded promising. "Is there anything I can do to help?"

"All any of us can do is stay out of their way and let them do their jobs. Speaking of which . . ." He nodded toward the stairs. "Why don't we go below and leave them to it?"

Even though she was miffed at him, she knew this was a perfect opportunity to work her wiles on her elusive husband—which she would do without a shred of shame now that he'd revealed his malevolent side by tossing Victor out. She'd have a chance to dazzle Bragen with her charm. If that didn't work, she'd resort to out-and-out seduction. "I think that's an excellent idea." Smiling, she followed him below deck.

The tiny porthole didn't offer much light, so Bragen lit a candle, then took a seat behind the desk.

Nichole slid into a chair across from him. "Do you want to play chess? Or another game?"

"Like what?"

She thought of all the games she knew how to play. All *one* of them. "Draughts?"

"I don't have a board."

"That's the only game I know." She perused the cabin. "There must be something else we can do to pass the time." She had a few ideas, but doubted he'd agree. Besides, the unfulfilled need running around inside her belly was gnawing her to pieces.

"I have a deck of cards. Would you like to learn how to play cassino?"

That wasn't what she had in mind, but it would have to suffice. "Is it difficult to learn?"

"Easier than chess. It's just a matter of winning cards by matching or combining those in your hand with ones exposed on the table."

"That doesn't sound too difficult." And it wasn't. It only took her two games to catch on . . . and beat him.

"Pure luck," he mockingly complained. "It won't happen a second time."

"We'll see." She gave it her best, but it wasn't enough.

Tossing in the last of her hand, she groused, "I know I'll win the next one."

"If you're that convinced, how about a wager?"

"I'm afraid my funds are sorely limited." Until she found Gabriel.

"We don't have to wager money."

"Then what?"

He shrugged a broad shoulder. "You choose what you hope to win, and I'll consider my prize."

She thought about it, then decided on something she loved to do. "If I win, I'd like to dance." *See if you can keep your hands off me then.*

"Here?"

"Right here in the cabin."

"There's no music."

"You can hum."

He chuckled. "So be it."

"Have you decided what you'd like your prize to be?" she asked, trying to check a satisfied smile.

Leaning back in his chair, he narrowed those beautiful dark eyes on her. "There are several things I'd like to wager, but only one I feel is appropriate."

She felt the heat from his smoldering look all the way to her toes. "And that is?"

"You tell me Gabriel's destination."

A secret smile pulled at her lips. "Very well, Bragen, you have a bet." She gestured toward the cards. "It's your deal."

He was both surprised and suspicious as he shuffled the cards. Then he became intent on the game. She knew there was only one way to stand a chance at defeating him—distraction.

While he dealt, she fanned herself under the pretense of being too warm, then loosened the laces holding her bodice together.

Bragen's hand stilled as he went to toss down the last card. For several seconds he held the card aloft, then lowered it to the desk. His accusing gaze met hers as he gathered his hand.

Undaunted, Nichole smiled as she laid down the first card, then straightened. The action caused her breasts to widen the gap secured by the dangling laces.

His eyes fixed on her chest. Absentmindedly, he threw in a card, not even looking at it.

She shifted, forcing the material to part even farther as she made her next play.

A hiss slid through his lips, but his attention never left her.

It didn't take long to beat him.

When he snapped his last card onto the surface of the desk, his eyes were still fixed on her breasts. "The next time we play cards," he rasped, "I want you covered to the chin."

She widened her eyes, trying to appear innocent as she traced a finger along her low bodice. "Whatever for?"

"Minx. You know very well why." He rose and held out his hand. "I believe this is our dance."

Unable to hide her satisfaction, she smiled and placed her palm in his.

To her surprise, he slipped an arm around her waist and pulled her close. "What are you doing?" Not that she minded.

"We're going to waltz."

Having only recently heard of the new dance, she didn't know the steps. "I've never—"

"I'll teach you," he murmured close to her ear. "Just relax and follow my lead." He began to hum a slow, lazy tune, his voice rich and mellow.

He settled her fully against him and started to sway, his body pressed to hers, his taut thighs caressing her own with each step he took. Their stomachs touched, their chests.

What a wonderful dance, she thought as tremors raced along her flesh.

He must have felt them, because his voice faltered before resuming its melodious rhythm. He spun her, glided, dipped, and by the time the dance ended, she was dizzy. She could feel the indecision in him, his determination battling with the urges of his body.

When Bragen released her, she caught the back of a chair to regain her balance . . . and her breath. All during the waltz, memories of that night at the Crimson Candle had danced through her head. Whether dancing or making love, the man knew what to do with his body.

"Nichole?" Bragen's husky voice broke into her thoughts. "Would you like another game?"

"No. I think that's enough games for tonight." She couldn't afford a loss . . . or another win. If she didn't find release soon, she was going to shatter into a thousand pieces. She wanted him to make love to her. Since her charm had obviously failed, she'd have to resort to her second choice— seduction.

"Then why don't we retire for the evening?"

That was exactly what she had in mind. Rising, she moved behind the screen and pulled her nightclothes from where they were draped over the top edge.

Bragen sat at the desk and watched, his expression unreadable.

He was trying not to be affected by their close proximity, but he was. She smiled to herself and slipped into her sheer nightdress, leaving the laces undone and her robe lying on the floor. There was only one way to deal with a stubborn man like Bragen.

Taking a fortifying breath, she summoned every ounce of courage she possessed, which wasn't much. What she was about to do was outrageous, idiotic, *scandalous*—but in this case, necessary.

She stepped out from behind the screen.

Bragen looked up—and froze. His throat worked, but he couldn't speak. He didn't need to. The hunger in his eyes said everything for him.

With deliberate slowness, he came to his feet, his hands clenched at his sides, his mouth drawn into an angry line. "I thought you didn't want to play any more games tonight." He raked her with a cold look, then turned and left the room.

Chapter 15

Few people were about for the noon meal the next day, and Bragen didn't say more than two words to Nichole. The contemplative look on his face made her nervous, along with the fact that he hadn't returned to the cabin last night. Was it because of her outrageous behavior? Heat stung her cheeks again when she thought about what she had done. But, she knew she'd do it again if it meant Bragen would be hers. Watching the hard set of his jaw now, though, she was sure that wasn't a possibility.

She rose from the bench. "I believe I'll return to our quarters and lie down for a while," she lied. "The roll of the ship, in this weather is unsettling my stomach." What she actually needed to do was take some scraps to Victor and escape Bragen's penetrating gaze.

"Yes. Get some rest. You're going to need it." He, too, came to his feet.

It was all she could do not to demand he explain that

comment. *Why* was she going to need rest? Because of him? Or because of the coming storm?

Bragen departed before her, which gave her the opportunity to empty their plates into one and avoid a trip to the galley. Her thoughts churned as she carried the full platter to Clay's cabin.

He answered on the first knock. "Thank God," he said when he saw the scraps. "The dog's been eyeing me for his next meal."

"Don't be silly," Nichole chided. "He doesn't look that way. He's such a pussycat." She held out the plate. "Come here, boy. See what I have for you."

The dog bounded off the bed as she set the dish on the floor. He attacked it with relish.

Clay smiled. "He's got a healthy appetite, I'll say that much for him."

"You would, too, if you'd been starved for most of your life."

"Yes, I suppose I would."

She studied Bragen's friend. "Clay? Would you do me a favor?"

"What's that?"

"Refrain from telling Bragen about Victor being in your cabin."

"Why?"

Good question. Nichole tried to come up with an answer without telling him she wanted to make Bragen jealous. At least she hoped he'd be jealous when he learned of her visits to his friend's cabin. "I'm not sure he'd approve." That wasn't a lie.

Clay watched her with intelligent eyes, then he smiled. "I don't think the animal's presence in my cabin would matter to Bragen one way or another, but if that's what you want, I won't mention it."

"Thank you." Now all she had to do was make certain Bragen knew she'd been in Clay's room. If he was going to accuse her of playing games, she'd show him how good she was at it.

She spotted Clay's gold cravat pin. It was shaped like a pirate ship, with intricately carved jade sails and tiny crossed bones of ivory. Because it was so unusual, Bragen would recognize it. "Do you mind if I borrow your pin? The laces on my gown refuse to stay tied"—she was inventing as she spoke—"and I don't have time to change. I'm going to meet Bragen on deck." At least that's what she intended.

"Take it."

She pinned it to her bodice. "Again, I thank you."

Clay watched her as she left the room, and she could have sworn she heard him say something about Bragen meeting his match.

When she emerged onto the deck, Bragen was there. "What happened to your nap?"

She fingered the pin. "I wasn't as tired as I thought I was."

He focused on Clay's jewelry but didn't say a word. Instead, he offered his arm. "Care for a stroll? After the storm hits, we'll be confined to the cabin for some time. The gale could go on for days."

Days? In the cabin alone with Bragen? Even the fates were on her side.

Bragen's temper seethed as he walked Nichole toward the bow of the ship. *You weren't as tired as you thought, huh? Did she think he wouldn't recognize Clay's pin?* Damn the man. Damn her. And damn himself for caring if Clay bedded the vixen. It wasn't any of Bragen's business. Still, the wrenching jealousy wouldn't leave his gut. It was an uncomfortable sensation, one he'd experienced only once before, the last time he saw Gabriel Bodine.

He refused to think about that fateful encounter. His hold tightened on Nichole's arm. "We can see most of the activity from here," he remarked when they reached the bow, trying his best to appear casual.

A gusting breeze feathered a golden curl near her jaw. The moist salt air brought a flush of color to her cheeks as she watched the crewmen at their various tasks. "What's he doing?" she asked, pointing a slender finger toward one of the sailors.

"He's using that strip of wood, called a batten, to reinforce and secure all the hatches against the coming storm."

"Is it going to be that bad?" Concern edged her voice.

Bragen didn't want to worry her, but she needed to know the truth. Her life could depend on it. "It's hard to tell. The sea's so unpredictable, we could be in for anything from a minor squall to a full-blown nor'easter."

Her face lost some of its color. "You know a lot about ships, don't you?"

"Some. I used to travel a lot with Clay and Gabe before—" He cleared his throat. "I spent a good deal of time on Clay's ships before I finally settled in the colonies."

"I thought you were from London."

"I am, originally, but I visited the Americas about ten years ago and fell in love with the country. During the war, I fought beside your brothers until I was wounded."

"Wounded?" Her gaze swept him. "Where?"

"At Camden."

She gritted her teeth. "Where on your person?"

"A few inches above my right thigh, but the scar's hardly noticeable."

"Did you return to the battlefield after that?"

"No." He couldn't keep the bitterness from his voice. "It was near the end of the war, so I went to England—to retrieve something I'd left there for safekeeping." *His wife.* "While I was there, I learned Gabe had gone to the colonies, so I went back to find him."

"Did Clay join the colonists' fight, too?"

"Yes, but in a different manner. He smuggled goods aboard his ships."

"How many does he have?"

154

"Seven. No, eight. He just purchased another one in Yorktown last month."

She gave him a confused look. "Why didn't you take one of his ships on this journey?"

"Six are loaded down with cargo and en route to various destinations. One's in dry dock, and the one he just bought is being refurbished to meet Clay's stringent requirements. Until we reach London, he's temporarily without a vessel at his disposal."

"He has a ship in London?"

"No. But his freighter, *English Maiden,* should arrive from Spain about the same time we get there. We'll use her for the rest of the journey." He gave her a suspicious glance. "You did say London was only a stop on the way to Gabe's destination, didn't you?"

"Yes." She changed the subject. "Didn't you say Gabriel had sailed with you and Clay, too?"

At the mention of Gabriel's name, Bragen's mood shifted from complacent to dark. "London is a main port, and Clay stopped there often to deliver or load cargo. On several occasions, we went with him for short journeys. Gabe and I even went to the colonies on one of Clay's vessels."

"Who is Meela?"

He tightened his hold on her arm. "Who told you about her?"

"You did. You mentioned her in your sleep one night."

He clenched his teeth. Those damned dreams. "Meela was my wife."

Nichole didn't look up. "Was she from England or the colonies?"

"America. She was the daughter of a Shawnee chief, and I don't want to discuss her anymore, Nichole."

Surprise flickered in her eyes before she started to ask another question. He had to stop her for his own piece of mind. "Listen. When the storm hits, the crew is going to be busy and water will be scarce. Bathing won't be possible, so you might want to make use of the tub while you still can. I plan to in a couple of hours."

She knew he was deliberately changing the topic. "Of course, Bragen. That's a splendid idea. I'll order my bath now."

Nichole held her chin aloft as she walked away from him, wondering about the previous Lady Blakely. An Indian. Were cultural differences what caused their marriage to fail? Had she returned to the colonies or was she in London? Would Nichole meet her there? She hoped not. The thought of coming face to face with a woman who'd once experienced Bragen's volatile lovemaking didn't set well at all; she'd better keep a close eye on him when they reached port. In fact, she wasn't going to let the man out of her sight at all if possible.

But until then, she needed to learn more about his first marriage.

After her bath, Nichole made for Clay's cabin.

He stared at her through the partially open door, his eyes heavy-lidded. "Is it feeding time again?"

"No," she answered truthfully, but she had gotten a pail of scraps to tide him over during the storm. She held the bucket aloft. "I brought some food anyway, though."

"How many times a day does this go on?" Clay still didn't open the door to admit her.

"Usually twice, but I thought he should have extra on hand—just in case."

Clay glanced over his shoulder. "Do you think you could come back in about ten minutes? I'm . . . not dressed."

"I'm sorry. Of course, I'll return later." The man was probably taking a bath. She rushed down the hall, only then realizing she had nowhere to go. Bragen was bathing in their cabin. She set the pail down and leaned against the wall. There wasn't anything for her to do but wait.

Only a few minutes had passed when she heard the sound of a door opening. She peeked around the corner. Her breath caught. The physician's daughter, Miss Wilson, was just coming out of Clay's room—*hastily lacing the front of her gown.*

Held motionless, Nichole watched as Clay pressed some coins into the woman's hands, then pulled her back for a very, very thorough kiss.

Miss Wilson left Clay's arms, then touched his lips with her finger. "I'll see you again tomorrow." She turned to leave, heading straight toward Nichole.

Grabbing the pail, Nichole ran for the cargo hold. She wasn't about to go back to Clay's quarters. Not yet. She was too embarrassed. No wonder the woman had such fine clothes.

Sitting in the dark, she leaned her head on the wall, trying to blot out visions of Clay and the redhead, only to have them take on the form of Bragen and herself. She could almost smell Bragen's musky scent, feel the way his hands and lips had touched her, excited her. She wanted to experience those magical sensations again.

She left the pail and headed for her own cabin. The need to see Bragen was strong.

When she opened the door, she found him standing in the center of the room with his back to her, his long, lean body beautifully naked and dripping with water.

He swung around, and she saw a damp towel hanging limply from his hands. It didn't quite reach the apex of his thighs—and he made no move to correct the oversight.

"What are you doing back so soon?"

She dragged her eyes upward. "I—I forgot . . ."

He waited several seconds, then arched a brow. "You forgot what?"

"What I came for." *But I know what I want, and it's standing right in front of me.* She took a step toward him.

"If you'll give me a couple of minutes, I'll get dressed and get out of here. Maybe then you'll be able to remember," he said, turning away to cover himself.

Nichole was too far gone to think rationally. Having seen

Bragen in all his masculine glory was too much. Something inside her ached for him. "Kiss me, Bragen."

He went still, then slowly turned his head to look at her. "Nichole, get out of here."

She couldn't move. She was held motionless by the muscle throbbing at the base of his brown throat, by the rise and fall of his chest with each harsh breath he took. She stepped closer. "You don't want me to leave." She trailed a finger over a flat male nipple.

It tightened into a hard pebble.

"Jesus . . ." He closed his eyes, but he didn't try to stop her.

Encouraged, and very, very aware that the man was her husband, she let her fingers roam through the silky hairs covering his chest, then explored his smooth, hot flesh.

A shudder ran through him, and a low, nearly inaudible groan slid past his lips. "You don't know what you're doing."

Oh, she knew, all right, but she couldn't stop herself. She leaned forward and brushed her lips along the same path her fingers had taken.

"Damn you." He caught her by the hair and jerked her head up. He glared for a heartbeat, then, as if unable to resist, he ground his mouth down on hers.

Their bodies merged, and he deepened the kiss, plunging his tongue between her parted lips. She met the intrusion with a hunger of her own, opening wider, pulling him deeper.

His fingers sought Clay's pin at her bodice, then tossed it aside. He sought her breasts, kneading, stroking, his thumbs teasing her aching centers until she thought she'd explode from sheer pleasure. Then he lowered his head and drew her into his mouth.

She cried out and pressed closer.

He suckled gently, then ravenously.

"Oh, Bragen . . ."

He moved to the other breast, while one of his hands

pulled their lower bodies closer together. She could feel the hard outline of his maleness, and it ignited a fire in her woman's core. She arched toward him.

His lips tightened around her breast as his hands worked her skirts upward.

She was trembling by the time his fingers found her bare thighs. His mouth returned to hers, hot and demanding. He stroked the curve of her bottom, the length of her sides, and the flat plane of her belly. Then he slid his fingers downward, parting her, touching her.

Flames seared the spot beneath his hand. She clutched at his damp hair. He deepened the kiss, and she thrust toward the sensations setting her ablaze.

He tore his mouth away and kissed her neck and ear. "Easy, angel. Relax and let me do the work." He swirled his finger over the sensitive spot between her legs.

Fire licked her flesh.

He stroked her again, robbing her of breath, of thought, of everything but him.

He returned to her breasts, taunting them with his mouth, while his hand continued its sensual magic.

It was too much. The feelings tumbled, one on top of the other, burying her beneath an avalanche of breath-stealing, mind-numbing pleasure. She cried out as jolt after jolt shook her, tossed her, smothered her, then at long last, buried her in a warm, contented glow.

Her forehead dropped against his chest, and she took great gasps to right her swirling senses.

Bragen wrapped her in his arms and just held her. "I've never known anyone like you, angel. So open and giving. So damned responsive." He kissed her temple, her ear, her jaw, and finally her lips. It was a slow, delicious kiss that reignited the blaze that had been waning in the pit of her stomach.

She slid her arms around his neck, and offered herself fully. "Make love to me, Bragen. Make me your wife in truth."

It was the wrong thing to say. He tensed, dangerously so, then stepped away from her. "So that's what this seduction is all about." He pinned her with a look that could have cut stone. "You'll never be my wife, Nichole. Not now. Not ever. Understand that and accept it."

The pain was so unexpected she flinched. "Why? Damn you, Bragen Alexander. *Why?* I know you care about me."

Unconcerned with his nakedness, he stalked across the cabin to put some distance between them. He took several harsh breaths, but it didn't seem to help. In a burst of frustration, he slammed a fist into the bulkhead. "You're wrong, damn it. I don't care about you. I don't care about anyone."

"Because you won't let yourself."

"Because I *can't* let myself!"

"Why? Are you afraid of being hurt?"

He was beside her in an instant, gripping her shoulders. "Yes, I'm afraid. I'm afraid of how you make me feel. I'm afraid of my dwindling control, but most of all, I'm afraid I'll fall in love with you."

Her heart took flight, and she softened her tone. "Would that be so bad?"

"Yes. Damn it, woman, you don't know me. You just don't know. . . ." He moved away from her, his eyes dark with pain. "I'm a murderer, Nichole. I killed my wife."

Chapter 16

Nichole stared at Bragen. He *killed* her? Disbelief warred with a sudden fear of the man she hadn't known very long, didn't know at all. "You murdered your wife?" Her voice was weak and uncertain. She took a step toward the door.

He didn't appear to notice as he jerked the towel around his waist and knotted it at the side. "Yes. At least I'm pretty sure I did."

It took a second for that to sink in, and some of her anxiety calmed. "What do you mean you're *pretty sure?* Either you did or you didn't."

He sat down at the desk and laced his fingers through his hair. "I wish it was that simple. But it isn't. I honestly don't know if I did or not. All I remember was finding my wife in bed with my friend. I went insane with rage, then everything went black. When I came to my senses, Meela was dead, and Gabriel was gone."

"Gabriel?" she breathed.

"Yes, Nichole. Gabriel Bodine."

She didn't know what to think. Gabriel had cuckolded his friend—somehow, that was not too surprising. He had stolen her jewels; she would never have imagined anyone but him betraying a friend like he had betrayed Bragen. And what about Bragen? Was he a murderer? *No,* her heart cried. He couldn't be. She crossed her arms to hide her nervousness. "Bragen, I know this will be painful for you, but I'd like to hear what happened. At least what you remember."

"Why?"

"Because, deep down, I don't believe you're capable of such viciousness."

He gave a bitter chuckle. "You and Clay are two of a kind."

She was relieved by that. Clay knew him better than anyone. "Will you tell me?"

Rubbing the back of his neck, he stared across the cabin. "There isn't much more to tell. As I mentioned, I was wounded during the last months of the war and spent several weeks in a New Jersey hospital. When I was released, my captain discharged me and told me to go home. My home was then in Virginia, with Meela's family, but before I could return, I needed to bring her back from England. I had sent her to London, to my childhood home, Royal Oak, to keep her safe." He gave a harsh laugh. "Ironic, isn't it?"

He rose and paced the small confines. "I didn't have enough time to send a message on ahead, and, a little selfishly, I guess, I wanted to surprise her, to see the look on her face when she saw me in the flesh. We'd seen each other only once during the war, and that had been four months prior to that day."

His hands curled into fists. "When I arrived at Royal Oak, the servants were gone, but I heard voices upstairs. That's when I found her and Gabriel *in my bed.*"

He arched his neck, the muscles working in his throat, and she could feel the devastation tearing at his soul. "What happened then?"

"I don't remember much—just Meela's scream and the force of my body hitting Gabe. After that, everything's a blank."

"Where were you when your mind cleared?"

He draped an arm above the porthole and rested his brow on his forearm. He stared out over the water. "Standing at the foot of the bed."

"Where was your wife?"

"In the bed. Her"—he swallowed—"throat was cut, and the knife I always carried lay next to her, covered in blood."

Oh, sweet providence. Nichole's stomach gave an uncomfortable twist, and she took a breath. "What happened after that?"

"A rider was cutting through the woods behind the house and had heard Meela's scream. He came to investigate and found me standing over her. I don't remember him leaving, but he must have, because the king's men came shortly after that, and I was arrested for my wife's murder."

He shoved a hand into his pocket. "While awaiting trial, the physician who'd attended me as a child came to the Tower of London to see me. He told me Meela had been pregnant when she died. I knew it had to be Gabe's child. And I was convinced I'd killed her until Clay came to see me. He was furious. He shouted to the heavens that I couldn't have done such a thing." Bragen gave a small smile. "We almost came to blows before he managed to plant a seed of doubt in my mind."

His eyes met hers. "That's why I have to see Gabe. He's the only one who knows what really happened that day."

It was all Nichole could do to keep from throwing up her hands. "I think it's obvious that Gabriel's guilty. Why else would he keep running from you all these years?"

"I've thought of that but it's possible, he saw me kill Meela and thinks I want to kill him, too."

"Oh."

"Or he could be avoiding me because I caught him in bed

with her and he thinks I'll challenge him. But I won't know until I talk to him."

"You expect him to tell you the truth?"

He smiled. "No. But I'll be able to tell. Control is not one of Gabe's virtues. His tongue gets loose when he's upset."

"What if he claims you did it?"

"Then I'll turn myself in. It's better to hang than live with the knowledge that I murdered my wife."

The image of that magnificent body twisting at the end of a rope chilled her blood. "You didn't."

"Clay doesn't think so, either."

"And what do you think?"

He shook his head. "I don't know. I guess it's possible. Bodine's always had a hard time controlling his temper as well as his tongue, but why would he kill her? It just doesn't make sense. Too, I can't help wondering if someone else might have come while I was unconscious."

"Do you have enemies in England?"

"I could. After all, I fought my own countrymen during the war when I took up the colonial cause." He raked his fingers through his hair. "God, I've been over this so many times, I think I'm losing my mind."

She could imagine he did. "How did you escape the Tower of London?"

"With Clay's help." There was anguish and the strain of uncertainty behind those midnight-colored eyes.

But Nichole knew Bragen wasn't a murderer. She recalled the gentle way he'd treated the child who had fallen out of the wagon on the street, his tender ministrations when he thought she was ill, and his reluctant protectiveness even though he'd been forced into an unwanted marriage.

He had a formidable temper, there was no denying that, but he never lost control. Not even with Ian McNall. Oh, he may have loosened a few teeth, but he hadn't done him serious damage.

Those weren't the actions of a brutal killer—not even one

who possessed a raging temper. She closed the distance between them and placed a hand on his arm. "You didn't kill your wife, Bragen. I'd wager my life on that."

"You may be willing to risk it, but I'm not." He stepped out of her reach. "Stay away from me, Nichole. You don't know me. Hell, I don't even know myself."

He flicked a hand toward the door. "Now get out of here so I can get dressed. And the next time you want to play your foolish games of seduction, play them with someone else."

Nichole knew it wouldn't do any good to argue, or deny his accusations, so she thought it best to leave. Besides, she still wanted to talk to Clay. Picking up the pin, she slipped out the door.

After retrieving the pail of scraps, she went to Clay's cabin.

"I thought you'd forgotten all about Victor," Clay said as he motioned her inside and closed the door. He flung a hand toward the dog. "He's been gnawing on my quilt for the last ten minutes."

The dog bounded off the bed to greet her.

"Hello, fellow," she murmured, then set the bucket down and watched him dive into the meal. So much for saving it.

Straightening, she faced Clay, trying her best not to flush. "I would have returned sooner, but I got sidetracked talking to Bragen about his wife's murder."

"What?"

"He told me everything, Clay, even that he thinks he may have done the deed."

"I'll be damned."

She perched in one of the wooden chairs. "Is that so surprising?"

"Coming from Bragen, it is. He's never discussed that day with anyone, including me."

"Then what makes you think he's innocent?"

Clay snagged another chair and straddled it. "I know him. Hell, I've known him most of his life. Bragen may have wanted to beat Gabe senseless, but he'd never have hurt Meela. He'd never hurt any woman."

She felt a measure of reassurance. "Were you there when he was arrested?"

"Right afterward. I'd just returned from a voyage and was on my way to see Morgan when I met Alexander and the king's men on the road to London. I went to the magistrate's office with them, and it damned near killed me to watch Bragen stand there in front of the official, in brooding silence, not even attempting to defend himself when the man questioned him."

That didn't surprise her. Bragen could be quite stubborn at times. "What do you think he'll do to Gabriel when he finds him?"

"I don't know. But if it were me, I'd run the cuckolding bastard through with a blade."

"Do you think Gabriel's capable of murder?"

"Possibly."

"Why do you say that?"

"He has no respect for women. His mother was a slut. When Walter, Gabe's penny-pinching father, was away, she brought countless men, young and old, to her bed. It didn't matter that her son slept right down the hall. She wanted the money. Gabe despised her . . . and that feeling carried over to all women in general. He considered even the highest born ladies whores—and he treated them as such." Clay met her eyes. "You were lucky we showed up in Charleston when we did. Otherwise, you might have learned firsthand just how cruel Gabe can be."

A fleeting surge of loyalty demanded she question the accusation. "Did you ever see him mistreat a woman?"

"Once. A harlot. Bragen and I had to pull him off her and calm him down."

Nichole was relieved she hadn't been subjected to Gabriel's brutality and never would be. She came to her feet. "You're right, Clay. I was fortunate." She scratched Victor behind the ear, then made for the door. "And just for the record, I don't believe for one second that Bragen killed his wife."

She stepped out into the hall—and ran smack into a wall of immovable male flesh—Bragen's chest.

His gaze moved from her to Clay's door, then back again. "Trying your hand at seduction again, Nichole?" He gripped her upper arms. "Tell me, how did it go? Was Clay any more receptive than I was?"

The dolt! She'd only gone to see Clay on *his* behalf, and it infuriated her that he was accusing her of such behavior. Her conscience pricked when she remembered her shameless actions with him earlier, but it didn't give him the right to demean her virtue. *Especially* not him.

She clenched her fists. Pain stabbed into her palm, and she realized she was still holding Clay's pin. She glanced down at the tiny ship, then back up to Bragen, her anger rising. "Clay was much more than receptive—unlike some I could name." Shoving past him, she slammed into the cabin. The man rubbed her the wrong way. And if she didn't believe he'd make her a wonderful husband, she'd push him overboard.

Exhausted, she sank down onto the bottom cot and stretched out. She didn't want to think about Bragen anymore, or Gabriel, or Bragen's first wife. She was tired of all this unrest. She just wanted her jewels, and to get on with her life . . . with or without Bragen.

Nichole awoke to a loud crash and a wildly pitching bed. She lunged to her feet and looked around in confusion.

The dressing screen had fallen. Her trunk had scooted into the center of the floor. Books, papers, and maps lay scattered everywhere, stained by an overturned inkwell.

The storm had struck while she was sleeping. But where was Bragen?

Grabbing her shawl, she raced toward the deck. In the companionway, she was tossed from side to side as the ship pitched crazily. When she reached the narrow staircase, she had to cling to the railings as she climbed.

A torrent of water blasted her in the face when she stepped onto the deck. She shielded her eyes in an attempt to see what was happening.

Through the rain, she saw the captain strapped to the wheel and crewmen holding onto the lifelines as they struggled with flapping riggings. The furled sails twisted and jerked against the slender poles that held them.

A movement overhead caught her attention. Bragen! She clamped a hand over her mouth to keep from crying out. He clung to a swaying mast, trying to gather a sail that had come loose in the wind. He wasn't wearing a shirt, and his wet buckskin breeches were plastered to his muscular legs, his black hair dripping into his eyes.

Clay was behind him, also shirtless, and clinging to ropes as he tried to roll the canvas back onto its mounting.

One slip and either man could be washed overboard. She turned away, too frightened to watch.

The cabin boy, Daniel, came into her line of vision, and she clamped down on a scream. He was clutching one of the lines for dear life, his lower body dangling out over the rail of the ship.

Frantically she searched for someone to help him. No one was close enough, and she knew her voice wouldn't carry over the howling wind. She spotted a line of rope nearby. One end was tied to a spot close to Daniel.

If anyone was going to help the child, it had to be her. With a daring she didn't know she possessed, she lunged for the rope and caught it just as her feet slipped out from under her.

It took her several seconds to regain her footing in her drenched skirts and on the rain-washed deck, then she dragged herself along the line until she reached the end tied to a hatch door, but she was still several feet from the rail that led to Daniel. If she was going to help him, she had to cross that distance without support.

Twenty feet, she guessed. Surely she could make it that far if she crawled.

Shaking with fright, she lowered herself to her knees, then took a breath and released the rope. She slammed her palms against the deck and lowered her face close to the planking. Water sloshed over her, but she held her ground, and inch by tedious inch, she worked her way over the wet, slick flooring.

A wave crashed over her, and she slid several feet. Scrambling, she came to her knees, only to be hit by another cascade of water.

She at last gripped the rail and hoisted herself up, then protected her eyes with her hand while she tried to gauge the remaining distance between her and the cabin boy.

He was gone.

"Daniel!" she screamed, running toward the spot she'd last seen him, her hand barely touching the rail in her haste.

She'd almost reached her destination when a rope cut across her path. It was drawn taut over the railing. Had it broken? Was Daniel hanging from the other end?

She grabbed onto the rail and hoisted herself up to see over the edge.

Daniel's frightened eyes stared back at her from where he clung to the tattered end of the rope several feet down. His frail body bounced off the ship's side again and again as waves slammed him into the ungiving surface.

She knew his arms couldn't hold out much longer. Curving one hand around the side of her mouth, she yelled down to him. "Hang on! I'm going to pull you up."

He shook his head furiously, but she ignored him. Holding onto the rail with one hand, she grabbed the rope with the other. But one arm wasn't strong enough to pull his weight. In fact, she doubted both would be enough, but she had to try.

She braced her middle against the teakwood and grabbed the rope with both hands. With every ounce of strength she had, she pulled, her arms shaking, her body quivering with the strain. Just as she felt the rope give, the ship pitched starboard.

A gushing wave slammed into her backside. Water crashed over her, consumed her. It stole her breath, tore her hands from the rope—and hurled her over the edge.

Chapter 17

Bragen had nearly reached Nichole when the wave hit. He clung diligently to the line as foamy saltwater whipped around him.

When the torrent receded, he struggled to his feet and searched the deck.

She wasn't there.

"Nichole!" he roared. He raced to the rail, scanning the swirling black water. When he didn't see her, he started to dive overboard after her.

"Bragen, no!" Nichole screamed. The words barely reached him through the wind.

He tried to locate her. "Nichole?"

"Down here! Below you."

A new surge of fear gripped him as he leaned over the rail.

Nichole clung to the end of a rope, one arm fastened in a death hold around the young cabin boy, Daniel.

Bragen was too horrified to move.

"What's going on?" Clay yelled. He stood nearby, hanging onto one of the ropes.

Bragen didn't waste time or energy trying to explain. He motioned him over, then turned and grabbed the rope. "Hold on!" he called out. Wrapping the hemp around one palm, he hauled back on the line. The weight of both Nichole and Daniel, along with their wet clothing, was more than he'd bargained for. The rope slipped.

Clay's helping hands came out of nowhere. "On three," he instructed. "One, two, *three.*"

Inch by inch, they raised the rope until Bragen was able to grab Daniel's arm. He swung him over the rail, then caught Nichole and hauled her straight into his arms. For several heartbeats, he just held her, trying to control the tremors racing through his limbs.

Clay inspected Daniel for damage. Seeing none, he dragged him toward the captain, holding to the stretched lines. There was no mistaking the anger on Clay's face.

Bragen gripped Nichole by the shoulders, angered, yet refusing to release her. He couldn't. The terror was too fresh. "What the hell were you doing out here?" His voice grated above the howling wind, and he wanted to throttle her for scaring him. He shook her. "Damn it, answer me!"

Rain poured over her face, plastering her hair to her head. Chill bumps puckered her flesh, and her teeth chattered. "I—I heard a crash and came up to see w-what happened. I saw D-Daniel go over the edge, but no one was close. I h-had to help him. A wave swept me over, b-but I caught the rope."

Rage, fear, and relief rolled through Bragen like a tidal wave. The woman had no idea how close she'd come to—"You little fool." He gave her another shake. "You damned near got yourself killed!" He wanted to turn her over his knee for scaring him. He wanted to kiss her until the image of her dangling from that rope faded.

Instead, he marched her along the line toward the hatch, then hauled her down to their cabin. Inside, he thrust her into the chair and scowled at her.

"B-Bragen, please. Don't be angry with me," she pleaded. "If y-you'd seen Daniel, you'd have done the same."

Knowing she was right didn't cool his temper any. The woman had no business on deck during a storm. He opened his mouth to give her a harsh, well-deserved putdown, but the anxiety in her eyes stopped him. She looked so small, so frightened, and so damned appealing, it took the steam out of him.

The ship pitched, and he caught the corner of the desk for support. "Nichole, what am I going to do with you? I never know how to react. Two seconds ago, I wanted to break that lovely neck of yours. Now all I can think of is comforting you."

She gave him a shy smile. "I like that idea much better than the f-first."

So did he, but he wasn't about to admit it. "You need to get out of those wet clothes before you catch your death." He considered helping her but decided he'd never survive it. Opening the door, he gave her a last order. "No matter what you hear, no matter what happens, *don't leave this cabin again.* Is that understood?"

"Yes, Bragen."

That sweet voice and childlike obedience worried him. "I mean it, Nichole."

"I understand."

Somehow he didn't believe her, but he'd already tarried too long. Captain Potter needed all the help he could get.

The uneasy feeling wouldn't leave Bragen as he made his way along the rolling companionway. Since the moment he set eyes on the vixen, she had never, *ever* been that meek. She had more spirit and more courage than any woman he'd ever known. More intelligence, more—"Ah, hell." Shaking his head, he sprinted up the stairs.

It took Nichole about ten minutes to change clothes and leave the cabin. She wasn't going above, but she was going to see to Victor, no matter what Bragen Alexander said.

Entering Clay's cabin, she found the dog curled in a

corner, shaking like a frightened child. Her heart went out to him. She knelt beside him and put her arms around his neck. "I'm here, boy. Everything will be fine now." She massaged his ear. "I know the storm's scary. It is to me, too. But I won't let it hurt you. I promise."

As if he understood her, he nuzzled her shoulder.

She smiled and sat down on the bunk. She patted the tick. "Come here, Victor. We'll be much more comfortable up here."

He sprang up beside her and curled against her leg.

Having never comforted an animal before, she wasn't sure what to do, so she covered him with the quilt, then placed a calming hand on his back and began to hum.

After a few minutes, his shaking subsided.

Encouraged, she stretched out beside him, then draped an arm across the covered lump. She continued to hum, her voice barely carrying above the wailing wind. She was completely exhausted. Her arms hurt, her head, and her eyelids felt so heavy. . . .

Bragen couldn't concentrate on anything. His concern for Nichole grew with each passing moment, and he knew in his gut she wouldn't stay in the cabin like he told her.

He darted across the slick deck and headed below. He had to make sure she was safe. Bracing himself on both walls of the heaving companionway, he staggered to their cabin and opened the door.

Nichole was gone.

Furious for not paying closer attention to his instincts, he slammed out the door. When he found her, he was going to tie her to the damn bed!

Some hours later, the storm mellowed and his anger had turned to genuine concern. He'd searched everywhere, the dining room, the gentlemen's parlor, the deck, even the cargo hold, where he figured she kept the dog. But Victor wasn't there, and neither was she.

A vision of the animal getting away from her and her

chasing it up on deck during the storm flashed through his mind, but he swiftly repressed it. The possibility was too horrifying to consider.

No. She had to be somewhere else.

But she wasn't. Not one crewman had seen her, not the captain, not the first mate . . . not Daniel.

Spotting Clay, he hurried toward him. "Have you seen Nichole?" Bragen had to raise his voice to be heard above the crash of a wave.

"Don't tell me you lost her again."

Bragen brushed his dripping hair out of his eyes. "I'm afraid so."

A smile tilted the corner of Clay's mouth. "She's quite a handful, isn't she?"

"She's a damned sight more than that."

Clay grinned. "Where have you looked?"

"Everywhere."

"Have you checked my cabin?"

Bragen's blood iced over. "Now, why would I want do that?"

"Because more than likely, that's where she is." Without further explanation, Clay returned to his work.

A knot formed in Bragen's gut, and his own words came back to haunt him. *The next time you want to play your games of seduction, play them with someone else.* But, damn it, he hadn't meant it. Whirling around, he ignored the safety line and stalked toward Cordell's cabin.

Without knocking, he swung the door open, and froze at the sight of Nichole fast asleep in Clay's bed. He darted a glance around the cabin for the dog, but it wasn't there. And she looked so content in Cordell's bunk. Fury consumed him. Damn her. Damn her to hell!

Unable to stand the painful sight, he slammed out the door.

Once in his own cabin, he slumped in the chair and buried his fingers in his hair. The pain of Meela's betrayal merged with Nichole's. When he'd found Meela in bed with Bodine, he'd been enraged and had wanted to beat Gabe senseless, but those feelings were nothing compared to how he felt now. He wasn't just angry. He was empty—as if a vital part of himself had been cut away. How could Clay do this to him? *The same way Gabe had,* a small voice answered.

No! This was different. Clay wasn't to blame. Bragen had made it known from the start that he wanted no part of the woman, because he was afraid; afraid of his feelings for her.

He stared at the rocking ceiling, trying to analyze the difference between that day three years ago and now. He had loved Meela, or at least thought he did, and when he found her with Bodine he'd been jealous. But he hadn't hurt the way he did now. He hadn't felt hollow and sick.

So what was the difference? Slowly, painfully, the answer came to him. He was in love with Nichole, in a way he'd never been with Meela. He'd cared deeply for Meela, he didn't doubt that, but he'd never let her touch his soul the way Nichole had. Even after Meela's death, he'd never felt the same, heart-twisting sense of loss he did at this moment.

As he watched candlelight flicker over the teakwood walls, he wondered how he could have killed Meela in a fit of jealousy when the hurt was far worse this time, yet he hadn't even confronted Nichole.

Clay's stubborn declaration of Bragen's innocence plagued him. Was it possible that Clay knew him better than he knew himself? Was it possible he hadn't hurt Meela at all? Only Gabe knew for sure. Only Gabe.

A loud noise woke Nichole, and she stretched long and lazily.

Victor untangled himself from the quilt and barked at the door.

She ruffled his ear. "It's all right, boy. It's just the storm." She came to her feet. "And I think it's time I went back to my own cabin." She nuzzled his neck with her forehead. "You'll be fine now. Besides, Bragen's bound to return soon." *If he hasn't already.* "You be good for Clay, hear?"

Victor wagged his tail.

Smiling, Nichole slipped Clay's pin from her pocket and set it on the desk, then headed for her own room.

She was startled to find Bragen staring out the porthole. By the stiff set of his shoulders, she knew he was angry. She gave an inward groan. He was going to be difficult about her disobeying his orders. She just knew it.

"Bragen, I can explain."

He didn't turn, but when he spoke, his voice dripped icicles. "Get your things and get out of my cabin."

Nichole sighed. He really was carrying this too far. "Don't be silly, Bragen. I'm not going anywhere."

He whirled on her, his eyes black and so cold they could have frozen the Atlantic. "Fine, then I'll leave." Shoving past her, he stormed out the door.

Nichole sagged against the bulkhead. The man was impossible. Well, fine. Let him smolder until he went up in flames. She didn't give a fig.

Nichole tried her best to remember those words when Bragen moved his clothes out of their room and pretended she didn't exist—which made for some long, boring days. But there was one consolation—Victor was able to stay with her.

She didn't know where her husband had been sleeping, and she didn't want to know. She might be tempted to go to him. Besides, if he was going to be so pigheaded over such a small indiscretion and not even allow her to explain, she didn't want to speak to him again. Ever.

Since most of the passengers still considered her tainted, and she had no acquaintances other than Clay and Bragen, she spent a lot of time in her cabin. She'd read every book in her trunk, and a couple she'd found in the desk drawer, Bragen's, no doubt. She'd unpacked her clothes and hung them in the wardrobe closet. She'd placed the statue Jason had sent her on the desk—a constant reminder of how her life had gotten so turned around. If Jason hadn't sent the statue and letter, she might very well be married to Gabriel now. She shuddered just thinking of how cruel he might have become once he learned she'd deceived him about her finances.

She was sure even Gabriel's viciousness couldn't have been more painful than Bragen's defection, though. Without his vital presence, the cabin felt empty. She knew she had fallen in love with him, and she was certain she shouldn't have done so—not that she'd had a choice, but his cool aloofness cut her deeply. She ached to see him smile, hear his laughter, watch his eyes sparkle with humor or grow dark with desire.

But she hadn't seen any of those things since the day of the storm, and if things didn't change soon, by the time they reached London, any chance she had of remaining Bragen's wife would shrivel up like a grape in the sun.

She had to do something soon. Something drastic.

Bragen threw down his cards. For the hundredth time, he hadn't been able to concentrate. The ache in his chest wouldn't let him. Damn it, he missed Nichole. He missed her wit, the way she made him feel good just watching her, The way her eyes brightened with excitement or lowered when she blushed. Jesus, he even missed her smart mouth.

Dragging in a breath, he rose. "Excuse me, gentlemen." He nodded to Prichard, Rupert, and the physician. "I believe I've had enough for today."

"Bloody shame," Prichard mumbled. "Was just about to break even. Lost a bundle to you, you know. Wife's only now speakin' to me again." He winked a puffy eye. "By the by, thank you for havin' Daniel sneak them bobs into the ol' gal's trunks. Saved me a passel o' trouble, you know. Speakin' o' missuses, I ain't seen yours around. She ain't ailin' again, is she?"

Bragen's mood turned black.

"No, Mr. Haviland," Nichole's soft voice called out. "I'm feeling just fine."

Bragen whirled toward the door to see her standing defiantly in the entrance. His heart took a giant leap. The gown she wore was a wine-colored silk that dipped so low, the dark pink flesh round her nipples was clearly visible. The material clung to her curves like wet red tissue.

Desire whipped through him.

Her hair hung loose, in shimmering gold waves, with tiny wisps brushing her smooth cheeks. He'd forgotten how beautiful she was. And he'd been miserable without her. Sleeping on the sofa in the gentlemen's parlor had been a lonesome affair.

He met her clear, sky-blue eyes, and the hunger he read in them tightened the coil in his abdomen. Not wanting to disgrace himself in front of the others, he lifted a hand in farewell, then strode toward her. "What are you doing here?" he hissed.

She stepped out into the hall, and Bragen followed. "Answer me, damn it."

Nervously, one hand fingered the lace on her bodice, while the other remained hidden in the folds of her skirt. "I needed to speak to you."

"We have nothing to say to each other." His speech was clipped. Standing this close to her was torture. Her scent and the heat radiating from her threatened his sanity. He desired her. No, he despised her, and he wouldn't let her get to him again. It hurt too much. He retreated a pace, hoping to put some distance between them.

She advanced. "Oh, but I do have something to say to you," she countered softly. Her hand rose from the folds of her skirt. "And you're going to listen."

He was too stunned to move.

She had a pistol pointed at his chest.

Chapter 18

Bragen didn't know whether to be angry or amused. The nerve of the vixen to pull a gun on him like some avenging angel—Clayton Senior's old flintlock at that. The thing hadn't worked in years, and Clay kept it only in memory of his father. "What's the meaning of this?"

"I said, we're going to talk. In our cabin." She motioned with the barrel. "Now."

Just the thought of being alone with her sent a thrill through him. Still, he was torn between wanting to turn her over his knee and wanting to learn the reason behind this foolishness. Trying to appear annoyed, he strode into the room they'd once shared. He'd expected to see the dog, since Daniel told him she had brought the animal to stay with her. But Victor wasn't there. "All right. What's this all about?"

"Take off your clothes."

"What?"

"You're going to make love to me, Bragen. Right here. Right now."

There was nothing he wanted more. That's all he'd thought about in the last weeks—hell, since the day he'd met her. But he couldn't shake the image of her lying in Cordell's bed. "You have the wrong man, Nichole."

"I do?"

"You know damn well you do. Don't play me for a fool, woman. I saw you in Clay's bed."

She was genuinely confused. "What are you talking about?"

"The day of the storm, I went to check on you and found you sleeping in Cordell's bed."

Her eyes filled with tenderness. "So *that's* what this is all about, and here I thought it was because I left the cabin against your orders." Her soft mouth curled into an indulgent smile. "Bragen, I was in Clay's cabin because of you. He agreed to keep Victor when you threw him out. I'd been taking food there, and that particular day, I went in because I knew Victor would be afraid of the storm."

He wanted to believe her, more than anything. "The dog wasn't in the cabin, Nichole." Crossing his arms, he smirked. "Any more ready lies, angel?"

Anger flashed in her pale eyes, and she tightened her hold on the pistol. "He was there, you jackass, but I see I'm not going to convince you. I'm not even going to try. I'm sick to death of defending myself." She gestured with the gun barrel. "Remove your clothes."

The uncertainty in her eyes and the slight tremor in her hand revealed how desperate she was. But desperate for what? For him to believe her? He studied her elfin face and saw her disappointment. Perhaps he'd been too quick to judge her. "Where was the dog?"

"Under the quilt. Now quit stalling."

He mulled her answer over for a moment and decided it was possible. The realization struck him hard. She and Clay weren't—Ah, hell. Still, he hesitated. If they made love, their marriage couldn't be annulled.

He damned himself for the pleasure that thought gave him. "What about the pin I saw you wearing? *Clay's pin.* Was that a mistake on my part, too?"

"No. I borrowed it to make you jealous."

The open honesty behind those words sank into his soul. There could only be one reason why she'd want to make him jealous. His pulse began to pound. He wanted her with a need that went far beyond sex or lust . . . and came straight from the heart.

Ignoring the voice inside his head that demanded he leave while he could, he lowered his hands to the laces on his shirt and pulled them free, then lifted the garment off over his head.

He hardened when he saw her eyes roam over his chest with hunger. His own went to the swells of her breasts.

He kicked off his boots, then released the buttons on his breeches. At her intake of breath, he stopped. A flush pinkened her skin, and her small white teeth nibbled her lower lip. He smiled. "Second thoughts?"

She lifted her chin. "None whatsoever. You may continue."

The witch. He'd give her something to suck in her breath about. He leaned on the desk and pulled off his buckskins, then tossed them aside. Naked, he straightened and planted his hands on his hips. "Now what?"

Her cheeks grew bright red. "I—I want you to make love t-to me."

"From here?"

She swallowed. "Of course not." She took a tentative step and waved the gun. "Lie down on the bed."

He stretched out on the tick and folded his hands behind his head, trying very hard to hide the desire tightening his loins. The struggle was useless. He was so hard he ached. "Shouldn't you take off *your* clothes? It's going to be difficult to carry through with this with them on."

She darted a glance toward the dressing screen. "Stay where you are. I'll be right back." She disappeared behind the barrier.

Unable to control a smile, he stared at the upper bunk, listening to the rustle of clothing and wondering what on earth had brought this on.

"Close your eyes," she said, peeking around the edge of the screen. "And keep them closed."

Checking the urge to shake his head, he lowered his lashes. "They're closed." He heard her pad across the floor and sensed when she stood beside him. A second later, her smooth, naked body slid down next to his.

His breath stopped. He swallowed. Hard.

For several moments, they lay there, neither of them moving. Inside—but at least not outwardly—he was a mess. His lungs burned from the strain of trying to drag in air, and the pounding in his chest intensified to the point of pain.

"Do something," she ordered in a husky whisper.

It took him a minute to control his voice. "What do you suggest?"

"I don't know. You're the experienced one."

"But I've never been 'forced' before. I'm afraid you'll just have to tell me what you want me to do."

"Oh, very well," she hissed. "Kiss me."

"May I open my eyes?"

"No!"

"Then how will I find you?"

"Oh, for pity's sake."

"It's a reasonable question."

"Very well, Bragen. I'll kiss you. Just don't move."

That wouldn't be easy. "All right." With a feigned sigh of resignation, he pursed his lips. "I'm ready."

There was a long pause, then soft, full female lips slid over his. She tasted like sweet tea and the honey-covered scones they'd had for supper. The scent of warm woman's flesh and lilac surrounded him, and it was all he could do not to deepen the kiss.

"You're making this difficult, Bragen."

Not nearly as difficult as you're making it for me. "I don't like being forced," he countered honestly, hanging onto his control by a thread. The moistness of her breath on his lips sent streaks of desire singing through his nerve endings. His whole body constricted with need.

She placed a warm palm on his stomach. "I've tried everything else."

The muscles beneath her hand grew taut. He'd dreamed of her every night for weeks, envisioned himself making love to her over and over again. Her closeness was more than he could stand. "You haven't tried asking."

There was a long pause, then her lips touched his ear. "Please make love to me."

Jesus. Did she know what those words did to him? He fought for calm and reason. "Not with a gun between us."

Silence filled the cabin. Waves slapped at the hull. Boards creaked. Candlelight wavered. Then the gun thudded quietly to the floor.

That small gesture touched a sensitive spot deep inside him. He raised his lashes to see her staring down at him, her eyes dark with longing. The last of his restraint shredded. His need overtook his senses, and he threaded his fingers through her silky tumble of hair, then slowly, gently brought her lips to his.

A tiny whimper shimmered over his mouth, and he pressed into her sweet, silken warmth. He stroked her tongue, her full lower lip, the smooth surface of her teeth.

She pressed closer, and he felt the stiff points of her breasts touch his chest. It started a fire he couldn't extinguish.

He deepened the kiss, sliding his hands down her bare back, learning her shape, the satin texture of her skin. He cupped her small rear and drew her astride him. His sex, hot and heavy, nestled against the softness of her belly, and a surge of desire hit him so hard he trembled.

It didn't matter what had transpired before. He wanted her more than any woman he'd ever known.

He nudged her back, wanting to look at her, feast on her. Creamy white breasts, full, round, and uptilted, beckoned him, the dusky tips beacons of temptation. He flicked his tongue lightly over one tight nub.

Her hands gripped his forearms, and she arched forward, offering him more.

He greedily took it, drawing her into his mouth. She tasted like lilac and musk . . . and woman. He closed his eyes, centering his full attention on the softness between his lips. His teeth grazed her, then he soothed her with his tongue. He suckled her again.

She pressed closer, her nipples hard and jutting.

Her response aroused him to a fevered pitch. He drew her deep into his mouth and nursed with hunger, burying his face in her soft flesh.

"Oh, Bragen," she breathed on a sigh. She curled her fingers into his hair, pulling him nearer still, her legs trembling against his sides.

He pleasured first one breast, then the other, but it was no longer enough. He needed more of her, all of her.

He caught her behind the neck and pulled her down to him, then took her mouth again and again, plunging deep in a rhythm his lower body craved. He tasted her ear, her throat, the gentle slope of her shoulder, then claimed a breast.

It still wasn't enough. He pulled her forward to straddle his chest, giving him access to the delicate flesh covering her ribs, the tempting dip in her side, the tiny recess centering her stomach.

He drew her up to her knees, and her fingers curled around the slats of the upper bunk. He explored her smooth stomach, her thighs, and the silky blond triangle that called to him.

"Bragen, you can't!" She tried to pull away.

He held her fast. "Oh, but I can." He eased his tongue between her moist folds. She shivered, and the aroma of her woman's scent filled him to bursting. He stroked her, then jabbed lightly and stroked her again.

She gave a low, shaky moan. Her spine arched in pleasure, and he covered her with his open mouth. His own passion slipped out of control. He pressed his tongue into her, while his thumbs met at the juncture of her thighs to continue the assault. He penetrated her in a motion that made his sex throb.

Her muscles tightened and shook.

He quickened the rhythm.

"Bragen! Oh, God!" She arched, her small body thrusting and twisting with the force of her climax. Still, he didn't stop. He pushed her on and on, drove her beyond mere satisfaction. He wanted her to touch heaven.

When her shudders slackened to light shivers, he lifted his head to stare into her exquisite face. Candlelight flickered over the golden curls that tumbled down her back and surrounded her glowing cheeks. Her lips were swollen with passion, her eyes half closed and dark with sexual gratification.

Her breasts, still tight with arousal, swayed with her uneven breathing. It quickened his own, and he knew he could no longer control his urges. He needed to be inside her.

Slipping his hands around behind her, he eased a finger over her damp core. She was ready for him. "Let go of the rails," he instructed in a heavy rasp. "I'm going to make love to you."

Her breath caught, and for just an instant, she hesitated, then she lowered her hands to grip his wrists.

By the way she responded to his touch, he knew—unless

she was a damned good actress—she was a virgin. He eased her over him, the tip of his sex pressed to her silken opening. "This is going to hurt, angel. But there's no other way. The pain will pass quickly."

"It won't hur—"

He plunged up inside her.

Smooth, tight flesh stretched to accommodate his size, but there was no barrier, no maidenhead. His momentary disappointment sank in a blaze of need. He withdrew, then drove into her again.

She met him thrust for thrust, her nails digging into his wrists as she took him deeper and deeper.

His world slipped away in a firestorm of white-hot jolts that had him rocking in spasms of pleasure so intense it bordered on torture. He was only vaguely aware of her cry of fulfillment, of her tightening around his erupting shaft as his own cresting pleasure tore free of its bounds.

He slumped back onto the mattress and let his hands fall away from her hips. Laboring for air, he closed his eyes and listened to the pounding in his chest. He didn't want to think about what had just happened, about what he'd just learned. Not yet.

"Bragen? Are you all right?"

No, he thought with a mixture of anger and sadness. Someone before him had introduced her to sexual pleasure. He knew it shouldn't bother him. After all, he was no virgin himself. But it *did* bother him.

He opened his eyes and stared into hers. The innocent look behind those thick gold lashes made him want to shake her. She was no damned innocent. Not by any means. "Who was he?" he demanded.

"Who was who?"

"The man who took your maidenhead."

She shrank away from him and left the bed, then snatched up his shirt and wrapped it around her. She didn't face him. "You're the only man I've ever been with, Bragen."

Disappointment struck him hard. After what they'd just shared, he'd hoped she wouldn't lie to him. But it didn't matter. He knew the answer. Hell, he'd suspected it all along. She had given herself to Gabriel Bodine.

Just like Meela.

Chapter 19

Nichole watched Bragen slip away from her. He didn't believe her. It was written all over his face.

She took a breath to ease the ache in her chest. He should have trusted her—or at least asked her to explain. But no, he'd drawn his own conclusions, convicted her without so much as a trial. The knowledge hurt beyond anything she'd ever known.

Just once, she'd like someone to believe her without her having to prove herself. She was sick of defending herself, of suspicion, and skepticism. *A man and woman can't have a life together if they don't trust each other.* She believed him, believed *in* him—even when he doubted himself. Why couldn't he offer her the same courtesy? Why didn't he just ask her?

Fighting tears, she stepped behind the dressing screen, then tossed his shirt over the top. "Get out, Bragen." She yanked on her own garments, refusing to see if he complied.

189

It didn't matter. If he wasn't gone when she was finished, *she'd* leave.

But he was.

Bragen stood at the bow, staring out over miles of open water. But his thoughts remained with Nichole. He couldn't explain it, exactly, but he felt as if he'd made some horrendous mistake. The edge to her voice when she told him to get out had been sharper than any knife, as painfully sharp as the knowledge that Gabe had taken her virginity.

But she said she'd never been with any man but you.

The thought startled him, forced him to pause and reconsider. Was it possible she'd lost her maidenhead in another manner? He'd heard of that, of women who'd injured themselves in an accident, though he'd never believed it.

He shoved his hands into his pockets, his feet spread to roll with the deck. But what if it were true? What if he'd misjudged her?

It wouldn't make any difference. Until he knew the truth about Meela's death, it just didn't matter. But he now had another problem. The marriage couldn't be annulled, and there was always the possibility of a child. The thought pleased him when he knew damn well it shouldn't.

And it was something they needed to discuss.

Sprinting back to the cabin, he'd just reached for the latch when he heard an unfamiliar sound. Concerned, he opened the door.

Nichole was bent over the chamber pot, retching.

He knelt beside her, his mind going over the contents of the meals served that day. Between eggs, ham, scones, and freshly killed chicken, he couldn't think of anything that would make her ill.

"Nichole, what's wrong?" he asked while massaging her back. He touched her cheek, testing for fever, but it was cool and damp.

"I don't know," she moaned, then lunged for the pot again.

When she'd finished, he dampened a cloth and washed her face, then carried her to the bed. "You stay lying down. I'm going to fetch the physician."

She was too weak to even protest.

When he returned with Wilson, the older man ushered him out into the hall. Bragen glared holes in the door. Then he worried. What if she'd contracted some deadly disease? It wasn't unheard of aboard ship.

Bragen swore and paced, and it seemed like hours before Mr. Wilson finally emerged from the cabin.

"How is she?" Bragen demanded. "Is she all right? What's wrong with her?"

Wilson smiled. "Take it easy, son. Your wife's fine. But I dare say it's a good thing you married when you did. Otherwise, you might have had some explaining to do when your babe arrived a month early."

"Babe? *What babe?*"

The physician lifted a graying brow. "Surely you knew your wife was pregnant."

Bragen could only stare at the man. Nichole was with child? *She's pregnant with Gabriel's child!*

Too numb to think, he handed the physician some coins, then headed topside. He didn't want to see her right now. He thought about everything that had happened since he met Nichole. He recalled the day they met at Miss Fender's and Nichole's determination to go after Gabriel. She must have known her pregnancy was a possibility even then. He remembered how she stowed away in his cabin, changed, and bathed—something an innocent wouldn't even consider.

He brushed the hair out of his eyes. But why would she tempt Bragen himself if she was so set on finding Bodine? The answer came with blinding clarity. She was running out of time and needed a husband. *And I've played right into her hands.*

His mouth tightened. It was all so clear: her willingness to marry a complete stranger, then her attempts at seduction. And now he knew why she'd been so determined to get into his bed. She couldn't afford to have the marriage annulled.

His hands drew into fists. She had planned it all. Since Gabe had skipped out on her, she'd been forced to find a husband . . . any way she could. God, what a fool he'd been.

She was going to have Bragen's child. Nichole shook her head as she slipped into a woolen gown. She must have conceived that night at the Crimson Candle. Of all of the men in the world, she had to get one of the most potent, and one of the most stubborn. He'd never believe the child was his. To his knowledge, they'd made love only once, and that was today. The only chance she had of convincing him was by telling him the truth, which was just what she intended to do—what she should have done in the beginning.

Dragging a brush through her hair, she tossed it on the desk and went in search of her husband.

She found him at the bow, staring out over the water. "We need to talk," she stated in a firm voice.

He stiffened, but he didn't turn. "Save it. I'm not in the mood for conversation."

"If you don't want to talk, fine. But I'm going to." She planted her hands on her hips. "The child is yours, Bragen."

He whipped around so fast he bumped into her. But the look on his face was anything but apologetic. Fury smoldered in his black eyes. "Is there no end to your lies?"

"I swear to you, Bragen."

"Don't." He held up his hand. "Nichole, I may not know a lot about women and childbirth, but I damned sure know I can't make you a month pregnant when we've only been together for an hour."

"I was pregnant before I got on the ship," she admitted. "By you."

He crossed his arms and leaned on the rail, his mouth a

mocking slant. "Since we met only the day prior, I'd like to know how."

"I was the woman in your bed that night at the Crimson Candle."

He started with surprise, then his eyes narrowed. "I'm well aware you overheard my conversation about the earbobs that first night in the cabin, and you've probably talked to Clay, too, and got all the particulars. I must admit, you're unusually thorough." He gave a disgusted snort. "But it won't work. I can see right through your lies. You needed a husband, and I was fool enough to fall in with your plans."

"I'm not lying!"

"Yes, you are. You lie about everything. You lied to the captain when you boarded the ship. You fabricated the tale about the seaman being tossed overboard so I could get to the brandy. You pretended to be ill to keep me in the cabin—which, in essence, is the same as lying. You even lied by omission when you didn't tell me McNall's blackmail had continued. But it won't work this time. You see, Nichole, there's a fact that escaped you. Even though my whore was a virgin—which I'm sure Clay told you—he forgot to mention the fact that she had red hair." With that, he turned and walked away.

"It was a wig!"

He didn't even slow his stride.

During the last week of the voyage, the sickness that assailed her every evening had at last given way to mere nausea, her bond with Victor grew, and she saw Bragen only once, and that was from a distance. The glower he'd sent her wasn't in the least encouraging. In fact, his black frown had warned her not to even consider approaching him.

She obeyed his silent command out of hurt and anger . . . and disillusionment. Too, she was angry with herself. Until Bragen had pointed out her penchant for lies—for the second time—she hadn't realized how often she fabricated.

It made her wonder if she wasn't at fault for everyone's distrust. Not a cheering notion at all.

But she'd never lie about the father of her babe. Bragen should know that, if he knew anything about her at all, which he obviously didn't.

She folded her arms on the ship's rail. What was she going to do? She might have escaped scandal because she was married, but she had no way to take care of herself, much less a child. Even her jewels weren't enough for that. And what was she going to do about Bragen?

"Captain says we'll reach port this afternoon."

Clay's voice startled her, and she jumped.

He didn't notice as he stepped up beside her and braced an arm on the rail next to hers.

"It can't be soon enough for me," she snapped, then winced at her waspishness. Clay hadn't done anything to deserve her sarcasm. "I'm sorry. I guess I'm getting edgy after so long at sea."

"Couldn't have anything to do with our brooding friend over there, could it?"

She saw Bragen standing by the captain, glaring at them. "His foul mood doesn't affect me one way or another." She tried not to grimace at the lie.

"What does he say about the babe?"

It was all Nichole could do not to roll her eyes. Was anyone left that *didn't* know about the child? "He says it's not his."

"I can see why. According to the physician, you were pregnant when you boarded the ship. But what I don't understand is why you just don't admit that Gabe's the father and be done with it. He was your fiancé, after all, and I'm sure Bragen would rather hear the truth."

"Bragen wouldn't know the truth if it slapped him in the face. Excuse me, Clay, but I need to start packing." With a brusque nod, she walked away. And as much as it pained her, she returned Victor to his cage until they transferred to

Clay's ship for the next leg of the journey, a voyage that would be tense and disagreeable.

When they disembarked in London, Bragen dutifully walked her to the Englishmen's Inn, a brownstone stationed near the docks, along the north bank of the Thames. It was a rather unassuming structure, and she knew why Bragen had chosen it. After his escape from the Tower of London three years ago, he was still a wanted man and needed to avoid the areas where people might recognize him.

The traffic and noise, the sickening odor of heavy smoke and fish brought back memories of her life in England, but she felt no melancholy. That life belonged to someone else.

Bragen ushered her through narrow doors that led into a lobby built of stone. At the high, polished counter, he paid for two rooms, then bustled her up the stairs and left her.

His distance hurt more than she wanted to admit, and it made her angry. She wouldn't live with that arrogant blackguard if he begged her! And, nice though a real marriage to Bragen might have been, she was tired of moping around over what would never be.

Bragen would be back. He had to, since she was the only one who knew Gabriel's destination. She knew, too, that once she'd given Bragen that information, he'd try to leave her behind. That wasn't going to happen. She needed to see Gabriel just as much as he did.

For just an instant she thought about telling Bragen about Gabriel's theft of her jewels, but decided against it. He wouldn't believe her. If only she'd told him sooner. . . .

Grabbing her reticule, she headed for the docks, determined to put past mistakes behind her and outsmart her pigheaded husband. She would find out if Clay's ship had arrived, and if so, she'd have her trunk loaded now. Then there would be only herself to worry about when the time came.

Nichole tried her best to be inconspicuous as she walked along Front Street, watching the afternoon sun attempting to peek through the thick overcast without much success.

Every so often, she'd stop at a shop along the way and pretend interest in their wares, while she covertly searched for an approachable seaman to ask about the *English Maiden* and where it might be located in the harbor.

A man with overlong hair and baggy clothes called out a lewd remark from across the street, then started toward her.

Frightened, she hurried toward the west end of town, to the safety of Piccadilly Street. When she saw one of the king's men standing in front of a millinery, she relaxed and slowed her pace.

She would wait a few minutes, then go back to the docks. Strolling along the boarded walkway, she stopped to gaze in various shop windows. One displayed a fine array of jewels. She admired a pearl necklace, then turned to leave. In the windowpane, she caught a reflection of the seaman from the docks.

He started toward her.

She darted inside the building. From behind a velvet backboard, she watched the sailor stop at the door, scratch his head, then shrug and walk off. She breathed a sigh of relief and straightened.

"May I be of assistance, madam?"

Embarrassed over her skittish behavior, she glanced around. "I'm not sure. I was interested in some new ear-bobs, but I don't see any I like." She retreated a step toward the door. "I'm truly sorry, but that's all I wanted." She stopped. "Unless, of course, you happen to know if the *English Maiden* has docked."

"No, I don't, miss. But, wait, please," the bespeckled storekeeper urged. "I have another tray full of jewels I just finished cleaning. Let me show them to you." He whirled around, his queue swaying.

Not wanting to offend the man by walking out on him, she waited, rehearsing a gentle refusal.

The man bustled around the counter carrying a silver tray laden with jewels.

She gave the contents a quick glance, then smiled at the curator. "I'm sorry, but I don't see . . ." Her gaze drifted back to the tray. There, in the center, lay the pearl earbobs Nick had given her. There was no mistaking them. An *N* for Nichole had been engraved in silver in the center of each pearl. She picked up her jewels. "Where did these come from?"

"A nobleman brung them in. Said the lady who once owned them had drowned in a shipwreck near the horn last year."

"Were there any other baubles?" *Like my locket?*

"No, miss. Not to my knowledge."

Nichole gnawed the inside of her cheek. The man didn't know the jewels were stolen, and she doubted he'd believe her if she told him so. She had absolutely no proof they belonged to her, proof she would need to convince even the authorities of the theft. There was only one way to retrieve the earbobs—the same way they had left her. "Didn't I see a necklace in the window that might match these?"

"I believe so, miss." The shopkeeper hurried over to the display.

Keeping her eyes on him—and with only a twinge of guilt—Nichole slipped the jewels in her skirt pocket. "I'm sorry, I don't have time right now. I fear I'm late for an appointment." She walked to the door. "But I'll return before you close."

Guilt pricked her as she hurried out the door and rushed toward the dock, keeping an eye out for the seaman who'd followed her. The theft wasn't the curator's fault, and as soon as she was ready to board the *English Maiden,* she'd send a note around, explaining why she took the earbobs.

Continuing her search for Clay's ship, she spotted a man

down the street who looked fairly presentable. Summoning her courage, she started toward him.

"Stop! Thief!"

Her heart jumped. She whirled around to see the winded shopkeeper racing after her, pointing in her direction.

A handful of men broke into a run—and headed straight for her.

Chapter 20

A pair of rough hands gripped her arms. "I got the tart," the man crowed. It was the same one she'd tried to avoid earlier. He smelled of sweat, ale, and foul breath behind decayed teeth.

Several more men crowded around her. Others up and down the street stopped to stare.

"Here, here. What's this, now?" The king's man she'd seen in front of the millinery nudged through the crowd. When he came abreast of her, he stopped and inspected her attire. He addressed one of the men holding her arm. "What's the meaning of this?"

"Crawford came runnin' outta his shop, sayin' she stole somethin'. We was just stoppin' her from gettin' away, Whitcomb."

Whitcomb returned his attention to her. "Now why would a high-born lady like yourself want to steal from a shopkeeper?"

"I wasn't stealing."

The shopkeeper, Crawford, shoved through the crowd. "That's her! She's the one who stole my jewels."

"I can explain," Nichole blurted. "The earbobs belong to me. They were stolen by the man who sold them to Mr. Crawford." She withdrew them from her pocket. "The *N* stands for Nichole. That's my name."

"Did you tell Crawford that?" Whitcomb asked.

"No."

"Why?"

"Because I had no proof."

"I see." He took the jewels and dropped them into his pocket. "Well, girl, until the magistrate returns from Sussex at the week's end to hear your . . . tale, you'll be a guest at the Tower."

Nichole shivered. The Tower of London? All the horrible stories she'd heard about the place came rushing back to her. She panicked. "Please. Don't do this. I was only trying to—"

"Silence!" He hauled her through the crowd, barely allowing her feet to touch the ground.

"Nichole has *what?*" Bragen roared, his furious gaze fixed on Clay.

"Been arrested for stealing," Cordell repeated. "They've taken her to the Tower."

Bragen couldn't stop a shudder as he recalled his own stay in that hellish place. Although the prison housed London's most elite criminals, and a goodly sum of money could buy a fair amount of comfort, the cells were damp, musty and cold—and confining. He slammed his glass of port down on the desk. Without another word, he stalked toward the door of his room at the inn. "Let's go."

"Why? So you can take her place? Or do you imagine the authorities have forgotten your arrest . . . and escape?"

Bragen swore and laced his fingers through his hair, remembering the night Clay had paid for his release and whisked him away on another of his ships, the *French Maiden*. "You'll have to go, then. I'll give you the money to bribe the guards so you can see her. I have to know she's all right."

"You know damn good and well I'm not concerned about the money. But I am concerned about her comfort for the next few days until I can arrange her escape."

"Escape?"

Clay gave him a disgusted look. "Bragen, we don't have time to wait for a trial, not if we plan to catch Gabe. We've got to get her out now. Or have you forgotten that she's the only one who knows where he's gone?"

No, Bragen hadn't forgotten that fact for an instant. "How long will it take to make the arrangements?"

"A couple of days."

"I'll see to her comfort, then," Bragen conceded.

"How?"

"I'll send a note to my manservant, Rawlins. Since I've been gone, he and his family have been taking care of Royal Oak. He'll see to her needs. You just find a guard willing to overlook her escape."

He tried not to think about the last time he himself had been at Royal Oak—the night Meela was killed.

When Clay left, Bragen snatched a piece of parchment and an inkwell from the desk and began to write his instructions to Rawlins.

The pen stilled as another idea came to him. He would write two notes, one to the servant, and one to Morgan Frazier. With his help, Bragen could take care of one horrendous problem.

"What are you doing in London?" Morgan snapped when Bragen opened the door to his room. "You damned fool. Are you trying to get yourself killed?"

"It's nice to see you, too, Frazier."

Morgan turned to allow room for his massive shoulders to pass through the partially open door. "I didn't come here to be nice. I came here to find out why I haven't heard from you in nearly three years—and why you're so anxious to get yourself hanged." He waved a huge hand. "I know you haven't been cleared of Meela's murder. I talked to the stipendary magistrate, Charles Coffland, over tea yesterday, just before he left for a meeting in Sussex. He mentioned the king's disapproval over the unsettled matter that's plagued the courts for three years."

Bragen winced. A stipendary magistrate was not only paid, but held his own court, and he had full jurisdiction over this area. Rubbing his forehead, Bragen got back to the problem at hand. "I need your help, Morgan. With a woman."

Frazier's sea-blue eyes darkened with amusement. "Since when?"

"Since I met Nichole Heatherton."

"Nichole?"

"She said she knew you."

"Very well."

Bragen slouched into a chair. "Then you'll understand what I'm about to request of you. She's been arrested for stealing, something I have yet to comprehend. Anyway, she has some information I need, and once I have pried it out of her, I want you to take her to Royal Oak and keep her there—by any means necessary—until I return." Bragen hadn't decided what he was going to do about his wife now that she was pregnant, but the decision could wait until he caught up with Gabe.

Morgan sat on the bed. "Now, why would I want to hold Nichole prisoner?"

"So Clay and I can get away on the *English Maiden.*"

"I should have known that rakehell brother of mine was in on this," Morgan snapped, but Bragen didn't miss the note of fondness in his tone. "Perhaps you'd better start at the beginning."

Even before Bragen finished, Morgan rose and began to pace the room, his eyes darting from one wall to another.

"Anyway," Bragen continued, "I left her at the inn this afternoon, and just recently learned of her escapades with the shopkeeper."

Morgan stilled. "Why would Nichole steal jewelry? From what I remember, she's never cared much about baubles."

"Who can understand women?"

"I won't even try. They're too complicated. But since this is so important to you and that pirate I call a brother, I'll see that the lady's entertained while you make your escape."

Bragen rose and shook Morgan's hand. "I knew I could count on you."

"There's a problem, though," Frazier announced. "If Nichole really doesn't want you to know Gabe's destination, I doubt you'll pry it out of her. The woman's stubbornness is phenomenal."

"It doesn't matter. If she refuses to tell me, I'll find out by other means, even if I have to question every seaman in port. Once she's out of the Tower, though, I want you to stay with her at Royal Oak until I return."

"Nichole's not going to like this."

"I know, but what choice does she have? If she's seen, she'll be arrested again. Besides, when she gets over being angry about us leaving her behind, she'll settle down and accept her fate."

Morgan chuckled. "Don't wager Royal Oak on that."

"Everything's arranged," Clay announced. "The guard's been paid, and I just talked to Morgan. He'll go in after Nichole when the time comes, then carry on with your plans."

Bragen breathed a sigh of relief. Any number of things could have gone wrong. "Then it's settled."

"Except for one thing," Clay countered. "Why are you doing this?"

"What?"

"Leaving her behind when you know how much it means to her to see Bodine."

Bragen had fought his own demons over that one, but he'd come to the conclusion Nichole was after Gabe for revenge. There just wasn't any other explanation. Gabe had taken her innocence, gotten her with child, and left her. She wanted her due, but she wasn't in love with him. She couldn't be after the way she'd responded to Bragen. "I'll bring him back to her. Besides, she doesn't need to make another journey in her condition."

All Bragen's reasons sounded good to his own ears, but he'd omitted one. No matter how much he tried to deny his emotions, he was in love with Nichole—and their situation was hopeless. He had to stay away from her, and he couldn't do that on a ship. "Come on, Clay. We need to talk to some sailors."

"Why?"

"Because I have the feeling that Nichole is going to give me as much information about Gabe's whereabouts as that water pitcher over there. And I need to find out which ship he left on. The *English Maiden* and crew won't do us any good if we don't know where to go."

Nichole stared at the brass tub the guard had just brought in to her, along with a satin quilt, two fluffy pillows, and a brush and mirror set. She didn't doubt that Bragen was somehow responsible for the amenities. Even a portmanteau full of gowns had been brought from the inn.

"A message for ye, gel." A guard shoved a sealed parchment under the heavy iron door. His leering face appeared in the small barred window. "Your lover must be missin' his piece already."

Heat surged to her cheeks, and she yanked the missive up off the floor. "You have the manners of a boor."

His cackle echoed down the corridor as he trudged back to his post.

Nichole broke the seal, and her pulse picked up speed as she read the bold scrawl.

Getting you out of there tonight. Be ready at midnight.
C.C.

Nichole felt tears sting her eyes. Even though the note was sent by Clay, she knew Bragen was involved. He wasn't going to leave her and go look for Gabriel on his own as she thought he would. She allowed herself to imagine what it would be like to be his true wife and raise his children. She touched her belly, cradling the small life within. No matter what happened, she would raise Bragen's child. But live with him? That remained to be seen.

Sniffing, she crumpled the parchment, then held it over the fat candle that had been included in the carpetbag. When it was engulfed in flames, she threw it on the floor and watched it blacken and shrink into a pile of ashes, much like her future would be without Bragen.

Get hold of yourself, she mentally scolded. Bragen Alexander was not the beginning and end of her existence. She did not need a man—not even *that* one—and there was only one thing standing in her way: Gabriel. Her dreams of a cottage and peaceful life were just that . . . dreams—until she recovered her jewels.

But thoughts of Bragen sitting across from her at the breakfast table, his hair tumbled from sleep, or riding beside her in a meadow, laughing as he pulled her to him for a kiss, or lying in bed, watching her with those dark eyes, would not leave her mind. The man had truly seized her heart.

"Ye have a visitor, gel," the guard's gritty voice called through the tiny window. The key grated in the door, then the heavy iron creaked open to reveal Morgan Frazier's enormous frame standing in the doorway. "Afternoon, beautiful. Thought you could use some company."

She smiled, knowing what it must have taken for him to come here. She held out her hands. "It's good to see you, but I must admit, not under these circumstances."

"I'm surprised you're still in here. I figured you'd have

found a way out by now," he teased, brushing his lips over her fingertips and doing his best not to show his discomfort at being locked in a cell.

"I'm working on it."

His chest rumbled with laughter, and his sparkling blue eyes met hers. "I don't doubt it." Then he turned serious. "What happened, imp? Why were you arrested?"

"I stole—"

"I know about the jewels," he interrupted. "What I don't know is why you took them."

Taking a seat on the hard bunk, she told him about Gabriel.

"That bastard." Morgan paced the cell, angered yet anxious, and she knew he would have to leave soon. The walls were closing in on him. "How do Bragen and Clay fit into this?"

If Morgan hadn't been one of the only people she trusted, she might have held her tongue. But he'd proven himself to her a hundred times over. She told him everything, even about the Crimson Candle.

"Hellfire," he rasped. "And Bragen doesn't believe the child is his? The man never *has* had any sense."

"No. And it doesn't matter. I don't care what Bragen thinks. I just want my jewels."

"Nichole, this is me you're talking to." He leaned closer. "Are you in love with him?"

"Yes."

"How does Bragen feel?"

She nibbled her lower lip. "I thought he cared, but now, I just don't know."

Morgan dipped his dark head in thought and started pacing again. "He wants to leave you behind, you know that, don't you? He's pretty desperate, too. He asked me to watch over you."

That didn't surprise her. "I figured as much. Not about you, but him wanting to leave me."

"At least staying in Bragen's home will be a hell of a lot

better than on a ship or in some prison. You'll be glad to know that since Clay bribed the guard, I'll be taking you away from all this tonight."

Disappointment hit her swift and hard. "Your brother bribed the guard?"

"Hoping it was Bragen, were you?"

"No, of course not."

"As long as it happens, I guess it doesn't matter who arranged it, hmmm?" He eyed the walls again, then lifted her hand and kissed it. "I'd better go; got things to do, you know." He winked, then slammed his huge fist against the iron door. The metal shuddered beneath the force. As he waited for the guard, he turned back. "Oh, one more thing. Bring that bag." He gestured to the portmanteau.

"Why?"

"Because, beautiful, I've decided you'll be going on a trip." He tilted his mouth into a roguish smile. "A voyage aboard the *English Maiden,* I believe."

"But I thought you said Bragen didn't want—"

"Let me worry about Alexander."

She folded her arms over her stomach. "Are you trying your hand at matchmaking, Morgan?"

"Yes."

"Why?"

He shrugged. "I want to see you happy, and I think Bragen can do that for you."

Chapter 21

When the guard closed the door behind Morgan, Nichole lifted one of her gowns from a peg on the wall and folded it neatly, reflecting on Morgan's words and Bragen's accusations about her numerous lies. She'd thought about those remarks late into the night and today, and as much as she hated to admit it, she knew he was right. She *did* lie—a lot. For heaven's sake, she'd even lied to Morgan just now, when she told him she didn't care what Bragen thought about the child she carried. She did care, very much.

No more. From this day forward, she would tell the truth, no matter whom it hurt, no matter how much trouble it caused her—except in an extreme emergency, she amended. She wanted trust, and there was only way to get it: she had to earn it.

Her resolution firm, she began packing the rest of her things, wishing Victor were here to keep her company. No, he was much better off in his cage, waiting to be transferred to Clay's ship, than in this smelly place.

By the time she'd finished stuffing the portmanteau, it had gone dusk. Her supper tray had been served and removed, so there was nothing left to do but wait.

It wasn't easy, and by the time the clock at Westminster Abbey struck twelve, she was so nervous, her mouth was dry. The guard would be coming for her soon, and she was scared. What if something went wrong? What if she were caught and Bragen sailed without her? She'd never see her locket or the father of her child again. So much depended on the next few minutes.

A key turned in the lock, and a guard she'd never seen before opened the door. He was gaunt, unshaven, and extremely nervous. "Come quick," he urged, his small eyes shifting with anxiousness. He darted a peek down the hall, then motioned to her with a skeletal hand. Grabbing the bulging portmanteau, she hurried after him.

The air in the corridor was foul and musky from dampness, but worse was the odor of expensive toilet water that mingled with the stench of chamber pots from the cells bordering both sides. She had to swallow to keep from being sick.

Footsteps thudded from around a corner in the corridor.

The guard jerked open an empty cell and shoved her inside.

Seized with terror, she plastered herself to the wall and listened as the two men greeted each other.

"Say, Davey, whatcha doin' here? Thoughtcha was to guard the south section."

The guard who was helping her cleared his throat. "Traded with Brummer. Got tired o' lookin' at the same ugly faces."

A disbelieving snort was the other man's reply. "Don't have to make up tales for me, Davey. If ye got a cully with the cash, just say so. Don't mean nothin' to me if ye need to line your pockets."

She heard Davey give a nervous chuckle. "I wouldn't do nothin' like that, Harry. I need me job too much."

Harry snickered. "Fine. Have it your way." His feet shifted as if he'd turned around. "But watch that gel in sixteen. Her fancy relatives, the Wentworths, talked to the constable when they found out she was arrested. Them upper-crust snoots don't want that one to escape. Said she's not nobility at all, but some bastard babe that was born to a whore in the colonies. They wanna see the chit swing for all the goods she stole from the Heathertons afore they died." He chuckled. "And with all them dandies can offer Coffland, he'll be givin' serious thought to hangin' the gel when he returns." His voice lowered meaningfully. "And he'd be right upset with a body if she suddenly disappeared."

Panic skipped through Nichole. She'd known the Wentworths hadn't liked her, but she never imagined it was to such an extent. Tears stung her eyes. She'd never, *ever* taken anything from the Heathertons. They were her family, for heaven's sake. What about Davey? Would he still allow her escape after what Harry said? Dear God, what was she going to do?

"I-I'll watch her real close, Harry." Davey's nervous wobble penetrated the cell door. "Don't you w-worry none."

Harry praised him. "Knew I could count on you, boy."

When the sound of Harry's footsteps faded, Davey opened the door and gripped her arm. "There's been a change in plans, girl. Ye won't be leavin' us this night."

Nichole tried to pull free. "Please, those things he said weren't true. I never took anything from the Heathertons. I swear I didn't."

"Tell it to the magistrate. He's the one ye need to convince." He dug his nails into her flesh and dragged her toward her cell.

"Is there a problem, Davey?" Morgan's voice rumbled from behind them.

Davey stiffened, and placed his free hand on the pistol

tucked into his belt. "Don't try nothin' funny, Frazier," Davey warned as he turned to face the big man. "I'll kill the chit where she stands."

Nichole didn't know whether to be frightened or relieved at Morgan's entrance.

Morgan smiled. "I don't plan to do anything, Davey, old chum. *He* does."

Davey whirled around. Before her eyes even had a chance to focus, a massive fist shot out and sent Davey sprawling. Nichole was jerked off her feet, and she landed in a most unladylike heap, her skirts and petticoats tumbling over her head.

She fought the lace and satin. Warm male hands hauled her to her feet and helped her right her clothes. Bragen!

"What are you doing here?" she demanded, more concerned for his safety than hers. "Don't you know what will happen to you if they catch you?"

"I have a pretty fair idea, and if you'll quit talking long enough, we'll get out of here before that happens."

Morgan, who had raced down to the end of the hall, motioned for them to follow.

"Bragen, they think I stole from the Heathertons. They were going to hang me!"

"I know. Clay talked to the constable this evening. That's why I'm here. We figured there'd be trouble."

"Where's Clay?" she huffed as he pulled her around the corner, her feet barely able to keep up with his long strides, the carpetbag bouncing into her leg.

He grabbed the bag and swung her up into his arms, then increased his pace. "He's waiting with the carriage."

Nichole looped her arms around Bragen's neck for support. Her fears dissolved under the comfort of his strength. She rested her head on his shoulder, enjoying the power protecting her with such fierce intent. He smelled of musk and ale and buckskin.

The instant they were free of the Tower, Bragen broke into

a run, then thrust Nichole inside a carriage manned by Clay and tossed the bag in after her. "Get her out of here." He slammed the door. "I'll see you at Royal Oak."

Royal Oak? Not the *English Maiden*? What had happened to Morgan's plans? Even as the thought formed, she knew. Bragen had somehow foiled them.

The carriage lunged into motion, and Nichole leaned out the window just in time to see several guards racing after Bragen and Morgan, who were running in the opposite direction, toward the docks.

They were leading the guards away from her!

Gunshots exploded, and Nichole's fear was so great, she was sick with it. Was Bragen hurt? Morgan? Oh, dear God. This was all her fault. If anything happened to either of them, she'd never forgive herself.

The carriage bounced along at a killing rate for several miles, through valleys and fields, along overgrown roads. By the time it at last wrenched to a shuddering halt, she had gotten anxiousness in hand. They would be all right. Bragen and Morgan were both intelligent men. They'd avoid the guards. She was sure of it. *Oh, God, please let it be so.*

The carriage door swung open, and Clay hauled her out. "Come on, woman. Hurry." He all but dragged her up some wide steps, fronting a huge, moonlit brick house surrounded by trees. White columns supported a long porch that protected floor-to-ceiling windows and massive oaken doors.

Clay hustled her inside. "Rawlins!"

A thin, wiry gentleman dressed in black wool appeared, completely unruffled by Clay's urgent command. "There's no need to shout, your grace. I've been expecting you. Master Alexander sent word of your pending arrival."

Your grace?

Clay was in no mood to explain. He shoved her forward. "See that she's shown to a room and made comfortable. I've got to go." He was out the door in a flash.

"Come, miss," Rawlins urged as he picked up the bag

Clay had tossed aside. "I'll show you to your room and prepare a spot of tea."

Nichole followed, still trying to understand why the butler had called Clay "your grace." And was this Bragen's home, Royal Oak? It must be—Rawlins did say Master Alexander, didn't he?

As they walked up a curved staircase, she glanced at some portraits lining the wall. One was of a much younger Bragen, and beyond that were two others who bore a striking resemblance to him. It *was* his home. Nichole stopped for a closer look at the strangers. "Who are they?"

"Master Alexander's brother, Christian, and his sister, Fiona."

"He's quite handsome." *Just like Bragen.* "And she's lovely."

"Yes, mum."

"Do they live here?"

"No. Mistress Fiona married and moved to France, and young Christian lives in Italy." He started up the stairs, but stopped at another portrait. "And these are the master's parents, Lady Elizabeth and Lord Winston." Before she could ask, he went on. "Lord Winston died eight years ago, and Lady Elizabeth purchased an estate near her daughter in Paris."

Bragen and both his siblings had inherited their mother's dark hair, she noted. But that beautiful mouth and arrogant bearing came from their father.

Rawlins led her into a room that made her bedchamber at Miss Fender's look like a closet. A massive four-poster, draped in wine-colored silk, sat beneath a ten-foot-high window. Matching settees and chairs were stationed before a huge white marble fireplace that danced with yellow flames. The armoire was big enough to house double the amount of clothes in her entire wardrobe. Yet for all its imposing size, the room was comfortable and inviting, the rich carpet soothing.

Rawlins placed her portmanteau on the bed, then turned

to leave. "After you refresh yourself, miss, I'll have my wife, Martha, prepare tea for you. She'll serve it in the parlor— the room across from the bottom of the stairwell."

"I'm not a miss, Rawlins. I'm Lady Blakely."

"Excuse the oversight, madam. Master Alexander didn't mention your identity in his note. Will your husband be joining you, also?"

"Yes. Bragen will be here." *God, I pray so.*

The butler sent her a sharp look. "Master Alexander, madam? He's your husband?"

"Yes."

"Then who is Blakely?"

Nichole felt cold numbness wash over her. "I was led to believe Bragen was."

The butler paled. "Well, perhaps—"

"There's no need to make excuses, Rawlins. I fear the cat has escaped the bag." *And I'm not the only liar around.* "Now, who exactly am I married to? And why did you call Clay *your grace?*"

"I think we should let Master Alexander explain."

"Rawlins, I'm now your mistress, aren't I?"

"Yes, your ladyship."

"Then answer me at once."

For a heartbeat, he was uncertain. Then he cleared his throat. "Master Alexander is Bragen Alexander Stanfield, Viscount Blackstone. And Master Cordell is Matthew Clayton Cordell, Duke of Westshire."

Blackstone. Nichole sat down on the bed before she fell. To protect his identity, Bragen had altered his name from Blackstone to Blakely. She shook her head. Alexander Stanfield and the duke of Westshire. She'd heard those names since she was a child. Alexander Stanfield was reputed to be one of the wealthiest viscounts in all of London. And Clay a *duke.* Good heavens. She'd made him share a cabin with her dog!

"Thank you, Rawlins. I think I understand now. And, I'll be down later for tea."

"Yes, mum." He nodded, but looked concerned when he left. It was easy to tell he was worried about how Bragen would react when he learned of their enlightening conversation.

She didn't give a fig how he reacted. Here he'd been so righteous about *her* lies, yet he'd been lying all along. No, she thought, Bragen had never told her he was Viscount Blakely. Clay did. But Bragen had lied by omission, hadn't he? Just like he had accused her of doing.

A tiny voice interceded. *He couldn't let his identity be known if he wanted to avoid the hangman.*

All right, she conceded. He did have a good reason for his tales, but so did she. Her very life had depended on it, too. After Gabriel's disappearance, and without her jewels, she had no way to even feed herself.

And it hurt that Bragen hadn't trusted her with his identity. Suddenly it was all too much for her—everything that had happened in Charleston, her forced marriage to Bragen, her pregnancy, that horrible cell, the Wentworths' treachery, the danger Bragen and the others faced because of her, Morgan's foiled plans for her to board the ship, and now this. . . .

She burst into tears.

Bragen was thankful for Clay's quick thinking. The Tower guards had been on Bragen's and Morgan's heels, chasing them through town, then into Hyde Park, when Clay had appeared out of nowhere in the carriage. They had dived inside under a barrage of musket fire.

At the inn where he'd been staying since he arrived in London, Bragen left Morgan and Clay to celebrate their night's victories, Morgan not yet over being caught talking to the captain of Clay's ship, which fouled up his plans for Nichole. The *English Maiden* would sail the next morning without her, but tonight, Bragen needed to make sure she was all right. Taking the coach they'd hired for her escape, he headed for Royal Oak, trying not to think about the gnawing in his gut at returning there.

Greeting his servants, he waved any questions aside until later and sprinted up the stairs, noticing that nothing had changed. What had he expected? Bleeding walls?

He heard Nichole's weeping before he even reached her room and opened the door to find her curled on the floor, her small body shaking and tears streaming down her beautiful face.

Pushing aside his unease, he hurried to her. Gently, so as not to startle her, he placed a hand on her back. "It's all right, angel. You're safe now."

She bolted up so fast, her head slammed into his chin. Then she was on top of him, plummeting him with her fists, cursing and crying, all at the same time.

He caught her hands. "What the hell's wrong with you?"

"You lying, sneaking, miserable, low-life cur! How dare you lie, accuse, and place yourself in danger! You could have been killed. And for what? To save me from a death that would have been preferable to this sham I call a *life?*"

"Nichole, take it easy."

"No! I won't. I've had enough. I just want to find Gabriel, recover my jewels, and get away from the lot of you."

Bragen gripped her shoulders. "What jewels? The ones you were trying to steal?"

She sniffed. "I wasn't stealing. They were mine. Gabriel stole them from me in Charleston."

He was stunned. "Is *that* why you've been so eager to find him?"

"Yes. Without them, I have no way to live. Miss Fender ordered me to leave her home by summer. The Wentworths were awarded the Heathertons' fortune. I'm penniless with nowhere to go."

Bragen was angered on her behalf. Had everyone set out to hurt her? First the Kincaids, then Miss Fender, Gabe, the Wentworths, and even himself. He pulled her into his arms and just held her. She was crying again—and so defeated.

"Hang on, angel," he soothed. "You've come too far to fall apart now. I'll make everything right if I have to shoot every one of the bastards who hurt you."

"Oh, Bragen. Those others don't matter. Only you do. I thought you'd been killed. Or worse!" She hugged his neck and buried her face in the curve of his shoulder.

He was still trying to figure out what was worse than death when she covered his mouth with hers. She clutched him tighter and pressed her tiny body hard against his.

His need for this woman staggered him. He forgot everything but Nichole, his beautiful, beautiful Nichole. He rolled her beneath him and thrust his tongue into her sweet warmth, lost in desire so strong he couldn't think.

When he'd heard about the Wentworths' plans for Nichole, he'd almost gone insane, and he would have done anything to protect her. But it hadn't occurred to him how she would feel when she saw the danger he'd placed himself in. Just thinking of how he would have felt if the situation had been reversed made him shudder. His hold tightened, and he deepened the kiss.

But kissing her wasn't enough. He needed to touch her, to possess her.

Her clothes fell away beneath his hands, then his own did, and they came together, each taking and giving with urgency. It was as if they couldn't get close enough, deep enough. Her nails bit into his back, and he revelled in the pain, in the savage beauty of their union. He plundered her mouth, her body.

He forged into her, deeper, faster. Each thrust a culmination of all his fear and passion. He couldn't breathe—didn't want to. He only wanted her closer, so much closer.

A low, agonizing groan tore from his throat as his body erupted in white-hot pleasure. Racking shudders shook every muscle in his body as his hot seed spilled into her.

He felt her stiffen, heard her cry of fulfillment, and sank deeper into blissful ecstasy.

Finally, slowly, the convulsions subsided, and he

slumped, gasping for breath. He rolled to the side, dragging her with him, holding her trembling body close to his. He didn't want to let her go, wouldn't. She belonged to him.

For several minutes, neither of them moved. They had a lot of things to discuss, he knew, but he wanted to hold her just a little longer. He closed his eyes and inhaled her sweet fragrance, enjoyed the feel of her warm skin next to his.

She was content to lie in his arms for a while before the questions became too much for her. "Are Clay and Morgan all right?"

"They're fine."

Her tears dropped onto his chest. "Thank heavens. I don't know what I would have done if something had—"

"Shh. Nothing happened." He kissed her ear, her damp cheeks, and her soft mouth, forestalling more conversation until later.

Her lips parted, and she slipped her small tongue into his mouth. The fires he thought were cooled leapt to life. He pulled her on top of him. She was so warm, so damned soft. He gripped her rear and pressed her closer to his swelling shaft.

"I want to love you," she whispered, "the way you loved me that night on the ship."

Before her meaning sank in, she slipped down his chest and circled his nipple with her sweet mouth.

He sucked in a breath.

She trailed her tongue over the stiff crest, flicking and suckling, the same way he'd done to her. His sex grew rigid with expectation.

Barely able to breathe, he closed his eyes and sank his fingers into her hair as she moved lower. She kissed his rib cage, her small pink tongue leaving a trail of moist fire.

She tasted the flesh on his stomach and abdomen while her hands explored the sides of his chest, his waist, his thighs.

Bragen's body began to pulsate under her shy ministrations.

Her lips came closer and closer to that part of him that cried out for her touch. But when her mouth closed over him, the thrill was so unexpected, he jerked with a surge of desire.

Anxious to give her the same pleasure, he caught her by the hips and pulled her around to him. He buried his mouth in her soft curls.

She gasped. A tremor ran through her, and she curved her hands around his thighs, then sank deeper over him, her lips and tongue bringing him to heights he hadn't known existed.

The sensations were so incredible he was fast losing grip. He was only aware of her mouth, of her nails digging into his thighs, of the firm, hard-tipped breasts teasing his stomach, of the sweetness beneath his lips.

He penetrated her with his tongue. She drew on him in retaliation, and a stab of pleasure pierced him like the point of a knife.

She increased the rhythm, grazed him with her teeth, then taunted him with her tongue.

He covered her fully, stroked her. She cried out, and the last of his control snapped. He couldn't take any more. He was so swollen he was about to explode. He dragged her beneath him and eased into the fiery haven he'd explored with his mouth. She was hot and tight, and he had to clench his teeth to halt his eruption. He wanted her pleasure first.

Drawing in heavy breaths, he began to move. He bent his head and caught her nipple, nursing it while his sex joined hers again and again.

She met him thrust for thrust, bucking and twisting in a pagan dance that set him aflame. Her fingers dug into his shoulders. She arched back, and a purely female groan slid past her lips.

He held her by the waist and drove her on and on while reaching for his own mind-numbing pinnacle.

It came with the force of a hurricane, whirling him into a ravaging swirl of pleasure so intense he feared he'd hurt her.

He cried out. He plunged one last time, then collapsed. His muscles went limp, and he slumped to the side, his arms listless as they draped across his wife's stomach. He couldn't do anything but close his eyes and gasp for air.

It was a long time before either of them moved or spoke. Their harsh breathing filled the silence. He became aware of the carpet beneath him, of the scent of wood smoke and lilac. Then his thoughts wandered in a direction that made him ache with sadness.

He and Nichole had no future.

Even though he loved her with his entire being, even though she was his wife, he knew Nichole could never really be his.

Not until he knew the truth about Meela's death.

Chapter 22

Nichole watched as Bragen rose and pulled on his breeches.

"We need to talk."

She slipped into her woolen gown and tied the front laces. The petticoats she ignored as she sat on the edge of the bed. "Why don't we start with your real name?"

That took him aback. "Who told you?" He sighed. "Rawlins, of course."

"Don't blame him. I made him tell me. And I want to know why you lied to me. You could have trusted me."

"I didn't lie. Bragen Alexander is my name. But few people know about the 'Bragen' part. I inherited that from an Irish ancestor, although I never used it. I was always called Alexander, even by my family. And I didn't tell you the truth because there was no reason for it at the time."

She nodded. "All right. I can accept that, but what about our marriage? Is it real?"

He gave her a lazy smile, then reached into the pocket of

his breeches and withdrew a folded parchment. "Read it." He tossed her the document.

She unfolded the paper. It was the marriage document signed by Captain Potter, and Bragen had used his true name. "You used your real name. Why?" she whispered.

He stared up at the scrolled ceiling. "I don't know why. It just seemed like the right thing to do at the time."

That wasn't the answer she'd hoped for. Setting the paper aside, she rose. "What about Clay? Why didn't he tell me—or anyone—that he was a duke?"

"Because he doesn't accept the title unless it suits him. In fact, he ignores his impressive rank and spends little time around those who are aware of it."

She shook her head. "Here you self-righteously accused *me* of fabrications while you and Clay were just as guilty."

"I had a valid reason, Nichole."

"So did I. Every time."

He arched a disbelieving brow. *"Every* time? I can't begin to think of a valid reason for you naming me as the father of your babe."

She wished he hadn't gotten around to that topic just yet. Defensively, she crossed her arms over her middle. "I didn't lie."

He walked toward her, wearing only his partially buttoned breeches. "You're still claiming you were the harlot at the Crimson Candle?"

"Yes. But I don't expect you to believe me."

He looked like he wanted to shake her. "Don't you think I want to believe you? But how can I? I *know* you overheard my conversation with Clay. I *know* you knew about my stay at the brothel. And I *know* you're nothing like the woman I bedded that night."

"It was me, Bragen."

Frustration hardened the line of his mouth. "All right. Let's get this settled once and for all. What color was the whore's dress?"

She winced at his word choice. *"I* wore a red satin gown that didn't reach my ankles."

His expression clearly said he wasn't impressed. Apparently red was a standard color for women of profession. "What about her hair? As I mentioned before, it was red."

"And I told you, it was a wig."

"Very well," he conceded. "We've established that the woman had red hair—or a red wig—and she wore a red dress. But what about her would distinguish her from other harlots?"

Nichole rose and paced to the window. "I was a virgin."

He considered that, his head bent, his gaze on the soft Bokhara carpet where they'd just made love. "I mentioned that, myself."

Anger made her voice quake. "And did you also mention of our brief conversation, where you wanted to know what was going on, and I told you 'explanations were extra'? Or that in my shame and humiliation, I slammed out the door without getting dressed?"

He stared at her for several chilling seconds, then exploded. "Son of a bitch! *You're pregnant with my child."* It was an accusation, not a question.

She couldn't tell whether he was pleased or furious.

He turned away from her and rubbed the back of his neck, his demeanor no indication of his feelings on the matter. "Why were you at the Crimson Candle, pretending to be a whore?"

"I thought I'd find Gabriel there."

Bragen whirled on her, his eyes flashing black fire. "You were going to *his* bed? Playing some sick game?"

The man really didn't have his head on straight. "No. I'd just discovered he'd stolen my jewels and was leaving on a ship at dawn. I was told he would spend the night in the brothel so I went to find him. Unfortunately, he wasn't there. But you were."

"Damn it. Why didn't you explain? Or at least *fight* me?"

"I'd had too much courage."

"What?"

"I drank some cognac. Too much, in fact, so I wasn't quite in control when you came in the room behind me."

He slumped on a settee near the fireplace. "I was in the same condition, and because of that night, and its consequences"—he looked pointedly at her belly—"we can't get an annulment or a divorce."

Did he have to make it sound like a curse? She'd hoped he'd grown to love her as much as she had him, but apparently he hadn't. Still, she wouldn't try to hold onto him. Doing so would only make them both miserable. "It's only a minor inconvenience," she pointed out, trying to keep the emotion out of her voice. The ache in her throat was almost more than she could bear. "After I recover my jewels, I'll move to a small cottage somewhere and have the babe. Then you'll be free to seek a divorce." She turned away. "Your freedom will only be postponed for a few months."

He said something ugly under his breath and began to pace again. Then there was silence. A long, breathless silence.

She stared at the wall, at a painting of a snow-covered forest, waiting for him to leave.

He came up behind her. "It may not come to divorce. If I'm guilty of Meela's murder, you'll be a widow." He massaged her still-flat abdomen as if he wanted their child to know his touch. "But if I'm innocent, there'll be no divorce. My son or daughter will be raised with both parents in attendance."

Did he realize what he was saying? She knew full well he didn't kill his first wife. They would stay married. But she wanted his love much more than his name and protection. "The child will suffer in a loveless marriage."

Bragen swept his lips down the side of her neck. "Who said it would be loveless?"

Chills trickled over her flesh. "I'm not talking about physical intimacy. I'm referring to matters of the heart."

He turned her in his arms. "So am I." He brushed his lips over hers.

There was no way she could resist him. With a resigned moan, she slipped her arms around his neck and gave in to the passion that held her prisoner.

He carried her to the bed and made love to her with aching tenderness, arousing parts of her body she never dreamed would be sensitive to a man's touch—behind her knees, the inside of her elbows, the length of her spine, the backs of her thighs.

A lifetime passed before he at last allowed her the release she all but begged for.

She curled into his side and rested her head on his damp shoulder. He smelled of leather and cheroots and . . . her. "I wish Gabriel hadn't stolen my jewels, but I'm not sorry I met you because of it." She drew circles in the hair on his chest. "I wonder why he took them."

"He's been on the run from me for three years. I imagine his finances are strained. He undoubtedly needed the cash to get away when he heard I was coming."

"Then he never planned to marry me at all?"

"I'm sure he did. It had been over six months since I'd lost track of him. I imagine he thought I'd lost him for good and was planning to settle down. To my knowledge, he's never proposed to another woman."

Bragen trailed his fingers up her bare arm. "I'm sure my appearance in Charleston is what forced him to steal your jewels and run. But you won't have to worry about them anymore, angel. I'll buy you enough baubles to sink Captain Potter's ship. Or if I'm not . . . here, you'll have enough money from my estate to purchase more jewels than you could ever wear."

"It's not the jewels. It's a locket."

He raised up on his elbow and stared down at her. The

leather tie in his hair had come loose, and the silky raven locks tumbled around his face. "What locket?"

"One that belonged to my real mother. There's a miniature of her and my father, Beau Kincaid, inside. I can't let that go, Bragen. It means too much to me. That locket is why I've been so desperate to find Gabriel."

His gaze came to rest on her lips, then he kissed her. "I'll get it for you, angel, if I have to search every country known to man. But I want you to stay here, while Clay and I look for Gabe."

"No."

"I'm not giving you a choice." The stern determination in his tone was unmistakable.

"I'm not giving you one, either," she countered, rising from the bed. She pulled the quilt around her. "If you don't allow me aboard Clay's ship, I'll stow away. And if that doesn't work, I'll find a different ship. One way or another, I'll get to Cape Town." The instant the words were out, she could have bitten off her tongue.

"Cape Town?"

"I'm going, Bragen."

He shot out of the bed, swearing as he strode naked across the room. He gripped the curtains edging the window and stared out for several minutes before he turned around. "I won't let you go. Not in your condition. I'll do anything to keep you and my child safe, Nichole, even if I have to set a guard on you night and day."

Threats or no, she had no intention of remaining in London while Bragen went after Gabriel. "All right, Lord *Blackstone.* You win. I won't try to board Clay's vessel or any other." And that was the truth. She wouldn't *try,* she'd *do* it.

He eyed her with suspicion, then gave her a slow, melting smile. "Liar."

Bragen watched the remainder of Clay's travel-weary crew board the *English Maiden* right after daybreak, but his thoughts were still with Nichole. They had made love late into the night, then slept before coming together again this morning. The six months it would take to get to Cape Town and back was going to be a long time.

If it is six months before I see her again, a small voice reminded.

"Do you think she'll try sneaking aboard?" Clay asked, striding up beside him.

Bragen braced his arms on the rail but didn't take his eyes off the boarding crew. "Without a doubt. I've known her long enough to be wary when she gives in without a fight."

"What are you going to do?"

Bragen nodded to a waiting carriage on the dock, where Morgan Frazier stood. Bragen had just released Victor from his cage and Morgan was holding him on a leash. "If—*when* —she shows up, your brother and that mangy dog are going to see that she gets safely back to Royal Oak."

Clay frowned. "I wouldn't trust Morgan too far, Bragen. She may be able to sway him to her purpose."

Bragen had known that when he had learned of Morgan's plan to sneak her aboard the *English Maiden* the night of her escape. But he also knew Morgan would keep his word to Bragen—if not for Bragen, then for Nichole. "No, he won't let her talk him into anything. I impressed upon him the danger to Nichole's health. She has no business making this journey with us."

"When do you think she'll try to board?"

"Now." He gestured to a trunk being carried aboard by two seamen. It was Nichole's trunk—and someone had cut holes along the side.

Clay swore. "What are you going to do?"

"Have the trunk nailed shut and taken ashore. By the time Morgan pries her out, we'll be in open waters."

When Morgan got the trunk open, and Nichole saw Bragen smiling at her from the rail of the moving ship, she was so furious, she could have screamed.

"It won't do you any good to fret," Morgan stated. "He did it for your own good, and I agreed to help him for the same reason."

She whirled on her big friend. "Why, you—" Her gaze landed on the dog standing beside him. "Victor, attack!"

The animal perked its ears, but didn't move.

Morgan grinned. "After Bragen brought him from Potter's ship, ol' Vic and I became friends while we were waiting for you, Nicki. You'll have to try something else." He caught her by the waist and set her in the carriage. "In the meantime, though, we need to get you to Royal Oak. I'd hate to have someone recognize you and be forced to rescue you from the Tower again."

"One prison's as good as another," she grumbled, leaning against the seat. "And I thought you were my friend."

"I am. That's why I won't allow you to endanger yourself or your child with this foolishness."

"Why should you care? Bragen doesn't."

Morgan snapped the reins, and the carriage lurched into motion. "Oh, he cares all right—much more than I'd figured."

Even with Morgan's constant guardianship—something she could have done without—the days passed at a snail's pace for Nichole. Because of Bragen's fear of her being seen and recaptured or boarding another ship, he'd instructed Morgan not to allow her off the immediate grounds, not even to take a walk. If it hadn't been for Martha, Rawlins's wife, Nichole would have gone mad. The woman was wonderful and so kind.

But, nothing, not even Martha's enjoyable company, stopped the emptiness Nichole felt with Bragen gone. She thought of him every day, and when she wasn't cursing him for leaving her, she missed him.

The months dragged by like years. Spring gave way to summer, and summer to fall. With each passing day she grew fatter. And the way she would cry for no reason at all made her miserable.

Morgan grew restless, but remained diligent in his responsibility. He never let her out of his sight for more than a few minutes.

But worse were the long nights in her lonely bed, a bed she again shared with Victor.

"Would you care for some tea, your ladyship?"

Nichole started and turned from the cold fireplace she'd been staring into for the last hour. "No, thank you, Rawlins. Lord Frazier and I finished supper barely an hour ago." And Morgan had gone to the creek for a swim.

"Very good, your ladyship." He bowed and turned to go.

"Rawlins?"

"Yes, mum?"

"Have you worked for the Stanfields long?"

"Since before the master was born."

She motioned to a chair across from her. "Please, have a seat. I'd like to talk to you a moment."

The older man was uneasy about sitting in her presence, but he obeyed. He perched on the edge of the chair, his spine rigid, his thin hands folded in his lap, his bony knees held together above his white stockings and buckled shoes.

"When was Bragen born?"

"The twelfth of September, in the year of our Lord, 1753. Right here in this house."

"That makes him thirty, doesn't it?"

"Yes, mum."

"Was he always so bossy?"

That brought a quirk of a smile from his wrinkled lips. "Yes. Even as a lad, he took things much too seriously. A day did not pass without him scolding Master Christian for not brushing his horse enough, or Mistress Fiona for riding her mare too hard."

"Bragen married young, didn't he?"

"I believe so. He was just twenty and two."

"What was Meela like?"

The servant's eyes clouded with admiration and remembered pain. "She was kind and gentle. A true lady."

Nichole was stunned. If the woman was cuckolding Bragen, why would Rawlins speak so fondly of her? "Rawlins, did you know that Meela was unfaithful?"

The man sucked in a shocked breath. "That's preposterous! Lady Blackstone would have never done such a thing. She *worshipped* the master."

He sounded so certain, she couldn't help wonder if a mistake hadn't been made. "How long were they married?"

"Five years."

"Did she live here the whole time?"

"Yes."

"And she never had gentlemen callers?"

Rawlins lifted his pointed chin. "That child never had any callers, period. She was ostracized from society because of her heritage."

The poor girl. The nature of her birth wasn't her fault, nor was her lineage anything to be ashamed of. "Did Mr. Bodine call?" He *was* here the night she died.

"He did. But Lady Blackstone refused to see him. She did not like that one. He made her uneasy."

"Did you know she was with child?"

"I most certainly did. I fetched the physician myself when she came down with a bout of sickness."

"If Bragen was fighting in the colonies, then how—"

"The master was able to take leave from the fighting, but he was only able to stay for a few days because the journey from the colonies was so long. That was four months before Lady Blackstone's demise."

"Do you think he killed her?"

Indignation flared in those tired blue eyes. "Absolutely not."

"Were you here when it happened?"

"No. It was the sabbath. Everyone but Lady Blackstone was at church. She had her own place of worship in the grove out back." Sadness marked his aged features. "If I had been home, perhaps I could have . . ." He swallowed, unable to go on.

"I doubt you could have done anything, Rawlins. Don't blame yourself."

"It is difficult not to, your ladyship."

She imagined it was. "Since you were at church, does that mean you weren't here, either, when Bragen arrived?"

"No. I did not even know he had returned from the war until Master Clay brought the news of his arrest."

"I see." And she really did. Bragen didn't kill his wife. But she knew who did. "Where is Meela buried?"

"At the edge of the grove."

"Does Bragen know?"

"No, mum. He never asked."

She hadn't thought he would. He'd been too hurt, too disillusioned, to approach the subject—he was even now. She rose and straightened the folds of her white skirt over her big belly. "Thank you, Rawlins. You've been most helpful."

He, too, came to his feet. "Would you care for that tea now, mum?"

"No, thank you. I believe I'll take a short walk before I retire."

Cool November sunlight filtered through the oak leaves and Nichole pulled her pelisse closer as she made her way into the thick woods. She'd gone only a few yards when she came to a small plot fenced in with short, white pointed stakes. The grave had been tended with care and had a wreath of flowers next to the headstone. Rawlins's and Martha's doing, no doubt. Being cautious because of her condition, she lowered herself to her knees and moved the circle of dried English daisies to read the inscription.

Mistress Meela Stanfield
Lady Blackstone
Died August 10, 1780
Age 20

Nichole felt the tears on her cheeks. Meela had been so young.

Hatred for Gabriel shook her. He had done this, Nichole was sure of it. Meela was uneasy around him; she didn't like him. For heaven's sake, she wouldn't even see him when he called. And if Bragen caught them together, then Gabriel must have been forcing himself on Meela when he walked in. But why? And how could she prove it?

Tracing the edge of the headstone, she cried for the young woman—and for Bragen. "I won't let Gabriel get away with this, Meela. I swear by all that's holy, I won't."

A soft breeze blew across her cheek. It felt like the gentle touch of a hand.

Drying her eyes on her skirt, Nichole struggled to regain her feet, but she didn't want to see anyone just yet. She would have enjoyed Victor's comforting presence, but he had gone to the creek with Morgan, so she turned in the opposite direction. She placed a hand on her back to soothe a twinge and strode deeper into the woods.

She didn't know how long she walked, or how far, until the sun slipped below the horizon, and it grew colder. Digging her hands into the pockets of her pelisse, she had just decided to return to Royal Oak when she spotted a deserted building in a small clearing. It was surrounded by oaks and poplars. Tall, ivy-covered columns sat below a balcony that spanned the front of the mansion, which appeared to have been grand at one time.

Curious, Nichole headed toward the house. She had almost reached the front steps when the thunder of hoofbeats startled her. She swung around to see a man riding across the field. Afraid of being caught snooping, she hurried to the side of the house as quickly as she could in her cumbersome state.

She made it into the trees, and slipped behind an oak that was barely wide enough to hide her. She peered around the bark to see who'd ridden into the drive.

The ground swayed beneath her feet. "Oh, dear God."

It was Gabriel Bodine.

Chapter 23

Gabriel spotted her, and his eyes flew wide with disbelief.

Nichole clamped a hand over her mouth to stop a cry. What was he doing here? Terror seized her. She panicked and bolted into a run. The damp ground sank beneath her boots and tree limbs snagged her clothes, but she couldn't stop—didn't dare. Gabriel was a murderer. She knew it! Her chest hurt from her labored breathing, as did her side and her stomach.

Footsteps pounded behind her.

She gripped the bottom of her stomach to ease the pressure as she accelerated her pace.

It didn't do any good. He was getting closer. Tears filled her eyes, until she was nearly blinded. Tree limbs cut her cheeks. Underbrush tore at her skirts time and time again.

The footsteps grew louder.

Fear spurred her into a full-blown run. Her foot shot into a hole. With a frightened scream, she pitched forward.

Hard hands grabbed her before she hit the ground.

Her terror exploded into hysteria. She fought the arms that held her, clawing and kicking. "No! Let me go!" She dug her nails into any flesh she could reach.

"Ow! Damn it, Nichole. Will you settle down?"

She froze. She'd know that voice anywhere. "Bragen?"

His cheek was next to hers, and he moved his lips to her ear. "Yes, angel?"

Long-dormant anger warred with happiness over his return. But the affair was taken out of her hands when he turned her in his arms and kissed her.

How could she stay angry with him when he was greeting her with such warmth, such aching tenderness? Six months had been a long time. Resigned, she slid her arms up around his neck and parted her lips.

He accepted the invitation with hunger. His hands swept down to caress her huge belly, her breasts, her bottom. "God, I've missed you." He held her a moment longer, then set her away from him. "Now, why are you out here *and running, in your condition?* Don't you have a brain in that—"

"Oh, my word. Gabriel!"

Bragen caught her shoulders. "What?"

She scanned the trees, but couldn't see anything for the growing darkness. "I saw Gabriel. And he saw me. He was chasing me. When I tripped and you caught me, I thought it was him."

"What!" Bragen roared. "He's here? Where?"

Bragen was frightening when he was enraged. "I-in a house not far from here." She pointed. "Back there."

"That conniving bastard." He released her and slammed his palm against a tree. "He didn't go to Cape Town. We found no sign of him at all. That sniveling whoreson's been sitting comfortably in his home—not a mile from my own—while I spent six long months on a useless chase across a continent." He whipped around to face her. *"What do you mean, he was chasing you?"*

"I—I stumbled upon a run-down estate—his, I guess— and I went to have a look at it. That's when I saw Gabriel riding up. I hid, but he saw me. I started running."

Bragen drew her into his arms and just held her. She felt a tremor run through him. "Are you all right?"

"I am, now that you're here."

"And the babe?" He slid a hand over her belly.

"Fine. Anxious, though. It kicks all the time."

As if to give truth to her words, the child stirred.

"I felt it," he breathed in an awed voice. "Our child moved."

Nichole hid a smile. She, too, had been overwhelmed the first time.

Bragen nestled her to his side. "Come on, angel. Let's get you to the house."

"What about Gabriel?"

"I'll take care of him. Right now, I want you safe and inside the walls of Royal Oak."

Morgan was pacing on the veranda when they walked across the wide, thick lawn surrounding the brick manor. Clay was sprawled in a chair near the door, looking quite grumpy. He and Morgan spotted them at the same time.

Clay jumped to his feet. "It's about time you showed up. We were just about to start searching for you."

"Damn it, Nichole," Morgan thundered. "Where'd you get off to? I was gone for only fifteen minutes."

"Enough!" Bragen commanded.

Nichole was surprised by the anger in her husband's voice. "I went for a walk—"

"And she ran into Gabe," Bragen spat. "That bastard's been here all along. She was running from him when I found her."

"I'll kill that son of a bitch!" Morgan bellowed.

Clay kicked the chair aside, his rage unmistakable. "Let's go."

"Martha!" Bragen shouted.

Rawlins's wife hurried out onto the porch. "I'm here, your lordship."

"See that my wife is made to rest until I return. And for no reason is she to leave this house." Without another word, he strode down the steps with Morgan and Clay on his heels.

Nichole was put out by his high-handedness, but in truth, after what she'd been through, she wasn't about to go anywhere.

"Come on, child, let's get you upstairs," Martha urged.

Nichole bathed and washed her hair, then brushed the heavy mass to a crackling shine. She donned her long white night rail that buttoned clear to her chin. But rest was out of the question. The men could be in serious danger.

All this time, she'd been within a mile of Gabriel. She should have remembered Bragen telling her that he and Gabriel grew up on neighboring estates. She should have checked his house. But what if he'd seen her before Bragen returned? Thank goodness for Bragen's orders to keep her on the grounds of Royal Oak. There's no telling what might have happened if Gabriel had known she was there. He might have tried to—*why was he chasing me?*

Trying to contain her apprehension, she grabbed a book and sat down in a chair by the fire, but the question wouldn't leave her thoughts. Had he recognized her and been trying to find out why she was here? Or had he thought she was a trespasser?

In exasperation, she snapped the book shut and tossed it onto a table. She couldn't concentrate.

Just as she leaned her head back to close her eyes, the door opened.

Bragen stepped in, defeat deepening the lines of fatigue on his handsome face.

But he was safe. "Did you find him?"

"No." He moved to the fire to warm himself. "The bastard wasn't at Acorn Manor. We searched his house and the surrounding area."

"Where did he go?"

"I don't know."

"What are you going to do?"

"Wait for him to return. Clay and Morgan broke into his house and are inside waiting for him now." He stood in front of the fire. His eyes were on her. "I'm going to join them in a few minutes. But I wanted to say a proper hello to my wife first."

Nichole's pulse leapt, but she couldn't respond, probably because her heart was in her throat. The man made her ache with wanting. Of course, in her condition, she would just have to keep on wanting.

He didn't move. He just kept watching her.

It made her nervous. Now that he could see her in the light, he probably thought she resembled a fat sow.

"Do you know how beautiful you are?" he asked. "To see you swollen with my child humbles me, yet it excites me. I want to protect you and love you, all at the same time." He closed the distance between them and laid a hand on her belly. "Take off your clothes, angel. Let me look at you."

He didn't wait for her to agree or refuse. He pulled her to her feet, then swiftly unbuttoned the front of her gown and lifted it off over her head. She blushed but was too stunned by the change in him to argue. This was a side of Bragen she'd never seen before. He was exploring her with such heart-stopping tenderness.

Desire darkened his eyes.

Nichole couldn't move. She could only stare into her husband's magnificent face. She thought of their volatile lovemaking the morning before he left, and a flush rose to her cheeks.

"Thinking about the last time we were together?" he taunted.

"Which part?" When had her voice turned so breathless?

"The part where I kissed you here." He slid his tongue over her lips. "And here." He stroked the tip of her breast. "And here." He found her woman's place and caressed it with his long fingers. "Is that the part you were remembering?"

Her knees went weak, and her voice came out in a whispered moan. "Yes."

"Me, too. Hell, I've thought of little else." He stepped back to pull off his shirt.

The sight of his muscled chest started a fire low in her belly. Every inch of that bronze flesh begged to be kissed.

He kicked off his boots, then lowered his breeches, inch by glorious inch. His heavy sex sprang free.

"See anything you like?"

Oh, she saw plenty, but she wasn't ready to admit it yet. She teased him. "I'm not sure. I think I need a closer inspection." With a shaky hand, she motioned to the bed. "Why don't you lie down so I can decide?"

Holding her gaze, he stretched out on the mattress. "Well?"

She knew she couldn't do anything in her condition, but she needed to touch him, to feel the warmth she'd missed. She ran a hand over his hair-roughened chest, then traced a flat male nipple. "This part isn't bad."

"That's what you think," he muttered.

"But," she continued, "to be a fair judge, I imagine I should be sure." She flicked her tongue over the small nub.

He drew in a sharp breath.

His response sent a stab of need straight to her center. She took a frustrated breath and slid her hand over his stomach. "This looks promising." She caressed the hard plane, moving lower with each sensual brush of her fingers before she dipped her head and kissed the recess in the center of his tight flesh. "Yes. Very promising indeed."

She smiled, and, with a boldness she didn't know she possessed, she reached out and trailed her fingers down his long length. "This part appears to hold great potential. But of course, I must be certain." She took him into her mouth. He was so hot, so smooth, so wonderfully male.

He gave a strangled groan and hauled her up. "Don't. Not

yet, angel. I'm too full of wanting you." He pressed her down next to him. For several seconds, he didn't move. He touched her with his eyes. Then he kissed her waiting mouth, sweetly possessing her. He kissed her jaw, her throat, the tops of her swollen breasts. At long last, he covered an aching crest, suckling with exquisite tenderness, while his hand explored the full shape of her belly.

There was such gentleness in him, it brought tears to her eyes.

He slid lower, moving his lips over the expanse of her stomach. He adored the tight flesh with his mouth, cherished it, while his fingers found the curls below. He taunted her with feather-light strokes.

She became dizzy.

He parted her curls to explore her, sending stabs of pleasure through every nerve in her body. Then he covered her with his palm, massaging her into a shivering state of arousal.

She grabbed the railings at the top of the bed.

He nudged her legs apart so he could reach her more fully. And reach her he did, clear to the center of her soul.

The explosion came, sweet and powerful, and she cried out at the long-denied sensation.

When she returned to earth, he was beside her, his hand resting on her swollen stomach, his eyes watching her face. "You take my breath away, angel."

"Bragen, you didn't—I mean—well, you didn't—"

"You're worried about my . . . er . . . welfare, is that it?"

She bit her lip and nodded.

Tenderness filled his eyes. "Watching you gives me pleasure, don't you know that?"

She flushed.

Victor gave a fierce, sharp bark from downstairs, just as a loud crash shook the walls. The barking continued as footsteps pounded the floorboards.

Bragen leapt off the bed and dragged on his breeches.

"Stay here." He jerked open the door and took a step—then froze in place.

The barrel of a musket was pointed straight at his chest.

Nichole cried out and yanked the sheet over her just as two of the king's soldiers backed Bragen into the room.

"Well, well, Lord Blackstone, aren't you a welcome sight. After three years, we figured we'd seen the last of you."

The man who had spoken cast a glance at her, then Bragen, assessing the situation. "Sorry for the inconvenience, milord. But you have a date with the magistrate. A matter of murder, I believe." His features hardened. "Get dressed."

Nichole was aware of three things at once: the authorities didn't know who she was, Morgan and Clay were still at Gabriel's waiting for his return, and Bragen was going to prison.

Bragen dragged on the rest of his clothes, then came to her side. He ran a hand down the hair falling over her shoulder. "I love you, angel. I always have." He kissed her. "And I need you to stay strong for me."

Then he was gone.

Her heart twisted into a painful knot. Bragen had just told her goodbye. No! Damn it, she wasn't giving him up without a fight. She crawled out of bed and grabbed the first article of clothing she could reach. She had to get Morgan and Clay. But when she reached the bottom of the stairs, Martha was waiting for her.

"Rawlins has already gone after the others," she announced, then thrust a cup of tea in Nichole's hand. "Come on, child. We'll wait by the fire."

Rawlins returned within the hour, but it was four in the morning before Clay and Morgan showed up, both looking haggard and worn.

Nichole struggled to her feet. "Is he all right?"

Morgan swore.

Clay couldn't meet her eyes. "While we were waiting for

Gabe to return to his house, that bastard was in town with the magistrate. When he was chasing you through the woods, he must have seen Alexander come to your aid. That lying son of a bitch headed straight for town to let the magistrate know Bragen was back. He told them he saw Bragen kill Meela. Gabe claims he ran after it happened and has been running from Bragen ever since because he was afraid Bragen would kill him, too. Coffland has set Bragen's trial for this afternoon. He was afraid Bragen might escape again, so he wants the hearing over with as soon as possible."

The room swayed.

Morgan was there in an instant, pushing her down onto the sofa. "Take it easy, Nicki. He's not dead yet."

Somehow, that wasn't very reassuring. "What are we going to do?"

Morgan didn't have an answer.

Clay rubbed the nape of his neck. "I'm going to find Gabe. I'll make that bastard confess if I have to beat it out of him."

Morgan swung on his brother. "Not without me, you're not."

Bragen's words came back to her. *I need you to be strong for me.* They had the most calming affect. "Neither of you will get anywhere with Gabriel. He knows how close you are to Bragen and wouldn't be fooled for a minute. But there is a way."

Clay stared at her for a full minute, then his eyes narrowed in understanding. "Don't even think about it, Nichole."

"Think about what?" Morgan asked, glancing from one to the other.

"Will you at least hear me out?"

"No."

"What?" Morgan was becoming really frustrated.

"Damn it, no," Clay repeated. "You're pregnant, for God's sake."

"My condition doesn't affect my speech."

"Will someone tell me what you're talking about?" Morgan grated.

"I'm going to talk to Gabriel," she said simply. "I know I can worm a confession out of him."

Morgan paled.

Clay took a different approach. "Damn it, woman. Gabe saw you with Bragen."

"True. But, he doesn't know the extent of our relationship. I'm going, *your grace,* with or without your approval." She fought tears. "Bragen is my life."

"I don't want to have to hold you prisoner, Nichole. But I will if that's what it takes. Bragen would never forgive me if I let anything happen to you." Clay's determination was pronounced in every hard line of his face. "Besides, even if you could manage to get a confession out of Bodine, what good would it do? Gabe would just deny it."

She was getting desperate. "Not if there were witnesses within earshot, such as yourselves and an official." She implored him with her eyes. "And you'd be there to see that nothing went wrong."

Morgan started cursing under his breath.

Clay clenched his teeth.

"If that isn't acceptable," she continued, "then you'd better lock me up now. But, if you do, know that *I will escape and go to Gabriel on my own.*"

Morgan slumped into a chair. "Bloody goddamn hell."

Chapter 24

Morgan had checked Acorn Manor to make sure Gabriel had returned from the magistrate, and he had, so there was nothing for them to do now but sit in the chilly open carriage and wait for Clay and the official. Nichole wasn't eager to see the king's man. He'd want to arrest her. Her only hope was to stall him until after she talked to Gabriel.

Her hand went to the small knife tucked into the pocket of her skirt beneath her heavy cape. It wasn't much protection, but if Gabriel became hostile, it might be enough to hold him off until Morgan and Clay got to them.

"They're coming," Morgan announced. He sent her a concerned glance. "Are you sure you want to go through with this?"

Now that the time was near, she wasn't as sure as she had been, but Bragen's life was in her hands, and she wouldn't let him down. Her whole future depended on the next few minutes. Gripping the edges of her cape, she nodded. "Stop worrying, Morgan. It won't be so bad." The lie made her wince. Yet she knew her conversation with Gabriel would also be tainted with untruths.

"What are you doing here?" The soldier who'd arrested her in town jerked his mount to a stop beside the carriage.

Clay edged his horse closer. "Sergeant Whitcomb, I'd like you to meet Lady Blackstone."

He ignored the introduction. "You are under arrest, madam." He reached for the pistol at his side.

Clay clamped a hand over the official's. "Not now, Whitcomb. I've already explained that she didn't steal those jewels, but after you've listened to her conversation with Bodine, if you feel the need to arrest her, then she'll go peacefully. But at least wait until after she's attempted to get the confession."

If there is one, Nichole thought. What if Gabriel saw right through her?

Whitcomb's chin wobbled in indignation, then he clamped his lips together and gave a curt nod.

Clay let out a breath, then spoke to her. "Knock on the front door and keep Gabriel in the entrance as long as possible. We'll go in through the rear and wait in the room next to the parlor. He receives all guests in there."

With her luck, he'd probably take her to the kitchen. "Don't be long." She was going to be as nervous as a horse in a snake pit.

Morgan climbed out and handed her the reins. He held on, concerned, then leaned forward and kissed her cheek. "I'll kill him before I'll let him hurt you, Nicki." He lightened the mood with a wink. "Besides, if anything happens to you, Alexander will give me firsthand knowledge of how Indians torture their captives."

Nichole wasn't smiling as she set the carriage into motion. She was too frightened. Puffs of steam rose from her breath, and she drew the long cape she wore close to her chest to ward off a chill that had nothing to do with the November weather.

She pulled in the reins to slow the horse's gait in order to give the others the time they needed. The wheels of the carriage bumped over the rough, unkept road and jarred her stomach. The twinge in her back started up again.

As the horse ambled out of the trees, Gabriel's run-down house came into view. The gray walls were faded beneath the falls of ivy that hung from the upper balcony. High, thick weeds and yellow grass covered the grounds, and the drive had all but disappeared. Layers of dust clung to the wood trimming the fogged windowpanes. Papers and broken pieces of wood and pottery littered the lower veranda.

Since Gabriel had been away for years in his attempt to escape Bragen, Acorn Manor had fallen into ruin.

Drawing the carriage to a halt, Nichole took a deep, fortifying breath and climbed down.

Gabriel swung the door open and stood with his hand on the latch. "Well, well, well. If it isn't my lovely bride-to-be. Such a welcome surprise," he cooed. "Such an unexpected . . ."—his gaze lowered to her chest—". . . delight."

She yanked the cape closer. He made her skin shrivel, and she was very relieved that she hadn't married him. And now that the moment was upon her, she didn't know how to broach the subject of Bragen. She had two choices. She could either blurt out her questions . . . or she could use the gifts God bestowed upon her and hopefully entice the truth out of him. "Did you think I wouldn't follow you, Gabriel? After all we meant to each other?"

He eyed her with suspicion. "Is that why you ran from me last night?"

She tightened her fingers on her cape. "I didn't want to, but I had no choice. Lord Blackstone threatened to beat me *again* if I so much as spoke to another person. I'd planned to sneak a message to you today to explain. But thank heavens, that horrible man was arrested, so I was free to leave."

He looked as if he didn't believe a word she said, yet he

motioned her inside, then led her to the warmth of the parlor. "How did you come to be in Alexander's company in the first place?"

She waved a hand, being very careful to keep her cape closed. "When he came to Miss Fender's, searching for you, I hired him to take me to Cape Town." She sent him a reproachful glare. "The place you *told* your maid you were going. I needed an escort. Of course, at the time, I had no idea he was such a monster."

He curled his lip, and there was no mistaking the mockery in his tone. "Did you tell him I stole your jewels?"

That took her aback. She hadn't expected him to admit it. "Yes I did. He wasn't going to bring me, so I had to say something. Besides, I was a bit miffed with you, even though we both know those baubles are of scant value. I had to see you. I just had no idea that awful man would—would— *claim* me as his own."

She lowered her lashes. "I was so frightened, and I missed you so much, Gabriel. After I learned how Lord Blackstone had been pursuing you all these years, I knew you left me only because you had to escape that maniac." She made her lower lip tremble. "But if I'm wrong, and you don't love me, then tell me now. I'll go away and never bother you again."

A cocky smirk brightened his square face. "Of course I love you, dear. Why, being married to you is all I have thought of since I was forced to use your jewels to get away from Alexander." He lifted her chin. "You do forgive me for that, do you not?"

Thinking of what this man had done to Bragen brought tears to her eyes, and she allowed them to fall. "Oh yes, Gabriel. I was so afraid you didn't want me anymore. . . ."

"Shhh." He covered her lips in a loose, wet kiss, and she tried her best not to flinch. "I will never leave you again." He stroked her hip. "In fact, I will post our wedding banns this very afternoon."

So he didn't know she was Bragen's wife. She gave a

thankful sigh that she hoped he interpreted as relief. "Truly? You still want to marry me even after what that man did to me?"

Gabriel moved to the sideboard to pour a drink, his stocky gait heavy, his blond hair tousled. "And just what was that?"

"He hurt me!"

Gabriel snorted with disbelief. "You are lying."

"I am not!" She threw the cape open to reveal her huge belly. "That savage raped me!"

Gabriel dropped the glass, and amber liquid splashed over his scuffed boots. *"What?* Bragen would not . . ." His voice died away as his gaze found her stomach. His eyes brightened with rage. *"You whoring bitch."*

He was across the room in an instant, gripping her shoulders. "You tramp, you allowed him to do this."

"No! I swear to you, he—he forced himself on me."

Gabriel struck her. "Lying whore! I have known Bragen all my life. He would never hurt a woman."

"He killed his wife!" she cried, clutching her stinging cheek.

"The hell he did. *I* killed that red bitch."

Nichole gasped. His admission both horrified and elated her. Bragen was innocent! She held onto her naive demeanor. "Don't say that. You had no reason to—"

"Yes, I did! Before that savage slut came along, Bragen and I were inseparable. She broke up our friendship. Then when he sent her here to England, every time she saw me, she would mock me. She treated me as if I were a peasant. She would taunt me, inviting me with those big dark eyes, flaunting herself in that clinging rawhide dress that left nothing to the imagination, then playing coy by refusing to see me when I would call. I would not stand for it. I took what she was offering. I knew she wanted it. But when Bragen came in on us, she started screaming, and I knew she would lie and say I was forcing her. Bragen would have believed her without challenge. He treated her like a queen! I *had* to silence her."

"The magistrate will be happy to hear your tale, Gabe," Morgan said, stepping into the room. He held a gun on Bodine.

Gabriel's reaction surprised them all. He caught Nichole by the throat and jerked her back against his chest. His thumb and forefinger dug into her flesh on either side of her windpipe. "Get back, Frazier, or I swear, I will kill her."

The pressure on her throat sent waves of nausea through her. She struggled in earnest. He dug his nails into her flesh, forcing her to gag.

"All right!" Morgan bellowed. He dropped his gun. "Just don't hurt her."

"Kick the pistol over here," Gabriel ordered.

Through a haze, she saw Morgan comply.

Gabriel took her with him as he bent to pick up the weapon, then the hand at her throat relaxed the tiniest bit, allowing her to draw in a breath.

He set the gun barrel to her temple and started edging toward the entrance. "If you so much as breathe wrong, she is dead."

Morgan didn't move a muscle—and she knew Clay and Whitcomb wouldn't dare reveal themselves, either—not if she was going to survive this. They couldn't take the chance.

The minute they were off the front steps, Gabriel shoved her into the carriage and grabbed the reins.

Nichole could only hold her throat and gasp for oxygen.

The carriage hit a rut and bounced wildly.

She cried out and grabbed the side to keep from being pitched out over the edge. The ground and trees became a blur as Gabriel whipped the horse into a killing pace.

Pain shot through her stomach, and she doubled over, clutching her middle. Tears spilled down her cheeks. Dear God, it felt like someone was ripping her open with a jagged knife.

Gabriel yanked on the reins and brought the carriage to a skidding halt at the side of the road. He leapt down, then caught her by the hair and shoved her ahead of him into the trees.

The pace he set was grueling, but, thank heavens, the pain in her stomach had temporarily subsided. He kept forcing her forward, through the woods, fields of waist-high grain, and across a river. At last they came to a cabin at the edge of a clearing—a hunting cabin.

Gabriel kicked in the door and shoved her inside. She hit the floor hard. Her head struck the leg of a stout table.

The crushing pain returned.

Holding onto her stomach, she rolled onto her side, barely aware of Gabriel shoving the door shut and grabbing a chair to wedge under the handle. The pain took her breath.

Gabriel didn't notice. He had raced to the window, his gaze wild as he scanned the area, the barrel of his weapon braced on the open ledge.

Nichole thought she was going to die, but just as the thought formed, the pain subsided into a dull ache. At last able to move, she sat up, staring at the single room, which held a dusty cot and rock fireplace. Another chair sat next to a sideboard that had doors hanging from broken hinges. Then she glared at Gabriel's back. "Bragen's going to kill you for this." She didn't even try to maintain her ruse.

Bodine didn't turn from the window, but the smirk in his tone was unmistakable. "He will have to outrun the hangman first."

"You won't get away with it."

"Of course I will, my dear. Just as soon as I have silenced Morgan Frazier, you and I will leave England . . . and Alexander will hang."

So he had it all planned out, did he? Not if she could help it. She stared at his rigid spine and inched her hand under her cape, toward the knife in her pocket. She pulled the blade free and struggled to her feet. She had to keep him talking. "What if they find him innocent? You know he'll come after you."

Gabriel didn't take his eyes off the clearing. "Oh, they will find him guilty, all right. I used his knife. And no one but you and Frazier even knows I was at Royal Oak that day."

Hatred filled her, and she was thankful he didn't know about Clay and the official hearing his confession. She started toward him, keeping her voice soft. "Bragen knows."

"They will never believe him." He leaned closer to the window, his eyes intent, his fingers twitching on the pistol's trigger.

She stopped behind him. For a heartbeat, she stared at his thick back, at the brown woolen coat stretched across his fleshy shoulders, but she couldn't do it. No matter what he'd done in the past—or planned to do—she couldn't kill a man.

But she could *wound* him.

Raising the knife, she aimed at his shoulder and brought the blade down with all the force she possessed. She heard the sickening thud of metal hitting flesh and Gabriel's scream. The knife was torn from her fingers as he spun around. She saw his crazed eyes, his knotted fist. Then everything went black.

A searing pain jarred her awake. It burned through her stomach like fiery claws. She took shallow breaths, trying to ease the discomfort. Nothing helped. It went on and on. She was going to die, that was all there was to it. Then, at long last, the fire subsided into a slow, aching burn.

She opened her eyes and saw Gabriel slumped in a chair, his eyes closed, his skin much too pale. He had taken off his coat and shoved a wad of material under the shirt that draped his wounded shoulder, and from the piece sticking out from his collar, she knew it was one of her petticoats. He must have taken it off her while she'd been out. Then she noticed the blood soaking the sleeve of his shirt. So much blood.

Bile climbed her throat, and she tried to sit up. She couldn't. Her hands and feet were each tied to a separate corner of the wood-framed cot. "Damn you, Gabriel. Let me up!"

He didn't stir.

"You low-life jackanapes! I said, release me."

Nothing.

A cold chill swept her. Was he unconscious? From loss of blood? She started to shake. Was he dead? Oh, God. No. "Gabriel? Can you hear me?"

Silence.

Noooo! "Gabriel, you've got to—" Fire ripped through her abdomen. A groan pushed up her throat. She twisted against the ropes cutting into her wrists. Against the pain. Even though it was cold, moisture beaded on her forehead, and she began to pant, trying to hold on. She couldn't have the babe *now*.

The pain eased, and she drew in great gulps of air, but something warm and wet startled her.

It gushed from between her legs.

Oh, God. No.

Chapter 25

Bragen didn't know what to think when a guard brought him from the cell and took him to Coffland's elaborate office. He was even more surprised to see Clay there.

The magistrate, with his heavy jowls and pale, feminine skin, motioned Bragen closer to the massive mahogany desk where he sat. "On behalf of the court, I would like to extend my apologies to you, Lord Blackstone, for any inconvenience we may have caused."

Apologies? All Bragen could do was stare, then he sent a look at Clay. The anguish on his face sent a stab of fear through Bragen. "What's going on?"

Coffland cleared his throat. "You have been exonerated of your wife's death. My sergeant, Mallory Whitcomb, was privy to Gabriel Bodine's confession."

Bragen was too stunned to move. He glanced at Cordell. Wariness clouded his eyes. "Clay? What is it?"

The duke met his gaze, and what Bragen saw there was enough to make him tremble. "Clay?"

"Gabe's got Nichole."

Paralyzed, he listened as Clay explained Nichole's plan and what had gone wrong. "When Gabe took her, Morgan followed, but he lost them when Bodine abandoned the carriage. He's searching for them now."

Something cold and ugly and numbing settled over Bragen. He couldn't say a word as he turned and walked out of the building.

Clay was right beside him. "I've got horses waiting."

Bragen mounted, every bone in his body taut enough to break. It hurt to breathe, to even think. Mechanically, he nudged the horse into a trot, then a frantic gallop. The ten-mile distance to Royal Oak felt more like a thousand.

A few of his senses had returned by the time they reached Frazier, standing next to a carriage, on the main road.

"Where'd you lose the tracks?"

Rage tightened the muscles in Frazier's face as he pointed to a thick grove of trees. "In there. He must have taken her on foot."

The terror Bragen had been holding at bay again tried to surface. He stepped into the shade of the trees and knelt, looking for disturbed soil, flattened leaves, and broken branches, all the signs that would indicate Gabriel's direction.

When he found them, he closed his eyes and gave a silent, heartfelt thank-you to God.

It took them less than an hour to locate the small clearing where the cabin stood.

"What are we going to do?" Clay whispered, afraid his voice might carry on the slight wind.

Bragen didn't even hesitate. "I'm going in after her." He started forward.

Morgan's big hand clamped down on his shoulder. "He'll kill her, Alexander. If he doesn't shoot you first."

Bragen's stomach clenched at the swift stab of fear for Nichole. "I've got to—"

A woman's scream curdled the air.

Bragen felt the blood leave his face. "Nichole!" He charged into the clearing.

"Goddamn it, Bragen!" Clay roared.

Bragen was running at full speed when his shoulder hit the door. It exploded under the impact, and he fell, rolling across the floor. He leapt to his feet and crouched, ready for battle. In frozen surprise, he stared at Gabriel. He was unconscious and slumped over a table. The sleeve of his shirt was dark with blood.

A cry came from behind him, and he whirled around to see Nichole tied to a bed, twisting in agony.

"Help me," she cried, tears streaming down her face. "The baby's coming."

"Ah, Jesus. Not *now.*"

Another chilling scream shook the cabin.

Morgan and Clay burst into the room—and skidded to a halt.

Clay saw Gabe, then swung to Nichole. He paled. "Son of a bitch."

Morgan was ready to collapse.

"Do either of you know anything about birthing a baby?" Bragen managed to shout through his horror.

Both men stared.

Clay at last found his voice. "I think you should untie her before it happens."

Bragen made short work of the ropes and pulled her into his arms. She shook so hard, she scared him.

"Please," she whispered in a tight, pain-filled voice. "Help me."

With a fear so great he thought he'd be sick, he turned to his friends. "Wait outside—and take that bastard with you." He nodded to Gabe's limp form.

When Morgan braced the door into place behind him, Bragen took off his coat and moved to the end of the cot. He lifted his wife's skirt. What he saw nearly sent him into a panic. A small head, covered with wet black hair, was pushing its way out of Nichole.

"Oh, God!" she cried, doubling into a sitting position. She grabbed Bragen's shoulders, her body drenched in sweat in the cold cabin, her fingers digging into his flesh as she moaned in chest-tightening agony.

He started to tremble. He didn't know what to do.

She let out another piercing cry, and, astonished, he watched a child slide out onto the blanket between her legs.

Exhausted, she collapsed onto the pillow.

At first, he couldn't move. Then gingerly, he picked up the tiny boy. For several seconds, he stared in wonder at the perfect, miniature human before he realized the child wasn't breathing. He shook him, but the babe didn't cry. Terror gripped him. No! Not after all this. The child had to live.

He held him up and gently patted the tiny spine.

Nothing.

He patted harder.

Still nothing. Desperately, he gave a swift smack.

The babe gasped and wailed in outrage.

Bragen was so relieved, he felt tears burn his eyes.

Suddenly, Nichole gave another gut-wrenching scream.

Startled, he swung his gaze, and to his horror, saw *another* child emerging. "Oh, bloody hell!"

Picking up his coat, Bragen wrapped his son and laid him at the foot of the cot. He had to—the infant was attached to Nichole. He turned just in time to see his daughter come screaming into the world.

Hearing the cries, Morgan and Clay came rushing in.

"What in the hell's going on?" Morgan's mouth fell open.

Clay gaped in shock.

"Give me your coat," Bragen ordered.

Cordell complied, never taking his eyes off the baby in Bragen's hand.

After he wrapped his daughter and placed her next to his son, he checked for more babies, and, thankfully, saw none. He scooted to the head of the cot.

Nichole's features were relaxed and soft. He pulled her

cape around her and kissed her sweet mouth. "It's all over, angel."

She opened her eyes and smiled. "What did we have?"

Bragen gave her a tilted grin and wiped a tear from her cheek. "A boy . . . and a girl."

Her silver blue eyes widened. "Twins?"

"Beautiful twins."

She lowered her lashes and chuckled. "I should have known."

When the children were separated from their mother and nestled in her arms, Bragen stared down at his family. He had come so close to losing them. His gaze swung to the door, and hatred for Gabriel Bodine consumed him. "Morgan, stay with Nichole. Clay, you get the horses." Trying to control his rage in front of the others, he picked up Nichole's knife and stalked out the door, then waited for Clay to sprint past him toward their mounts. He turned on his former friend. Gabriel would pay for what he did to Nichole . . . and Meela.

Bodine was sitting on the ground, tied to a tree. His bloody arm hung limp, and he was groggy, but awake.

Any friendship he'd ever felt for this man was dead. "Do you know what an Indian would do to a man who hurt his woman?" Bragen asked in a quiet voice, belying the fury tightening every muscle in his body.

Gabe's eyes flickered with fear. "Stay away from me, Alexander."

Bragen crouched in front of him. "He would start by castrating him." He waved the point of the knife near Bodine's groin, then pressed the tip against the seam of his breeches.

"No!" Gabriel screamed and tried to dislodge the blade. He kicked out.

Bragen jammed his knee down onto Gabe's ankles and held them in place. He smiled, loving the scent of the man's fear. "Is that what Meela said when you killed her?" He pressed the point of the blade deeper, piercing the material.

"Or what Nichole said when you tied her to that damned bed—when she was in labor?" Bragen's hand shook with the need to ram the blade home.

Gabriel's eyes darted around in panic. He whimpered. "Please. Oh, please, Alexander. I did it for you! For our friendship. I wanted things to go back to the way they were before Meela came between us. And I only took Nichole to stop you."

"To stop me from what, Bodine?" It was becoming harder and harder to keep his voice level.

Gabriel fixed on the knife between his legs. "From hurting me," he croaked.

Bragen tightened his fingers around the handle. "It didn't work." With extreme slowness, he began pushing the blade into Gabriel's testicles.

"Oh, God!"

"Alexander, don't," Morgan said from behind him. "Not this way." He placed a hand on Bragen's shoulder. "No one wants to see that bastard tortured more than I do, but not when you'll suffer because of it. And you will—once the anger has passed." He knelt down. "Let me take him to Coffland."

Bragen was torn between Morgan's logic and the need to watch Bodine writhe in agony. He hesitated, then released a slow breath and withdrew the knife. "Nichole needs a physician. Get him when you take Bodine."

Morgan relaxed.

When Clay returned with the horses, Morgan loaded Gabe onto one and headed for town.

Bragen gathered his wife and children.

Riding into the yard of Royal Oak, cradling Nichole in his arms while Clay carried the babies, Bragen was surprised to see a messenger at the door, handing a letter to Rawlins.

He reined in and dismounted, shifting his wife to a more comfortable position. "Who's that from?"

"Mr. Jason Kincaid."

"Take it to the parlor. I'll read it after Nichole and the children are settled."

Rawlins snapped his head up. "Children?"

"Twins," Clay announced, showing him the two babies.

Rawlins inspected the bundles, then Bragen's and Cordell's coatless forms, and sniffed. "I'll fetch wood for the fire."

When everyone was situated, Martha was cooing over the children, and the physician was in with Nichole, Bragen joined Clay in the parlor for a brandy while he read the letter.

"What did Kincaid have to say?"

Bragen stared down at the pages. "There're two letters. One from Jason, and one from Nick." He crushed them in his hand.

"What is it?"

"They want Nichole to come home."

The physician was just closing the door when Bragen started up the hall. "How is she?"

The thin man with a bald head gave a dry smile. "She's fine, but she needs rest."

He pressed several coins into the man's hand. "Thank you."

"You're welcome. And I'll check the children before I leave."

Nodding, Bragen opened the door to his wife's room.

Nichole looked beautiful lying there in the bed with her shimmering gold hair haloed around her head. The covers were drawn up, leaving only her neck and shoulders visible. She was wearing a prim white nightgown.

He knelt beside her and brushed a lock away from her cheek. "Our children are beautiful, angel."

"I just can't believe I had twins. I never even considered . . ." She shook her head.

Bragen lifted her slim hand in his, so thankful for the warmth nestled in his palm. He loved her beyond his own life, and would do anything to make her happy. As much as it pained him, he knew the Kincaids were right. Nichole had been forced into too many things. It was time she made a choice of her own.

He kissed her fingers. "Your brothers want you to come back to Virginia."

"My brothers? What are you talking about?"

He straightened the wrinkled pages of script. "Captain Potter returned to the colonies a few months ago, and he met up with one of Nick's captains. He mentioned the forced marriage he'd performed between Nichole Heatherton and Lord Blackstone. Word got back to your brothers, and they wrote to you here."

"Why?"

"Because they love you and want to make up to you for what they did. Damon confessed to the mishap at the stables, and Nick's cabin boy exonerated you about the accident on the docks." He read her the letters.

She didn't say anything for several seconds after he'd finished, then she met his eyes. "What do you think?"

"I can't help wondering if they aren't right. Maybe you *would* feel differently about us if you had a chance to think—to decide your own fate."

"I see." She held out her hand. "Would you give me the letters, please?"

Fearing her decision, he handed them to her.

She tore them to shreds. "Get this through that thick head of yours, Bragen Alexander Stanfield: I love you. And not Jason or Nick or a whole damned army is going to make me leave you. You're my life."

Bragen's eyes misted. "I love you, angel."

"I love you, too. And just as soon as I'm able, you won't need words of reassurance. I'll *prove* it to you."

He touched her cheek, her sweet mouth. "You already have."

Epilogue

Bragen grinned at Clay and Morgan as they mounted the steps at Royal Oak. They all looked like hell after the last three days, but their efforts had been worth it. Even Clay's black eye, Morgan's swollen jaw, and Bragen's own split lip had been worth the price.

When he opened the door to the bedchamber, he found Nichole sitting in a chair, nursing their son. The sight humbled him.

She looked up, her eyes filled with hurt, then she lowered her gaze. "I see you've finally found your way home."

"No, I haven't. Not yet anyway. Our home is in Virginia, or will be by the time we arrive. I posted a letter to a solicitor three days ago." He knelt in front of her. "I have nothing to keep me here, and I know you'd like to be near your family."

Her eyes softened just the tiniest bit. "What about your family?"

"We'll visit them."

"Where have you been, Bragen?"

He stroked his son's silky head. "I had some matters to clear up."

"For three days?"

He rose and spread his hands out in front of the fireplace. "Thank God that's all it took. I was afraid it would be longer."

She set the child in a cradle next to the chair, a cradle he recognized as his own. Rawlins must have brought the infant bed down from the attic. Their daughter was in Fiona's cradle. Victor was stationed protectively between them.

Nichole came to her feet. "What are you talking about?"

He sent her a sly smile, then withdrew a velvet packet from his breast pocket. "This." He handed it to her.

She unwrapped the parcel and let out a small gasp. Tears shimmered in her eyes as she stared at her locket. "Oh, Bragen. How?"

He grinned. "I got it in the Waterfront Tavern, an establishment near the docks where a gentleman can get much more than just spirits."

"What?"

"Now, before you trounce on me, let me explain. You see, Gabe had given your locket away to a—well, you know. All we knew was that the woman worked in a tavern on the docks. Anyway, after we learned about its whereabouts, we headed there.

"Unfortunately, we had to search several establishments before we found the right one. And let it be said, some of the patrons in those places aren't very friendly." He smiled and touched his cut lip. "But we got what we went after."

Her chin trembled. "I don't know what to say."

He nuzzled her ear. " 'Thank you' would do for now."

"Thank y—" She burst into tears.

"You're welcome, angel." He cradled her in his arms and held her while she cried, loving her more than his own life. He'd give her the rest of her jewels they found at Gabriel's later.

Right now, he just wanted to hold her.

Dear Reader:

Your opinion is important to me. Please let me know if you enjoyed *Wayward Angel*. You can write to me at the address below.

Sincerely,

Sue Rich

Sue Rich
c/o Pocket Books
1230 Avenue of the Americas
New York, NY 10020

P.S. Your self-addressed, stamped envelope would be greatly appreciated.